The Garden Party

The Garden Party

Sarah

CHALLIS

headline
review

First published in Great Britain in 2011
by HEADLINE REVIEW
An imprint of HEADLINE PUBLISHING GROUP

1

Cataloguing in Publication Data is available from the British Library

ISBN 978 0 7553 5675 1 (Hardback)
ISBN 978 0 7553 5676 8 (Trade paperback)

Typeset in Bembo by Palimpsest Book Production Limited,
Falkirk, Stirlingshire

Printed in the UK by
CPI Mackays, Chatham ME5 8TD

Headline's policy is to use papers that are natural, renewable and recyclable
products and made from wood grown in sustainable forests.
The logging and manufacturing processes are expected to conform
to the environmental regulations of the country of origin.

HEADLINE PUBLISHING GROUP
An Hachette UK Company
338 Euston Road
London NW1 3BH

www.headline.co.uk
www.hachette.co.uk

For dearest Caro

Chapter One

SOMETIMES WHEN ALICE Baxter couldn't sleep, which was often these days, she found that great cinematic scenes floated into her head from nowhere, and the idea for the party first came to her as she lay in bed in the half-light of a grey spring dawn. Suddenly, she could see the whole thing as if she were watching a film, with the parts that in real life would need attention brought up to scratch. The garden, for instance, was awash with bright summer flowers and the lawn was a startling emerald green and neatly mown in alternate silvery stripes, unlike the worn-looking March grass she saw through the kitchen window as she stood at the sink.

There was a small white marquee set behind the house, accessed through the dining-room French windows and lined with the sort of silky, blush-coloured material that transforms a tent into a palace and casts a flattering glow on the complexions of the guests. There were elegant little gilded chairs drawn up to a long table draped with white linen and set with gleaming silver and glittering glasses.

And all the family were there with champagne flutes in their hands: Charlie, her eldest son, tall and dark as her husband, David, had once been, and his clever little wife

1

Annie, and their boys Rory and Archie; her second son, Ollie, loud and energetic, with his wife Lisa, and her children, Agnes and Sabine, from her previous marriage to a Frenchman. She saw her daughters: Marina and her partner Ahmed, and baby Mo; and Sadie and her current boyfriend Kyle, and her daughters Tamzin and Georgie; and her sister, Rachel, in a navy two-piece and a lot of gold chains.

They stood with bright, expectant smiles on their faces, all turned towards the house, waiting for her and David to make an appearance, and here they came, hand in hand, laughing happily, stepping out of the French windows like eager contestants on a game show. David was wearing a blazer, something he had never worn in his life, with an unfamiliar pink shirt and tie, and Alice was looking quite unlike her usual self, with her hair styled into a sleek bob and at least twenty-five pounds lighter than her present weight, wearing a navy linen suit with white piping and a white collar. That suit was a surprise – how had she dreamed up such an unexpected garment? She certainly had nothing like it in her wardrobe. For the last ten years or so, as her waist thickened, she had favoured stretchy skirts and easy-fitting tops, but here she was in something tailored and chic and evidently expensive. And it could be done, she told herself, if only she had the willpower to take herself in hand, lose the weight and get a more adventurous haircut. She had had the same style for the last fifteen years, trimmed every six weeks by her cleaner's daughter, Diane, while sitting in her own kitchen with a beach towel round her shoulders.

A transformation was perfectly possible. It was not too late. Women of sixty were always being told they could turn back the clock, develop a better dress sense, take up running half-marathons or learn a foreign language, and even wear a bikini on holiday, although that particular idea made her shudder. There was no excuse for having slipped comfortably into what she knew she had become: dull and matronly.

Now back to the vision, because Charlie was stepping forward, and he too looked tidier and better groomed than usual in a lightweight suit – he was a history teacher and didn't bother much about his appearance – and he was tapping a glass with a fork from the table and asking for quiet so that he could begin his speech. Alice had been to enough similar occasions to know what he would say, but he went beyond the expected and spoke so warmly of his parents that she and David, still hand in hand, looked at one another in delighted surprise and gratitude. What seemed even more unlikely was that throughout his speech there was no dissent or arguments or interruptions, the younger children all crowding round with smiling, happy faces and even Mo, a fractious, squalling baby, chuckling and waving his arms about. Roger, the old Labrador, was there, looking less portly and refraining from sniffing crotches in his usual party manner, but posing alertly, with his dear old greying face lifted towards them.

The scene was like a vision from on high, and Alice found she could pause and replay it as she chose. Each time she ran it through her head she became more convinced that it was quite possible to turn the dream into reality. It would take a lot of goodwill and hard work, and quite a lot of money, but it was worth it for such a special and beautiful occasion.

She sat up in bed and switched on the bedside light.

The party scene disappeared, but not the residual excitement. She looked with wakened eyes at her shabby, comfortable bedroom furnished with old, so-familiar pieces of furniture; at the bedspread with the egg-shaped ink stain and the colour faded by the sun that streamed through the window. Everything about her was so worn and marked by years of family life. Her gaze settled on the hatbox on top of the wardrobe, containing her two wedding hats, and on top of that the shoebox in which she kept treasures left over from her children's childhood years: first teeth, first shoes, little curls from first haircuts tied with coloured cotton. This is what I have become, she thought, like this room, that box – a repository of the past. We have a family history that started with me and David, where we have come from, what we have become. It's all prized and beyond value and it needs celebrating.

She and David had never been ones for splashing out on anything much – certainly not giving parties. From the penny-pinching days when they first got married, living quietly and modestly had become their modus vivendi. Having four children was their biggest extravagance, and what marked them out from most of their friends. A large family was the preserve of the well-off and confident, or the feckless poor, not ordinary, careful people like them, although Sadie, their fourth child, was not planned. She had simply happened. When Alice had found she was pregnant again, there had been a week or two of shock before the delight took over.

With the serenity of motherhood upon her, she knew they would manage somehow on David's pitiful salary as a university lecturer. It would be difficult, but they would get by. David had been less sanguine, because he was pessimistic by nature. He had sat with his head in his hands for a week or two, but then Alice's parents had bailed them out with a loan to cover the mortgage on their house, this very house that they still lived in, and everything was all right again.

Naturally, with a fourth baby, extravagant parties were never on the agenda, and Alice and David were not the sort of people who ever wanted to be the centre of attention. The great milestones in their lives to date had been celebrated quietly, but that didn't mean, thought Alice, that they shouldn't push the boat out for once. After all, they had a family to be proud of, and they were still married after forty years, which was an achievement in itself these days. As for being sixty, well, that was something that had crept up on her almost unawares. The busy years had flown by until suddenly here she was, drawing a pension and applying for winter fuel allowance while still feeling inside exactly as she had at twenty-one when she and David, both university students, had got married.

Now she was so wide awake she might just as well get up and make a cup of tea. She felt for her slippers with her bare feet, and when she found them noticed with her fresh eyes how extremely shabby they were. The mock sheepskin had turned grey and bald. That was another thing she could take in hand – she could throw out everything that was past it, threadbare, worn out. It was high time for a bit of spring-cleaning.

Passing the door of the bedroom she still thought of as belonging to the boys, even though they had left home years ago, she heard David's rhythmic snoring from within. Since he had retired from the university last year, he had developed strange sleeping patterns, staying up late and lying in in the morning – like an old teenager. One evening when she was washing up and tidying the kitchen before going to bed he had said, without looking at her, 'I'll sleep in the boys' room tonight. I can stay up late then, and read if I want to,' and she had known that something had come about, something important, but all she had said as she swirled the water round with the silly brush was, 'Okay, if you prefer.'

She had never told him that she felt put out by this new arrangement because it seemed to her less like consideration and more like rejection, as if he actually preferred to sleep alone. If she was honest, they both slept better as a result, and there was a luxury in having the whole bed to herself and being able to turn on the light or listen to the radio when she wanted. But there was a tug of loneliness in sliding her hand across the cold side of the bed and finding it empty.

Going downstairs, she thought again about the party. A small doubt had already asserted itself, because she had to admit that she had been misled before by what David called her flash-in-the-pan ideas. In fact, all her life she had been guided by inspirational visions of how she imagined things might be, usually followed by a process of slow disillusionment and final acceptance that her daydreams had been misleading. She remembered how, even as a quite small child, she would dream about an approaching Christmas, or a birthday party, and how very often the reality would be a disappointment. In her head her sticking-out party dress with its velvet sash would be the prettiest and she would win Pass the Parcel, whereas the truth was that she was a stout little girl who looked comical jammed into an organza frock, and she was so shy and reluctant that she was overlooked by adults when they handed out prizes.

But the more she thought about it, the more sure she was that her idea for an anniversary celebration was a good one. As soon as she judged the moment was right she would break the news to David. She did not expect him to be enthusiastic, but obviously she would have to have his support. She would need to deploy the tactics of a politician to get his approval. To begin with he wouldn't take it seriously. He would think of it as another of her harebrained schemes, best ignored until it went away. He wouldn't be able to visualise it as she could. He wouldn't be able to imagine the whole family gathered in the garden on a lovely summer day to celebrate both her birthday and their fortieth wedding anniversary, or how it would provide them with happy memories to last them into their old age.

In the kitchen, she waited for the kettle to boil and rubbed Roger's warm tummy with her foot as he snored in his basket. She knew what David would say. That was one of the things that happened after years of married life. You ended up being able to write the script for many situations. His first objection would be on financial grounds. He would say that they couldn't afford it and what was the point of spending a lot of money on a grand family gathering when they could have a barbecue or something simple, sausages stuck in rolls and cans of beer. Yes, thought Alice, already arguing with him in her head, and the kitchen would be hot and chaotic and they would have to carry everything back and forth to the garden and then there would be all the dirty plates to deal with, and she would be in the middle of it all in her old jeans with her midriff bulge and her face red and shiny with effort and her hair untidy.

He would say what was the point of getting them all together when the journey would be long for two of the families and there would not be enough room for them all to stay. He would say that it would not necessarily be a happy get-together. Agnes and Sabine were now eleven and thirteen years old and would be bored, and Lisa and Annie had never been the best of friends. There had been one or two 'situations' in the past, at christenings or Christmas, where there had been a bit of an atmosphere and some pointed remarks exchanged. He would say that it would be uncomfortable for Ahmed, the newest recruit to the family. He would be overwhelmed by the Baxter clan en masse and Marina seemed to look for an opportunity to take umbrage. She always had been huffy – even as a small girl flouncing out of rooms and slamming doors. He would make all these objections and a lot of others and a few would have some truth to them, but that didn't alter the fact that Alice knew that the celebratory nature of the party would overcome any of these minor difficulties and they were sure to have the most wonderful day.

The real reason for David's inevitable objections, she thought, fishing for the tea bag in her mug with the end of a fork, was the fact that he was apathetic and often morose these days. He had been retired from the university for a year and did not have much to show for it. His last decade of lecturing had been fraught with frustrations and disenchantment and he was the first to admit that he had limped towards the finishing post, worn out and demoralised. The sad thing was, thought Alice, that he had never

8

really recovered any vigour or appetite for life. He hadn't done anything in the garden, for instance, in which she thought he might have taken a bit of interest. He hadn't painted the peeling window frames or cleaned out the gutters. He hardly bothered to get dressed before midday, wandering about in his drooping boxer shorts half the morning, displaying his thin old man's legs. He often did not bother to shave, and badgery-coloured stubble sprouted on his chin.

He was depressed, she supposed. It hadn't been easy for him to adapt to being at home all day, but then he had complained so bitterly about his job that it was reasonable to suppose he would be glad to do anything other than sit through the endless departmental meetings, moaning with his other old codger colleagues about the new head of department and the woeful collapse of academic standards.

He wouldn't talk about how he felt. His face took on a pained expression if she pointed out that he seemed a bit low. He perceived it as criticism, which it was, in a way. As well as voicing concern for him, what Alice was really saying was 'Why aren't you a more cheerful companion?' and even 'Is this how it is going to be for the rest of our lives?'

She had once talked about it to Ollie, who was a doctor, and he had said, 'I shouldn't worry too much. Dad's always been a miserable old sod. It's become a habit. He's cheerful enough with other people. It's you he takes it out on.' And this was true. David reserved his most gloomy behaviour for when they were alone at home together. He always had, and he wasn't alone among husbands, Alice knew that. Quite a few of her friends said their men were exactly the same; even those who were married to life-and-soul-of-the-party types said that they were moody at home. Thank goodness she still worked, and got out of the house to her part-time job as a receptionist at the doctor's surgery.

Taking her mug, and a piece of paper and a pen from the muddle of stuff that collected beside the telephone, Alice made her way back to bed to plan the party.

David heard her pass his door. It was really annoying that she made so much noise in the morning, he thought irritably. She seemed unable to turn a handle properly. She always turned and pushed at the same time, so that the shutting mechanism rattled and the door banged open. She thought he could sleep through anything and did not seem to concern herself that it might disturb him when she made tea at an unearthly hour.

He thought about the physical distance that had recently developed between them, when for years and years they had shared the same bed. As students it had been a mattress on the floor, when Alice had been a gangly girl with long legs in miniskirts; then a small double bed with a dip in the middle in the first flat they rented together. A cheap king-sized bed followed when they moved into this house. It had seemed embarrassingly enormous in those days. He used to think that his parents, who slept side by side so tidily in a small double bed for their whole married life, eyed it with distaste when they came to visit.

Into that bed each of the children had been gathered as milky babies, and then as toddlers, scarlet-cheeked with fever or sobbing in the grip of a nightmare. As they got older they had still climbed in every morning and squabbled and giggled and fought one another for space, kicking out with their lovely smooth, unblemished feet. What had happened to that bed? wondered David, turning over and bunching the pillow under his head. Ah, yes, Alice had read a magazine article about how you should have a new bed every decade and insisted they threw it out and bought a new one ten years ago. That was another of her annoying traits. She got ideas into her head and wouldn't let them go.

He wondered if he missed lying beside her and thought he probably did. A single bed was a lonely place when you were a grown-up, but in some ways David wanted to feel lonely. Sometimes he felt tired of being part of his family, pulled this way and that by them all. At least when he had a job to go to he had some sort of escape route, an independent existence that they weren't part of, somewhere where they couldn't get at him to suck him dry with their demands and expectations.

Now he was at home all day, he had to give explanations, justifications for how he passed his time. Alice was always leaving him notes, making suggestions. Paint the bloody windows was one of them. The thought of buying paint and brushes and turpentine and then all the scraping and filling of rotten woodwork made him feel worn out before he even began. No way was he going to take up DIY to please her. She treated him as she had done the children on a wet day in the holidays – finding him things to do, making bright suggestions about how to pass the long hours. She'd be giving him pocket money next and making him a bloody star chart for good behaviour.

He turned over again. With any luck he would go back to sleep, the deep early-morning sleep that would render him unconscious until well after Alice had left for work and he could have the house to himself again. In which to do nothing useful at all.

The party idea continued to grow. Alice thought about it as she drove to work through the splashy wet countryside and parked in the lane behind the doctor's surgery. The first twenty minutes of the day were given over to general organising and chatting before the telephones started to ring, but this morning she listened distractedly to Margaret's complaints about the computer system.

Margaret, one of her fellow receptionists, was what you would call full-figured if you were being kind, and wore very tight skirts and low-cut spangly T-shirts for someone in her fifties. She had a lot of auburn hair done up in various combs with tumbling bits escaping as if she was fresh from a sex romp. This morning her black skirt looked all right from the front, but when she turned round to move some files, a slit was revealed almost to her rump. The backs of heifer-like knees are not really attractive, thought Alice, on anything other than cows or small children.

When Margaret first started work at the surgery, Alice had wondered whether Deidre, the practice manager, would have a word. Instead, after a week or two, she had sidled up to Alice during a coffee break and asked her if, as senior receptionist, she would bring up the subject of appropriate clothing for the workplace in an informal way. Alice had firmly refused. She judged that Margaret was not someone you offended lightly, and after all, she had to work beside her.

Instead she told Deidre that she thought maybe Margaret's appearance cheered people up as they queued for repeat prescriptions or to make another appointment. She wasn't exactly what you expected to see through the sliding glass window when you came to the doctor feeling miserable with a chesty cough or a suspicious rash. In the end nothing was said and everyone got used to how she looked and after a while expected her to look like a cabaret artist.

Would she invite Margaret to the party? She tried to imagine her there in one of her dressy outfits and teetering high heels. She dolled herself up exotically for the practice Christmas dinner, which was held in a local Indian restaurant. Last year she had looked like a belly dancer in harem pants and a tight silver top. Yes, she decided, she would like Margaret to be there, because she was an important part of her life and a real friend.

Alice hadn't really begun to work out the guest list, and as she totted up names in her head she realised that there would have to be a line drawn somewhere or the marquee would be bigger than the garden itself. She even had a wild thought of extending the whole thing into a sort of street party, because she would like to invite both sets of neighbours as well. There were the Bakers on one side, both retired teachers, with a heavy, flat-footed grown-up daughter, Mandy, who still lived with them after her own marriage faltered twenty years ago after only two months.

On the other side was John Pritchard, long widowed, who had recently found a new partner, a divorcee in her seventies whom he had met on a Saga holiday to Egypt. He had come round to show them his holiday photographs, and there Carol was in all of them. Alice had screwed up her eyes and peered at the rather imposing, colourfully dressed figure. There was even one of her on a camel in front of the pyramids.

When she finally met Carol in person, Alice wasn't altogether sure about her. She was such a change from Betty, John's wife, who had been unrelievedly beige in both dress and outlook. She was tall and brightly blonde with a muscular frame and wearing a trouser suit. She looked better in trousers than John, who recently had let himself go and allowed his Terylene slacks to ride up over his old man's pouch of tummy, which made them too short in the leg and gave him an elderly, wading-bird look.

Carol proved to be an energetic, free-range talker who steered every subject back to herself. Alice could see David growing restless and then desperate, and after a short while he had risen to his feet and when he could get a word in edgeways mumbled, 'If you will excuse me, I have to . . .' and backed out of the room. Alice heard him going upstairs and had to pretend that he had some work to do on a paper he was writing. John, meanwhile, sat silent in his armchair balancing a mug of tea on his knee, looking shell-shocked. He was like a country that had been overrun by an occupying army and had offered no resistance.

Alice started her computer and made a new file, which she titled 'Garden Party', and throughout the morning she surreptitiously added and deleted people's names. Family first, of course. Her sister Rachel, and her husband and children and their partners and children. She would draw the line at cousins. How quickly the list grew. Then she added the neighbours, and close friends. Soon the list was far too long and she had to think again. Even if half of them couldn't come, it was getting out of hand.

'What are you up to?' asked Margaret, passing behind her chair. They were not supposed to work on personal things on the office computers, but Margaret was addicted to internet shopping and chat rooms and between them they had reached a sort of understanding of what they felt was permissible when things were quiet.

'Planning a party,' said Alice with a little smile. It was the first time she had said the word out loud. 'Well, hardly planning it yet. Sort of thinking it through.'

'A party! I love a party!' Margaret did a jiving movement and wiggled her hips.

'Well, this is rather a special year for us. It's our fortieth wedding anniversary in November. Yes! Really! We let David's sixtieth birthday go past without a celebration two years ago and it's my sixtieth in June, so I thought it was time for a celebration.'

'A long-service medal, more like. How have you managed to stay married that long? Six years is my record, and I partied, I can tell you, when my divorce came through.'

Margaret paused to answer the telephone and studied her computer screen to book an appointment. Yes, Alice thought, it *is* an achievement, and she felt a little rush of pleasure in the acknowledgement that their marriage *was* worth celebrating.

'What sort of party will it be?' asked Margaret, putting down the telephone. 'A meal out somewhere nice? Black tie for hubby and a posh cocktail dress for you?'

'No, I thought we'd do something at home. A proper party, though, with a tent and everything. A marquee, I mean.' A tent sounded like Boy Scouts.

'Oh, lah-di-dah!' said Margaret, pulling a face. 'You should retake your vows. People do that these days, with their kids as witnesses. I've seen the pics in *Hello!*, although God knows who stays married long enough. Half those celebrities seem to do it, just before they split up.'

'Oh, no, we wouldn't want anything like that. David would hate it.' It had been hard enough to get him to have a church wedding in the first place. He maintained that he hated all the mumbo-jumbo and the dressing up. 'No. This is more for the whole family. Getting them all together. It's not just about us.'

'A family get-together would be my idea of hell. I can't be five minutes in the same room as my sister without wanting to slap her.' Alice tried to imagine wanting to slap her own sister, Rachel, who was even fatter than she was, and a county councillor, and couldn't do so. She often thought that Rach was the one person in the world she could happily live with if anything happened to David. In fact, she would be much nicer to live with than David in many ways. Sometimes they went on holiday together and got on so well and laughed so much that their husbands sulked.

'I suppose the first thing I must do is find a date that suits everyone. A Sunday I think would be best.'

'Don't do that. Just tell them all what day it will be and say you want them there. You'll never suit everyone.'

Maybe Margaret was right, but being so assertive was not Alice's usual style. She looked at her office diary. She would need to take time off before the party and she had already got a week of holiday booked in May, attached to a bank holiday weekend. She left the school holidays to the practice staff who had younger children. At the end of the week was Sunday 6 May. That would be it. That would be the day of the party. All that was left was to tell David.

David had just got out of bed. It was ten thirty and he felt as if he should eat something but didn't fancy any of what he knew would be in the fridge. Breakfast seemed a pointless meal when you were in the house all day. You needed to be going somewhere to justify eating it. He boiled the kettle and made some coffee and sat at the kitchen table and looked at yesterday's newspaper. He couldn't be bothered to go and collect today's paper from the hall, because the news hardly varied from day to day and neither did it matter whether he was up to date or not. He used to enjoy an exchange of views on current affairs while he was still at the university, but when there was no one to annoy, what was the point of having any views at all?

Later he would turn on his laptop and read the news online and browse through the pop-up advertisements and check his e-mails, which would all be rubbish as usual. Stiffy in a Jiffy. Enlarge Your Manhood. Candy sent you a message on Facebook. Bigger You Make It Big. This was the strange virtual world of the lonely time-waster. Or empty time-filler more like. He imagined all the sad, disappointed stay-at-home men, staring at screens and tapping the keys in search of solace and satisfaction. God, it was depressing, this shadowy, dirty-fantasy country of the internet. When he was young, retired men fancied pigeons or worked on allotments or shuffled up the street to the library with their books to return in a string bag. In those days at sixty you were expected to be old and past it. There was no shame attached.

He had discovered to his relief that internet porn was not an attraction. When, out of interest, he typed in Office Babes or Hot Black Pussy the resulting images left him unmoved or faintly repulsed. At least in that area he had nothing to hide from Alice.

He finished his coffee and put the mug in the sink. The thought did not occur to him to place it in the dishwasher, any more than he would have noticed that the floor needed sweeping or that he had left the cutlery drawer open when he had looked for a spoon. He glanced out of the window. Grey clouds jostled across a tin-coloured sky. He could tell that the morning was cold and uninviting just by looking. No point in going out, then. Without much further thought he mounted the stairs and went back into the room in which he now slept and where he had set up his computer on the table scarred by years of abuse by the boys as they struggled with homework. The points of knives and compasses had pitted and gouged the surface like Braille. Sitting at the table in his underpants, he switched on his laptop and waited while it flickered and whirred. He hit the e-mail button, and there it was, below a message from Amazon – an e-mail from an address he didn't recognise, titled 'Hi! Is that you, David?'

By the time Alice got home, heaving supermarket bags out of the car and banking them up inside the front door, and shouting into the quiet house for some help in unloading, she was tired and faintly cross. A sharp pain had developed at the base of her neck and her shoulders felt stiff.

She was in the kitchen by the time David appeared. 'Oh, there you are!' she said unnecessarily.

'Why? Where did you think I was?'

'Oh, I don't know.' How irritating he could be. 'Can you help me with the shopping? I've done something to my neck.'

He turned obediently to bring bags from the hall and heave them on to the counter. Alice started to unpack, thinking, I buy it, I lug it home, I put it away, I get it out again, I cook it, I wash up afterwards, and on it goes, I suppose, until I am carted off to an old people's home, like a pit pony brought up to the surface and put out to grass in retirement.

'What have you done to your neck?' David enquired dutifully. 'I expect it's working on a computer. You know the average head weighs . . .' but Alice wasn't listening, he could tell. She seemed to find the number of tins of chickpeas in the cupboard more interesting.

'I can't understand it,' she said, staring at the shelves. 'I seem to go on a sort of buying jag and every time I'm in the supermarket convince myself that we need something like chickpeas and buy another tin. I mean, how many times a year do I make something with chickpeas? I've got five tins here and I bought another one today. A little while ago I couldn't stop buying Worcester sauce. Look, we've got three bottles.'

'Perhaps you're turning into a Mormon. Subconsciously.'

'God, I hope not. Aren't they a bit weird? Why do they buy a lot of chickpeas? Is it their religion?'

'They are preparing for the end of the world. Stocking up.'

'If it's the end of the world, why would they need chickpeas?' Alice couldn't imagine the sort of Armageddon that would require her to plan the next meal.

'They practise polygamy, or at least they used to,' said David, as if in answer. Alice, who often thought that she could do with a wife, sighed and put the kettle on.

She doesn't even notice, thought David, that I have had a fairly radical haircut. That afternoon he had been to the most expensive hairdresser in the nearby town and paid more for a haircut than he considered morally defensible. It was a chunky, short style that the girl said made the most of his thick hair. She was a pretty girl, younger than his daughters, with a shiny black bob and long fringe. She said he was lucky to have such a good head of hair and had rubbed some stuff on the palms of her hands when she had finished and smoothed them lightly over his head, almost like a lover's caress, while her boobs nudged his shoulders.

He watched Alice make two mugs of tea and then push one towards him. She sat down at the table holding hers between her hands and started to read the paper upside down. She still hadn't looked at him properly and he felt suddenly self-conscious, standing there waiting to be noticed. It was better to say something.

'Notice anything different?' he asked, gesturing with his hands, palms up.

Alice looked. 'Goodness!' she said. 'What have you done? Where has your hair gone?'

'Well, I had it *cut*!'

'I can see that. Why?'

David felt she was making fun of him. 'Why do you think? It was too long, wasn't it?'

'Yes, but why the revamp all of a sudden? It's good, actually. Makes you look younger. Where did you get it done?'

'The Studio.'

Alice made a startled face. 'Goodness!' she said again. 'You did push the boat out. I thought you disapproved of paying more than a couple of quid for a whiz round with the dog clippers.' She rose and went over to where he was leaning against the counter and reached up, ruffling the top of his head as if he were a large child. 'I like it,' she said lightly. 'You look quite, um,' she searched for the word she wanted, 'modern. Cool. You know, as if you were presenting a television history programme or something.' She turned away to massage the back of her neck with her hand.

David felt pleased. The awkwardness had gone, and Alice had convinced him that he did indeed look better. He felt like the sort of man who might have once modelled rugged sweaters in an outdoors setting. His mother had had a book of knitting patterns like that at home when he was a boy. In those days the models were allowed to grip a pipe between their teeth while resting one foot on a stile. Perhaps at his age and because his hair was now silver, he was more like one of the older models pictured seated in an armchair reading a book, with crossed legs and a cup of tea to hand, or maybe concentrating on making a ship in a bottle. How innocent were the pursuits of men back then. Had knitting patterns disappeared, he wondered, along with wool shops?

Funny, thought Alice, as she started to wonder about supper, that David should have had his hair cut today. He had unwittingly fulfilled one of her party requirements, to tidy himself up. He didn't look at all bad. It was annoying really that men aged so much more gracefully than women and remained attractive as they got older, with minimum effort. She thought of all the waxing and buffing and wrinkle

21

banishment that women were exhorted to practise after the age of about twenty-five; the cellulite worries, upper arm and thigh insecurities and tummy and bottom hatred that took up so many waking hours. As far as she was aware, David had not given more than a moment's thought to his appearance for the whole of his adult life. There was a narrow range of clothing that he had always worn and would continue to wear, and a much wider range that would not be considered. He had never worn a tracksuit, for instance, or a pair of sandals or a patterned sweater or a novelty tie. It was about knowing your look, as the fashionistas would say, and David certainly did that in an unswerving way.

It had been on the tip of her tongue to bring up the subject of the party after the haircut conversation, but she had thought better of it. She had decided that the best course of action was to e-mail the children and run it past them first and then present David with a fait accompli. After supper she would start up her old laptop and send them all a message.

David had disappeared again. She could hear the sound of the television news from the sitting room. She got a bottle of wine out of the fridge and poured two large glasses. She and David were the sort of middle-class drinkers that the health police had got it in for, as the frequent trips to the bottle bank bore witness to.

'David!' she called. 'Drink?' There was no answer, so she took the glass through to him. She was surprised to find the television on but the room empty. 'David?' She went back through to the hall and looked up the stairs. The door to his room was firmly shut. Oh well. She put the glass down on the table beside his armchair and went back into the kitchen.

Upstairs, David was checking his e-mails again. He didn't know why exactly he should feel furtive but he did, even more so when he heard Alice calling him. There was a message from Sandra Supersize You, and Shelley said Will You Attend ME, but apart from that nothing. He switched off and sat for a moment, thinking. He should not expect an immediate reply. Perhaps he had been a bit hasty, a bit too keen-seeming to have replied at once. Oh well, too late now. E-mails were dangerous like that. One tap on a key and they were on their way, arriving silently and secretly, one hoped. Not that he felt he was being secretive. He just wasn't going to tell Alice, that was all.

Chapter Two

IT WAS ANNIE, Charlie's wife, who opened the e-mail from Alice. She read it twice and then laid her head wearily on the table beside her laptop and shut her eyes. Her instant reaction was that the one thing guaranteed to create lasting discord and disharmony was to collect the whole of any family under one roof – or tent. She was tempted to delete the message and pretend that it had never arrived, but that would be pointless. This proposed party wouldn't go away just to oblige her.

It was half past ten in the morning and the house was quiet. Rory was at his primary school and she had dropped Archie off at nursery, and the precious three hours before she had to repeat the whole process and collect him again were supposed to be dedicated to getting an article finished for the in-house magazine she edited for a chain of DIY superstores. It was a crap job – how could you write a shout line like 'Step Up for Summer!' to accompany an article on store safety and the use of folding ladders without feeling suicidal – but at least it was something she could do at home without farming the boys out to childminders.

She raised her head to read the e-mail again, hearing Alice's girlish, excited voice in her head. She had already fixed a date and would expect everyone to be there on a Sunday in May. 'I want this to be a really special day,' she wrote, 'not just for David and me, but for all of you, too.' Annie sighed. How could Alice really think that was possible when she and Charlie would have to make a 150-mile round trip with two small children and then keep them under control for what sounded like a formal party with a sit-down, grown-up luncheon? What was Alice *thinking* of?

It would be her, Annie, who would do the childminding, while Charlie would drink too much, egged on by Ollie. She would have to bear the cutting remarks of Lisa, and fond as she was of her, the depressing hopelessness of Sadie embarked on a new relationship with another useless man, while Tamzin and Georgie were sidelined yet again. Marina would behave as if she was the first woman ever to give birth, while Ahmed would sulk as he always did when he wasn't the centre of attention. To cap it all, she would have to drive all the way home with fractious, overexcited children and a pissed husband.

It was amazing that Alice, who had reared four children in swift succession with little help and not much money, could apparently fail to remember the true nature of what life was like when kids were small.

Annie leaned back and gazed out of the Velux window at the square of grey sky above her head. After Rory was born and they couldn't afford to move, they had converted the attic into what was supposed to be an office, and this was where she had set up her computer and box files and tried to create a work-like atmosphere. Because they had lost storage space as a result, one end of the narrow room was filled with a miscellany of cardboard boxes and camping equipment and Charlie's hardly used exercise bike and other stuff that couldn't be thrown away but was hardly ever remembered or used. It got her down, this distracting mess. It reminded her of the half-life she seemed to be living, suspended between the worlds of work and motherhood and finding neither at all satisfactory.

She stared at the thick swab of sky, so loaded with moisture that it clung to the window like fuzzy grey felt, and gave herself up to a familiar morose inertia. She couldn't write a word when she felt like this. It was as if a giant hand had her by the throat and stifled any breath of imagination or inspiration. A weight of tiredness pressed down on her eyelids and she longed to close them and rest her head on her desk again.

She felt utterly bleak and wished that she could find a crumb of comfort somewhere. She could remind herself that Charlie and the boys were all healthy, that they had enough money, a house of their own, that no terrible tragedy had devastated their lives, but she knew this blue-sky thinking wouldn't work. It never did. It seemed that there was something in her very nature that would drag her down to this leaden grey place from which she struggled to emerge.

She hated this predisposition to gloom. What had happened to the bright, funny, energetic girl she had once been? It's this sodding job, she thought angrily, staring at her computer screen with hatred, and Charlie, too, with his preoccupation with his own work, teaching history at a well-known, highly academic grammar school, treating her as if she had been handed the lucky ticket when she gave up work she loved as a magazine editor after Archie was born.

'Doing anything nice today?' he would say as he picked up his briefcase in the morning.

'I'm taking Rory swimming after school and Archie's got a party this afternoon.'

'Hmm. Well, have fun!' He didn't listen anyway. She could have said, 'I'm chucking Archie out on the central reservation of the M3 and feeding Rory tranquillisers before I fly off to the Caribbean with the grumpy twenty-stone man from the post office,' and he still would have said, 'Well, enjoy yourselves. Bye, boys!'

She had enough self-awareness and intelligence to know what the matter was. The syndrome was universally recognised and well documented. The dissatisfied stay-at-home mum was a much-discussed species. Every magazine she had ever worked on ran frequent articles about women who found staying at home and rearing children to be mind-numbingly boring and frustrating. She did not need anyone to explain to her the origins of her despair. She was bored, undervalued, lacking in job satisfaction, riddled with guilt and feelings of failure. She hated not earning her own money, hated child-based friendships with people with whom she had nothing in common. She hated the grind of domestic chores, hated the endless buying and cooking of bland, boring food, half of which she would scrape into the bin or sweep up from the floor, hated the horrible plastic toys with vital small componenets she had to pick up or search for day in day out, hated the colouring pens left without their tops to dry up, hated the mess and the clutter and noise that crowded her out of her life.

Worst of all, she hated herself for resenting her own children; loving them fiercely, devotedly, but often hating being with them. How unnatural was she that the best thing anyone could do for her was to take her children off her hands? How shameful was her inabililty to make life any more fun for them than it was for her? This was their *childhood* that she was messing with, for goodness' sake. These were the formative years that would shape the sort of people they became. Raising them was the most important job she would ever do and she was an abysmal failure at it. She was terrified that they would grow up dysfunctional, emotionally warped, because she could not act like a proper mother.

It was *could* and not *would*, because she tried, she really tried. Every single day she tried, and some days were better than others and she felt that she might just get by, and then she struck a patch like today when she could hardly bear to get out of bed in the morning to start another day of pretending that everything was all right.

Pretending to Charlie was the most difficult, because to him of all people she could never admit the devastating truth that family life was anathema to her. And neither must the women at the school gate nor the boys' teachers nor her family nor Charlie's family, and most especially not Alice, know the extent of her hopelessness.

Annie thought of Alice, of her square, capable hands and her broad, kindly face. She thought of how easily the boys climbed on her lap and hung round her neck, how she heard her laughing with them in the kitchen, how she didn't seem to mind the mess they made or how naughty they were about going to bed. Alice was a natural mother and grandmother and Annie felt judged by comparison and found woefully lacking.

She was shocked at how hostile she felt towards her

mother-in-law. She hardly deserved it, she knew, but she resented that Alice embodied everything that she herself apparently could not be – the warm centre of a loving family. Or that was what Alice would have you believe. It was how she saw herself, because if Alice *wanted* everything to be fine, then it was fine, and there was a conspiracy amongst the others to go along with her delusion. There was nothing dark allowed into Alice's life. She failed to accept any suggestion that the Baxters were anything less than a perfect family.

This party, for instance. This celebration. What was there to celebrate? The fact that she and David had stuck together in what was clearly a pretty hopeless wreck of a marriage? Or the pride they took in their four children, who in reality were only just holding their lives together?

Annie felt a pang of remorse. How unfair she was when she was in this frame of mind; how unable to be generous or charitable or optimistic or even basically kind. Alice didn't deserve this opprobrium. Alice had always been kind and patient and supportive of her.

Self-dislike is so wearing, she thought dismally, and so paralysing. She couldn't write anything when she was in this state – not even something as banal as 'Watch Your Step!' with ten bullet points to drive home the Health and Safety prerogatives in the appropriate use of the equipment, the first one being 'Know When to Use a Ladder!' If you couldn't work that out for yourself, then surely you shouldn't be allowed out unaccompanied. 'Last year,' she had just typed, 'there were 14 deaths and 1,200 major injuries resulting from incorrect use of equipment.' Really, she should take this seriously, but she couldn't. At the same time she had also discovered that there were six serious injuries and one death related to incidents with dog bowls. Dog bowls! The world was going mad.

She sighed and looked at her watch. There was only an hour left before she would have to leave the house and walk the half-mile to the nursery to collect Archie, and that would be it for the day. She had asked a whey-faced child called Dillon back for lunch because it made it marginally easier if there was some sort of distraction, if it wasn't just her and Archie finding each other mutually unsatisfactory.

She read the e-mail again. 'I am writing to ask you to keep this day free to come and celebrate – all of us if possible – at a very special party we are going to organise to mark some important milestones in our lives. I intend to have a marquee, champagne, a buffet lunch provided by caterers, and maybe even dancing.' Annie pondered on this, noticing the change of person from 'we' to 'I' as Alice expounded on the plan. This idea had been cooked up by her alone, that was obvious. David was probably not even in on the planning. So what were the milestones? David's retirement? It was a family joke that he was pathologically gloomy about his work but also that giving it up hadn't brought much relief. David liked being gloomy. Was that worth celebrating? He was over sixty already and Alice would be sixty in the summer, so perhaps that was the reason for the party – but then what was so great about sixty? It was a nothing age these days. It wasn't old enough to be wonderful in any way. It just marked the start of the downhill slope towards deafness, eyesight going, hips needing replacing, memory loss, inability to work a new mobile telephone or download music on to an iPod. Annie heard all about it from her own mother, who was also still bitter after a twenty-year-old divorce from her father.

Oh, perhaps that was it! A wedding anniversary! She knew that David and Alice had been married since they were students – maybe they had reached one of the big noughts. She would have to check with Charlie. Being still together was an achievement, she had to accept that. She thought again of her mother, living alone in a small flat in Bexhill and eaten up with jealousy that her father had remarried and had a second family and was apparently happy – and it was her who had walked out on him! Annie remembered it well, because it had happened while she was in her first year at university and finding life hard enough to deal with as it was. Her mother had told her that she had waited until she had left home to tell her father that she wanted a divorce, which had made Annie feel responsible in some weird way.

But as far as she could judge, David and Alice were only together because she put up with him, which not many wives would do, certainly not of Annie's generation, and she derived some perverted satisfaction in being long-suffering and martyred. Did they love one another? Annie couldn't tell. She didn't seem to know about love any more. She didn't know if she loved Charlie. She often thought she didn't, and sometimes she hated him. She had been such an authority on the subject at one time. 'Ten Ways to Know This Is the One', she used to write in articles for the magazine. 'Fifty Ways to Show Him How Much You Care'. That had once been her world. Full of romantic certainties.

There was no point in even trying to continue work now. She would have to finish writing about stepladder

31

safety this evening when the boys were in bed. She switched off the computer and stared again at the unbroken grey slab of sky above her head until her mobile rang.

'Hello?'

'Annie? It's me. Alice!'

'Oh, hi!' Annie tried to make her voice bright, but it sounded leaden even to her own ears.

'Are you all right?'

'Yes, yes. I'm fine.'

'You haven't opened the e-mail I sent this morning?'

'I have, actually.'

'And?'

Annie tried to breathe normally. She could hear the excitement in Alice's voice, the expectancy.

'Yes! Well! Great! Very exciting!'

'You do think it's a good idea? Because I just thought, well, why not? Why not, for once in our lifetime, push the boat out and have a celebration. We never have, you know, not once. There's always been something else going on, some worry, or no money, or something, and I just thought, let's do it! And I have just had an idea. What do you think about a bouncy castle or one of those trampoline things that you can hire? For the children. I know Lisa's girls might think they're a bit too old, but the boys would love it, wouldn't they? And Tamzin and Georgie. It would entertain them while you enjoyed your lunch. What do you think? Because I saw an ad in the local paper and I should really get on and book it.'

Annie held her forehead with her spare hand as a wash of guilt swept over her. Alice was so kind, so thoughtful, so guileless in her enthusiasm, while she was a witch, shrivelled inside, her mind full of black bile.

'Anyway, I can't talk because I am at work, but I just wanted to run it by you. You are all right, are you? You sound a bit, well, down.'

Annie made a great effort. 'It's a fantastic idea. The boys would love it and I'm fine. Don't worry. I've just had a difficult morning wrestling with stepladder safety!'

'Oh, I see.' How could she? thought Annie. 'Well, I'm glad you like the idea. I haven't told David yet. I'm gathering support first. I must go. Give the boys a hug.'

Later, assembled outside the door of the nursery school, Annie stood with a gaggle of other mothers and a few bored au pairs talking into their mobile telephones or listening to their iPods. She knew a few of them quite well, swapping children on a fairly regular basis, but none were what she thought of as proper friends. One or two had buggies with babies strapped inside and looked hollow-eyed with exhaustion. Most were dressed in jeans and waterproof jackets and trainers with long shapeless hair caught up in elastic bands. Some who used the footpaths to the village were never out of rubber boots. Only the au pairs had any freshness or allure.

For years, all her professional life, Annie had judged other women by their sense of style or admired them for their glamour. Hers was the world of 'Ten Ways to Update Your Wardrobe', 'Key Buys for this Season', 'The Essential Coat'. She thought of the hours spent with the fashion editors arguing over future trends or the latest lipstick colour, and here she was in tracksuit bottoms, a sweatshirt, a woolly hat and a three-year-old parka, looking like a refugee or someone living in a hostel.

There was an excited flurry of activity inside the building before the double doors were thrown open and the mothers surged forward to collect their children and sign the register. Annie saw Archie sitting on the floor struggling with the Velcro strap on his shoe, which he had on the wrong foot. Dillon was standing patiently waiting, already in his rain jacket with the hood up, as if expecting the worst, his pale face peering out like a small nervous animal, his little paws clasping his school backpack.

Annie knelt beside Archie, and he looked up and beamed and put his arms roughly round her neck. 'I've made you a picture!' he said, almost shouting. 'Look!' On the floor by his school bag was a large square of mauve sugar paper with dried beans and macaroni stuck in what looked like a random pattern with some painted lines between.

Annie swapped the shoes to the right feet. 'What is it?' she asked, peering sideways. Archie had no artistic ability whatever as far as she could see. She dreaded the artwork that piled up everywhere, too awful to do anything with but impossible to throw away.

'Can't you see? Look! It's our house. See? That's you in the garden.' Annie saw a stick figure with a large round head and a big loop of smile. Archie was like Alice. He had drawn what he wanted in real life.

She bent to kiss the top of his head. 'It's lovely, darling. Really lovely! Thank you very much.' She stood up. 'Come on,' she said, taking Dillon's hand. 'Let's get home and have lunch, shall we, and then this afternoon, if it doesn't rain, we could go to the play park.'

It was Sabine who opened the e-mail sent by Alice to her mother. The first thing she did when she got in from school was to go to her bedroom and switch on her laptop. She was nearly thirteen and preferred the world she could enter via the internet to what was going on in her real life. It was two years since she and her sister Agnes, two years her junior, had been moved from their school in France to live in Wiltshire with their mother's new boyfriend, who was now her husband and their stepfather.

Their real father stayed in the village outside Bordeaux with his new wife, who was co-director of his wine exporting company. Sometimes Sabine tried to work out all the steps in her life – stepbrothers and sisters, step-mothers and fathers, step-aunts and uncles, step-cousins and step-grandparents. Now, Jacqui, her father's new wife, was expecting a baby, and that would be another sort of step, or maybe a half-baby something or other.

The baby coming made her mother very upset. She didn't like it mentioned and Sabine never told her that she was secretly excited about it, and so was Agnes, and that they didn't mind Jacqui and looked forward to going home when they went back to France in the holidays. Lisa didn't like them still thinking of the house in Pompignac as home. 'This is your home now,' she told them. 'Your home is with me in England.'

They were allowed to call Ollie 'Ollie', and not Daddy, and she was glad of that, and he didn't try and pretend that he was their father, and that was good too. She didn't mind him at all, really. He was funny a lot of the time, and not too bossy. He didn't make a lot of rules about things, like their mother did. She was always talking about what was 'acceptable', and it was mostly to do with giving her and Ollie what she called 'space'. It wasn't acceptable to just walk into their bedroom – Sabine supposed that they might be shagging – and it wasn't acceptable to interrupt them when they were eating dinner together, or to play music too loud or leave their stuff lying about in the sitting room.

Sometimes Sabine thought that their mother would prefer it if they weren't there at all, but then she made a great fuss when they went back to France and cried a lot and tele- phoned and texted and wanted them to talk on Skype as if she couldn't live without them.

Her mother didn't like anything to do with France any more. When people said, 'Ah, Bordeaux! That's a lovely city; a lovely part of France,' she always said, 'It's different when you live there,' and 'We're all glad to be back in England. You don't know how lucky you are living here, unless you've tried living abroad.' But Sabine liked France. She liked being half French. It gave her status at school for one thing – it marked her out as being a bit exotic and she liked that, whereas Agnes wouldn't speak a word of French and just wanted to be the same as everyone else. Sabine was pleased when people said she looked French because she was small and dark and skinny with large brown eyes; they never said that to Agnes, who was tall and golden- haired like their mother.

Sabine read the message about the party because she and Agnes and their mother shared the same e-mail address – although she had set up a Hotmail account of her own that her mother didn't know about. Her mother liked to keep an eye on who she and Agnes were in contact with. It was part of wanting to oversee their relationship with their father – Sabine knew that. Once she had sent him an e-mail complaining about something or other and saying she wished she was back in France with him, and her mother checked the 'sent' list and there was a terrible scene.

Sometimes Sabine felt unequal to what her life seemed to demand of her. She didn't know how to be the sort of daughter she felt her father wanted, at the same time keeping her mother from getting upset. She heard her talking to her friends on the telephone, saying that it was 'incredibly difficult' and how Jean-Louis was 'using the girls', and she knew that her parents were still wrangling in the French courts about the divorce settlement.

Sometimes Sabine forgot about it all and felt as if she was just an ordinary English schoolgirl and worried about ordinary things like school assignments and whether Delaware Hastings still liked her, but on the whole she couldn't forget. She had to worry in advance about the next school holiday and the arrangements that would have to be made to get her and Agnes out to Bordeaux, and the tension and unhappiness before they went and the silent drive to the airport with her mother holding Agnes' hand so tight that it hurt; and she had to worry about the past, about the things that had happened that had made her mother so unhappy and were never to be forgotten, and that were often mentioned in reference to her father, and, of course, to Jacqui.

She read the e-mail again and felt glad. She liked seeing these particular steps – Ollie's parents. They didn't seem to expect anything of her at all and were always pleased to see her and Agnes whatever else was going on, and they were allowed to do what they liked when they were there – read, or go shopping, or take Roger for a walk. Granted, it wasn't exciting stuff, but it was kind of easy and fun. Last time she and Agnes had cooked an entire meal, and they had made meringues that hadn't worked, and Alice had helped to turn them into îles flottantes and David had three helpings.

So they were having a party. Sabine tried to imagine it. Her mother complained about Ollie's family, saying there were too many of them – there were so many of them that she couldn't always get them straight. She said she felt swamped. She didn't like it when they telephoned, especially his sister Sadie, who she said never rang unless she wanted something. Sabine especially liked Sadie. She made her laugh. She was tall and quite fat with curly brown hair and she was always doing things like picking up stray dogs or getting into fights with people who made her angry, like some young man who cycled on a pavement and nearly knocked over an old man.

Sadie had two daughters, Tamzin and Georgie, who were younger than her and Agnes. They were lively and a bit wild, shrieking with laughter and the next minute quarrelling. Sabine wasn't sure who their dad was. He wasn't around anyway.

She supposed that Charlie, Ollie's brother, would be there because he was the eldest, with Annie, who didn't smile much, and their two little boys, whom she and Agnes were asked to look after. They were naughty and didn't do what they were told. They threw things and stuck out their tongues and made Tamzin and Georgie laugh by saying rude things. They would all be there at the party, she supposed.

She heard steps coming up the stairs and then the door of her bedroom opened. 'What are you doing?' It was her mother's voice.

'Nothing. There's a message here from Ollie's mum, asking us to a party.'

'A party?'

'Yes. A big one. You'd better have a look.' She got up and moved over and her mother sat in her place. Sabine leaned on her shoulder and looked at her mother's hair, which was deep gold, like clear honey, and tied back in a ponytail. It hung down her back like a streak of amber. Her father had loved her hair. Sometimes in the evenings he used to sit on the sofa and brush it so that it spread out like a shawl on her shoulders. Jacqui had very short dark hair, like a boy.

Lisa read the message and sighed. 'I suppose we'll have to go,' she said. 'It sounds as though Alice is making a big deal of it.' She looked up at Sabine. 'Do you mind, darling? It'll be a whole day. It will be boring for you and Agnes.'

'No, I don't mind. I like going to Ollie's house. I like his mum and dad. They're cool.'

Lisa laughed. 'Cool? Well! I wouldn't have called them that. Can you be cool and sixty?' She stood up and pointed to the pile of clean, folded clothes she had put on the bed. 'Put those away, there's a good girl. Have you got much homework?'

'A bit. I'm just about to start.'

'You're a good girl, Sabine. Come here,' and Lisa pulled her daughter towards her in a hug. Sabine loved her mother's tallness and strength and the smell of her. She smelled of soap and fresh air, like washing from the clothes line that had been in the sun all day. Sabine had always thought she was too big and strong to ever be hurt, and yet her father, who was smaller than her by several inches, had managed to do just that. Sabine remembered the nights that her mother had come into her bed to sleep, her face hot and her hair wet with tears, her strong, big, soft body taking up most of the space.

Lisa aimed a kiss at Sabine's forehead and went out. Sabine closed the door behind her and went back to her laptop. She would just check her Hotmail account and send her dad a message. He hardly ever replied, but she liked to think of a connection between them as the message sped on its way, like a very thin line stretching from her bedroom in Wiltshire across the hills and green fields, across the choppy grey water of the Channel and south, south, down into the sunshine of beautiful France and all the way to the grey stone house in Pompignac.

Sadie read Alice's e-mail and rang her mother straight back at work in the surgery.

'What's all this about, Mum? Why are you forking out on a posh party? I'd have done the catering for you and saved you thousands.'

Alice, on the other end, aware of the hush in the waiting room where she was sure her voice could be heard, thought of Sadie's cooking – always inspired and delicious but haphazard in presentation and usually served from the saucepan. 'That's lovely of you, darling, but I want this to be a special day for you as well,' she said. 'I don't want any of us to even have to go into the kitchen.'

'What does Dad say about it all?'

'I haven't told him yet.' Alice lowered her voice even

further. 'I wanted to get your support first. You know what he's like. He'll be against it at the start and then enjoy it more than anyone else.'

Sadie wasn't so sure. 'Do you think he will? Getting us all together? Wouldn't you rather celebrate all this stuff by going off on a really good holiday, just the two of you? Spend the money on that.' She had a vision of the family camping holidays they had all endured as children, and how her mother had gallantly cooked sausages and kept cheerful with rain dripping down her neck and four whining kids to cope with. Surely, now that it was possible, she'd prefer to go and stay in a luxury hotel somewhere warm rather than throw this party for them all?

'No, I wouldn't. What would be the point? Dad and I prefer a simple life — we don't like luxury. It makes us feel uncomfortable. And anyway, this is about all of us — the family — not just about Dad and me. I want you all here to celebrate. To celebrate our lives together.'

Sadie tried to picture it, but it was beyond her to imagine anything other than a peace camp or a sort of Glastonbury gathering, with the guests lounging about and smoking dope, whereas her mother wanted them smartened up and on best behaviour and with everything set up in a grown-up way. Sadie didn't have the imagination for that sort of thing. On the whole her life was not subjected to much advance planning — it just rolled along and she responded to what turned up. Still, she told herself, if it was what her mother wanted, she deserved their co-operation, and Sadie determined that they would give it to her. She suddenly saw her role in all of this. She would be the one who made it happen. She would drag the others along with her if necessary.

'Well, Mum, if it's what you'd really like. I know someone who hires out giant teepees. I could give him a call. He'd give me a good price.'

'Thanks, darling, but I want this to be traditional. I want a proper white marquee with a peach lining.'

'God, Mum, that's not really us, is it?'

'But why shouldn't it be? For once. Doing things properly. In style.'

What is 'us', anyway? thought Alice as she put down the telephone. Why should things always be worse than how she dreamed they'd be? Why should they always be smaller, cheaper, meaner, shabbier, less fun, less romantic? For once, just once, she was going to insist on the very best.

Sadie, who was sorting vegetables for an organic box scheme in a cold shed on a farm at the end of a deeply rutted and muddy drive, thought about the party. Not since she was a child and at the jelly and orange squash stage had she had a celebration of her own – not that she would have wanted one. Even when she had married Tom, the girls' father, she'd only gone from the registry office to the pub with a few friends. She'd been so far gone with pregnancy that she wasn't up to doing much else. She'd celebrated her divorce three years later by getting extremely drunk with her two best girlfriends. That was the sort of party she liked – one that just evolved and ended up with someone ringing for a takeaway, and a terrible mess and a hangover the next day.

She counted pearly mushrooms into brown paper bags, deftly twisting the ends to hold them closed. What was it exactly that her mother was after? She supposed she could understand the birthday party, although she couldn't really see what was so special about being sixty. Then there was the wedding anniversary – forty years, apparently – and her dad's retirement.

Sadie used to find it almost impossible to think of her parents' lives as anything other than the background to her own, which, naturally enough, she judged to be much more interesting and eventful. Now, as her own children were growing up, she realised how much she and her brothers and sister took their parents completely for granted. It was hard to think of them as individuals, with the same sort of needs and emotional ups and downs as she herself experienced. The details and workings of their marriage had never interested her. It was just woven into what she thought of as 'my family'. Perhaps her mother was right to feel that they had reached a sort of milestone that should be recognised.

All that money, though. It seemed a terrible waste. At the moment Sadie was extremely hard up. Kyle, her partner, who was five years younger than her, was a herdsman on the farm where the organic vegetables were grown, and where Sadie worked too while Tamzin and Georgie were at school. They had a tied cottage, picturesque to look at, but a small, dank place in which to live. It was set just off the stockyard where twice a day the dairy cows stood about waiting to be milked.

Sadie still had a large lump of student loan to pay back, although a fat lot of good her degree was to her. Women's Studies didn't really equip her to do anything very much, which was what her father had argued at the time when she was first going to university. 'For heaven's sake study something that will help you get a job!' he'd argued. 'You're a good scientist – do Chemistry or Pharmacy or Natural Sciences. You could get a well-paid job in the pharmaceutical industry or with a multinational oil company.' God, he'd made her angry – deliberately winding her up when he knew that she considered both industries the work of the devil.

She'd modified her views a bit since then. Now she had to be more practical. It was no fun being on the dole or doing low-paid boring jobs, and anyway, there was little work around where she now lived with Kyle in the middle of Dorset. She helped out on the farm, which was something. She enjoyed working in the polytunnels with the warmth on her back, or hoeing outside between the rows of chard and spinach. It meant that she could trudge down the long drive every morning and afternoon to meet the school bus, and there were jobs she could do when the girls were at home too. They often had to amuse themselves while she was busy in the packing shed, and they could be quite useful, picking over the fruit or putting eggs into cartons.

She tried to imagine being with Kyle for forty years. She'd be nearly seventy. An old woman. What would have become of them? She couldn't think that far ahead. When her parents were her age, they had four children and lived in the house where they still lived. Her father was already in the job at the university from which he had only recently retired. All that certainty. All that monotonous certainty.

How could she know what she would want in five years'

time? How could she know where life would take her and what would be right for her then? Kyle was great. They were in love. He had helped her so much to regain her self-esteem after the bashing that the breakdown of her marriage had given her. He loved her for what she was, overweight and chaotic and warm and funny and good in bed. Unlike Tom, a struggling musician, who was tired of her almost as soon as they married and who started to play around when she was pregnant again so soon after Tamzin was born. Tom didn't do pregnancies or babies. He wanted full attention on himself.

Anyway, thought Sadie, as she checked the box list and added a knobbly, muddy parsnip, if a party is what Mum wants, a party is what she'll get. I'll see to that. I'll get the others on side. When she considered her brothers and sister, she couldn't imagine any of them showing the sort of encouragement that she now felt her mother deserved.

By the end of the day, the only household Alice had not managed to contact was that of Marina and Ahmed, and she would try to reach them tomorrow. She felt satisfied that the organisation of the party was now under way. Responses had ranged from tentative to enthusiastic, but nobody had said that they thought it was a bad idea. As she shut down her computer when the last patient had tottered out of after-noon surgery, she felt as confident as was possible, given her natural tendency towards uncertainty.

'I don't know why you're so anxious about what they'll think,' said Margaret, applying lipstick before she drove herself home to an evening with her cats, as far as Alice knew. 'They should be glad to get asked to a posh do like you're planning. Everyone loves a chance to dress up!' She spoke as one who firmly believed this to be the case.

'Well, I hope so,' said Alice, changing into her driving shoes. 'But, you know, sometimes it's hard to know how people will see things. Often it's not quite as you do yourself. The next thing is to tell David.'

'He'll be all right about it, don't you worry,' said Margaret, patting at her hair combs. 'Although it ought to be him doing all this for you, not the other way round.'

'If it was up to him, it would never happen. Not in a million years.'

'He must know how lucky he is having a wife like you. He should be glad to celebrate the fact that you've put up with him for all these years.'

Alice felt touched by Margaret's loyalty, although she knew her remark was misjudged. It would never occur to David to think himself lucky. She was his wife and that was that. He would think it was more good judgement on his part in choosing the sort of sensible, steady girl who was unlikely to cause any bother or upset. That was his view of women, really. That on the whole they were a lot of trouble.

Would she consider that she was lucky in having him as a husband? Of course she would. He had so many good qualities, the most important of which was that he was honest and absolutely trustworthy and dependable. Straight as a die, people said of him. And he was still attractive. She thought of the new haircut and how it enhanced his craggy face. He was a handsome man, and the best thing was that he was quite unaware of it. If anything, she was the lucky one.

David had passed a restless day and had nothing to show for it. He had spent most of the morning on his computer, checking his e-mails every few minutes. There were no new messages other than invitations to enlarge his penis by three inches. What he was now anxious about was that perhaps the reply he had sent hadn't got there. Maybe his network connection was malfunctioning. Perhaps it was permitting incoming messages but losing outgoing. He thought about it, and then sent off a couple of messages to former colleagues asking them to forward him a lost telephone number. One of them was sure to respond and then he would know that all was well with the system and that the delay in receiving a reply was because Julia wasn't as excited about getting back in touch as he was, sad old man that he had evidently become.

He was taken by surprise when at half past four he heard the sound of Alice's key in the front door, and he jumped up, startled, glancing at his watch. Where had the day gone? He couldn't admit that he hadn't even taken Roger for a walk – just shoved him out into the back garden every few hours.

Guiltily he turned off the computer and went to the top of the stairs. He could hear Alice in the kitchen and he wondered briefly whether he had cleared up the remains of his lunch. He didn't think it was likely. A strategy came to him that generally worked, and he hurried down the stairs and into the kitchen.

'Sorry about the mess,' he said, before she could say anything. She was putting things away in cupboards with her back to him. 'I had someone – one of my old PhD students – suddenly ask me to look at a paper. I've been working on it all day.' Liar, liar, pants on fire, he thought.

47

'Oh, I see. I suppose I'll have to forgive you then.' Alice's voice was light and unmenacing.

'Would you like a cup of tea?' he offered.

'Oh, yes. That would be nice.'

'How was your day?'

'Okay. Fine. Actually . . .' Alice took a deep breath and turned towards him. 'Actually, David, there is something I want to talk to you about.'

Irrational fear overtook him. How did she know? Was there some means by which she could access and read his e-mails? Did she know that he had passed the day in a state of arousal because Julia had come into his life again?

'I was thinking we should have a party – not until the spring, but a proper party to celebrate our birthdays and our wedding anniversary and everything. Invite all the family and the neighbours and some of our best friends. A proper do with a marquee and caterers. What do you think?'

He looked at her blankly. She had caught him completely on the back foot.

'Well? Say something.'

'It's a bit sudden, isn't it?' was all he could think of to say.

'Sudden? What do you mean? How can it be sudden when the date I have in mind is in May – two months away?'

David felt she was staring at him in an unnatural way. 'Well, if it's what you want,' he said uneasily. 'If you think it's a good idea.' He filled the kettle at the sink, glad of something to do.

There was a strange atmosphere in the kitchen and Alice could not put her finger on what it was that lay unsaid between them. She looked at her husband curiously.

'Really?' she said. 'I thought you'd make a fuss — put up a bit more resistance. I know parties aren't really your thing.'

'How do you know what my thing is?'

'I should do after all these years!'

Her words sounded smug and patronising to David. He finished making the tea feeling rebellious. Let her think what she liked. What had Julia said? 'I remember you as being the most attractive man in the department . . .'

'You don't mind, then?'

'No. Have a party, if it's what you want. If it will make you happy.'

Taking his mug with him, he went out of the kitchen and Alice heard his feet on the stairs. Well, she thought, *that* hadn't gone as she had expected. So he didn't mind. He had accepted the idea without a murmur. She sat at the table to drink her tea and wondered why his answers had left her dissatisfied rather than pleased. Of course, in an ideal world he might have said, 'Darling! What a wonderful idea!' or 'You deserve the best party in the world!' but both those reactions were so unlikely as to be absurd. It was more the fact that David hadn't raised any objections that upset her. It felt as if an important step in the party planning process had been left out. Maybe by supper time he would be back on form and she would be given the chance to parade the argument she had so carefully worked out in her head.

Sitting there, she felt affronted that he had simply acquiesced, taken his tea and walked away. It wasn't good enough.

It wasn't giving her idea for a party the respect or attention it deserved. Picking up her mug, she went out of the
kitchen and up the stairs. She was not going to allow him
to retreat like that. She would give him her reasons for
having a party whether he wanted to hear them or not.

Chapter Three

SADIE LAUNCHED HER campaign by telephoning Marina, with whom she had a relationship that had not really changed much since they were small. Sadie was still the baby sister as far as Marina was concerned, despite the fact that she had led the way by several years in more recent life-altering events such as getting married and becoming pregnant.

She telephoned her office number because she was too impatient to wait until the evening. Marina answered instantly. She was an investment banker with a City bank, and the tone of her work voice implied there was no time for chat, but such a notion was lost on Sadie, who had more than enough time for everything. That morning, in fact, she had sat on her doorstep with a mug of coffee and gone to sleep in the quite warm spring sunshine while her four speckled chickens pecked in the dirt round her feet.

'Hi! It's only me.'

'Sadie? Has something happened?'

'No. Do you mean something bad?'

'I mean you never telephone me at work.'

'Well I needed to speak to you. Should I have made an appointment?'

'Don't be silly. What do you want?' Sadie could hear a pen tapping on a desk. She could imagine Marina in a City suit, swivelling in a desk chair away from listening colleagues.

'Have you spoken to Mum?'

'No. Why? There *is* something wrong, isn't there?'

'No, there isn't. For goodness' sake. She's planning a party, that's all.'

'A party? What do you mean – a party?'

'Marina! What's the matter with you? You know what a party is.'

'What sort of party? What does she want a party for?'

'That's exactly it. She wants a big family party. A posh one with a tent and caterers and all that stuff. It's her sixtieth and they've been married for forty years and Dad's retired, and I suppose that she feels there hasn't been that much in the way of celebration so far.'

There was a silence while Marina consulted the in-box of her computer.

'I've got an e-mail here. I haven't had time to open it. Okay, so what's the deal?'

'Deal? I just want to make sure that you will be supportive. Of Mum. It means a lot to her.' Sadie could tell from Marina's voice that she felt wrong-footed, as if Sadie was getting at her for something indefinable. Well, it wouldn't hurt her to feel guilty for being so preoccupied that she neglected her own family. If Marina had a bad conscience, it wasn't Sadie's fault.

'Yeah, okay, I get it. Well, I'll give her a ring.'

'Exactly.'

'What do you mean, "exactly"?'

'Marina, you're doing it again. I mean yes, exactly. Give her a ring and say yes, and how lovely.'

'I don't need you to tell me what to do. Since when have you been so considerate to Mum? When I think of what—'

'Marina! Stop it! We're not six years old!' Sadie felt pleased with that. Her sister had always accused her of being childish, and it was good to turn the tables. 'I just wanted to make sure that your reaction was favourable, because I happen to think that it is really important that if this is what Mum wants, we should all do our best to make it happen for her.'

'Okay, I hear you. I shall have to check with Ahmed. It will be a long day for Mo . . .'

'Marina! Just say you'll be there.' Sadie enjoyed this unusual feeling of superiority.

'All right, all right. I just don't like being steamrollered, which is what this feels like. There are some other con-siderations here as far as I'm concerned. Anyway, I can't talk now. I'll give you a call this evening.'

Like hell you will, thought Sadie. Marina didn't get home before seven o'clock and then she had to squeeze in her quality time with Mo before he went to bed. Sadie could not remember the last time her sister had telephoned her to have a chat of any sort unless it was to ask her advice about some aspect of childcare – advice that was generally ignored.

Sadie sometimes wondered why she felt hostility towards how her sister chose to manage her life, when generally she was a pretty laissez-faire sort of person. She supposed it was a kind of jealousy – which surprised her because she didn't consider herself a jealous person either. The truth was that she was envious that Marina was so bloody well-off. She must be taking home well over a hundred thousand a year, Sadie reckoned, while she and Kyle were scraping along at less than a quarter of that, and although she resented admitting it, because it felt like a contradiction of everything she stood for, money did make a huge difference.

She sometimes felt tired of having nothing left over for things like clothes and holidays, and she worried that Kyle felt burdened by supporting her and the girls while their father fought paying proper maintenance.

Sadie went back to sitting on the step and thought about Kyle. He was wonderful, in every way. He had come into her life when she was at her lowest ebb and carried her away in his strong farm worker's arms. Not literally, of course. She was far too hefty for anyone to do that. She still found it amazing that he loved her and that three weeks after she met him she had moved out of the horrible flat in Yeovil and into his cottage on the farm. For the next six weeks she had to ferry the girls to and from their primary school, a forty-minute trip each way, but she managed to get them places in the village school by the time the summer term began, and after that life settled down.

That was nearly a year ago and things were still good, although maybe not quite so romantic as before, but then you couldn't expect that sort of stuff to last. Real life wasn't like that. They still loved each other and that was the main thing, and got on well and didn't row, which was good for the girls after all the upsetting scenes they had witnessed.

Sadie felt a heaviness in the region of her heart. Maybe it was sadness or regret or contrition, she didn't know which. Of course she wished that things could be different. She wished that she hadn't made a mess of things, that she hadn't made people unhappy, but there was no point in dwelling on the negative. She was lucky in lots of ways. She had Tamzin and Georgie, for one thing. She suddenly had a vision of their anxious little faces, of how they had clung to her hands on the first day at their new school. She would make it up to them, she had promised so many times. She would make sure that they were always safe and happy. However, this thought did not bolster her spirits because she knew that it was not always possible. She was no longer the confident girl that she had once been. Her marriage and subsequent divorce had seen to that. Shit did happen.

There was the new baby as well. She had told Kyle last night, and although he hadn't been exactly thrilled, she knew that given time he would be glad. He just had to get used to the idea. She couldn't help but smile when she thought of their baby growing inside her. The seal on their relationship. The baby that would make them into a proper family. Goodness, though, it would be easier if they had a bit more money coming in, and that was why she envied Marina.

That evening Sadie telephoned what she still thought of as home and Alice answered.

'Have you heard from Marina?'

'Yes, she rang this evening. Poor thing, she sounded exhausted. She'd only just got in. Ahmed had put Mo to bed and was cooking supper.'

'Well, he is a kept man, so why shouldn't he?' said Sadie. 'If he was a woman it would be taken for granted that he should.'

'Sadie! That's not fair. Ahmed is not "kept". He's doing everything he can to get work. It's not easy being a Syrian journalist in London.'

'Well, that doesn't stop him from looking after the baby.'

Alice sighed. She felt too weary to argue. She had just finished clearing up after supper and was looking forward to sitting down.

'Did she say anything about your party?'

'Yes! That's why she rang. She said they'll be there and she's happy to help.'

'Good. I told her she better had.'

'Oh, you've talked about it already, have you?'

'Yes. I rang her today. I'm right behind you on this, Mum. I'll get the others on side, don't worry.'

'Well, that's good.' Alice wondered how quickly Sadie would put everyone's backs up. It was a talent she had, good-natured and well-intentioned though she was.

'Have you told Dad yet?'

'Yes, I have. Amazingly, he is quite happy with the idea.'

'Really? That's a bit out of character. A bit of a surprise.'

'Yes, it was to me. I don't know how actively *helpful* he'll be, but he doesn't oppose the idea in general. So now I can begin planning and organising. I'm going to start ringing round caterers and getting quotes for the food.'

'It'll cost you a fortune. Much better to let me do it. I could cook a salmon and a ham and all that summer party stuff.'

'I know you could, darling, and it's really kind of you to offer, but I want this to be a party for you too – for everyone.'

'Well, make sure that the food is locally sourced and ethically whatever. Some catering firms buy their chicken from Thailand and Korea, and are very dodgy about refreezing defrosted party puddings.'

'Of course. Only the best!'

There was a pause, and for a moment Sadie found she wanted to tell her mother about the baby, that when the party took place in May she would be four months pregnant, but something stopped her. There was a nagging fear that maybe this baby wasn't the best idea, that from a financial point of view they weren't in the best position to provide for another child and that what Kyle had said last night about it being a fucking disaster was true in more ways than one. Not telling what was on her mind was an unusual experience for Sadie, who was open and direct by nature and whose relationship with her mother, even when she was a tempestuous teenager, had always been close.

I'll tell her later, she thought. After I've seen the doctor. No point in getting her worked up until I know for sure.

But the truth was that she did know for sure, and it was something else that she couldn't quite explain that was restraining her from passing on the news.

Alice put down the telephone, already worrying about Sadie, who she felt was not quite herself. It was so hard to know how things really were for her younger daughter, who seemed to blunder through life, full of enthusiasm and optimism, until something happened to bring everything crashing round her ears and she was left in a depressed, broken heap. Alice had doubts about her relationship with Kyle, who was a nice enough boy but, at twenty-four, too young to take on Sadie and the girls. When she saw them together he looked almost like Sadie's child rather than her partner.

As for Tamzin and Georgie, well, she couldn't allow herself to think about what their lives had been like and what they had been through. She and David had done what they could, having the girls to stay for quite long periods when Sadie had made them homeless by moving out of her marital home, and she often had them after school if Sadie was off somewhere. It was such a good thing that they were close enough for her and David to be useful. They were such funny, cheery, bouncy little things, brown as berries with tangled gypsy hair since they lived on the farm, and generally seemed untouched by the lack of stability in their lives.

They could be wilful and naughty, though, especially with their mother, almost as if they sensed that they could punish her for being a single mother. Once, Alice had driven up the appalling muddy drive and when she had drawn up in the farmyard the cottage door stood open and had heard spine-chilling screams coming from inside. With terror in her heart she had jumped from the car and run in to find Tamzin lying on the sitting-room floor in a paroxysm of rage that Sadie, at the kitchen sink, was studiously ignoring.

'Whatever's the matter?' Alice had cried. 'Tamzin, what's happened, darling?'

'Don't "darling" her,' said Sadie, not turning round. 'She's having a tantrum because I've told her she can't go riding on Saturday.'

'Oh dear, but why not? She loves it, doesn't she?' Comet, a short-legged hairy pony at the local riding school, was one of the things that Tamzin was most enthusiastic about.

'Because, Mum, she can't always have what she wants. You taught us that, didn't you? I can't take her on Saturday because I'm going to a willow-basket-making workshop, and Kyle will be at work.'

Alice was silent. Shouldn't Tamzin come first? she wanted to ask. Hadn't she had enough taken from her in her short life? Surely Sadie could see that the fact that she minded so much was an indication of how important it was for her. She knelt beside her granddaughter and took her hand. 'Shhhh! Shhh! Don't cry like that.' Tamzin looked up at her, her face scarlet with emotion and great sobs racking her little body.

'Comet will be waiting for me,' she croaked. 'I look after him on Saturday mornings. I fill his hay net and groom him and everything.'

'Well, someone else can do it this week, can't they? He won't starve just because you're not there,' said Sadie.

'Sadie! Can't I take her? I don't mind coming over and picking her and Georgie up. David can collect them later from the riding school and they can stay the night with us.' Alice knew that she shouldn't interfere, but she couldn't help it.

Grudgingly Sadie had agreed, turning round, wiping her hands on a tea towel and finishing them off on the backside of her jeans. The idea of a night off was an enticement, as Alice knew it would be. 'But honestly, Mum, you're just reinforcing the idea that a tantrum pays off.'

Alice had let that go. In a way Sadie was right, but as a grandmother her instinct was to try and compensate for the deficiencies of Tamzin's childhood.

Upstairs, David wedged a wad of newspaper under the door and turned on his laptop. It seemed to react more and more slowly now that he was impatient to get online. With half an ear he was listening for Alice. She would be going to sit down any moment and would wonder where he had got to. It was unusual for him to be back up in his room in the evening, when they generally sat together in the sitting room and read the newspaper or watched the television. He could only allow himself a minute or two to check his e-mails. He already felt shaken by the earlier conversation he had had with Alice. It was stupid of him to react defensively when of course she knew nothing – how could she? By behaving strangely he was drawing attention to himself, which was the last thing he wanted just at the moment.

He was so strung up that he jumped when he heard the telephone ringing downstairs and then Alice answering it. He guessed it was one of the girls – Sadie, probably. Marina had already telephoned earlier. He could hear the faint sound of Alice's voice and guessed it was something about this party idea that she had just chucked at him. Well, he would go along with it. It would divert her attention for one thing and also, when he thought about it, he couldn't work up much opposition to the idea. Opposition required more vigorous involvement than he felt capable of at the moment.

At last the screen cleared to show his e-mail in-box. Nothing new. Not even a message from Lindy wanting to talk hot. He had already received replies from his old colleagues – one short, the other chatty, both giving him the telephone number he had pretended to have lost – so he knew his system was working. He hadn't replied to either. He couldn't put his mind to it or even summon up the old jocular common-room language. He tried 'send and receive' again – still nothing. He revisited the original message that he had received that morning and then read his reply. Had he got it terribly wrong in interpreting Julia's message as provocatively flirtatious? She used no punctuation whatever, which he found confusing and would normally have irritated him, but now he thought it refreshingly young and unrestrained, and the opening '*hi*' – that was youthful too. He had 'hi'd' her back in his reply, which he now read again.

Hi, Julia.

Of course I remember you. How could I not? You were a breath of fresh air in the department, and I was extremely sorry to see you go. I am afraid that university politics being what they are, no amount of pressure on your behalf had any effect on the decision. Thank you for all the nice things you said about me. Are you sure this is not a case of mistaken identity?! I would be delighted to help you in any way – well, within legal constraints, of course! I think, as you suggest, that it would be best to meet to have a chat. I shall wait to hear from you. Since my retirement, I am available most days, although evenings would be more difficult. I am sorry to hear about your marriage. It can't have been an easy time for you.

Anyway, we can catch up when we meet. I look forward to hearing from you.

Then came the difficulty of how to sign off. Julia had put '*lol*' and signed off '*Julia (ex-peters now fairfield)*, with a smiley face – the sort of thing his daughters might have done. In the end, he had just put '*David*'. Anything else seemed undignified.

Reading through what he had written, he felt that he couldn't have expressed himself better, but he could certainly have been more professional in tone – treating Julia as a senior lecturer would the research student she had once been. He could have been more truthful, too. From a departmental point of view she had been pretty hopeless and her research definitely second rate. It had been no surprise that she had been unable to get funding to continue.

It was true that she had been a breath of fresh air, or at least an unsettling influence on the staid atmosphere of the department, where the average age was at least fifty and there were only two full-time female lecturers. Julia was in her mid-thirties, a mature student, and desperately keen and eager but always demanding attention and needing special consideration because life generally seemed to connive against her. As far as David could remember she had a difficult journey each day in to the campus, and her husband lost his job, or her mother was ill, or she was desperately searching for a new flat and the sale of her present house had fallen through. There always seemed to be some sort of crisis going on. She was often late to meetings and arrived pink-faced and distressed and needed to stay on afterwards to have a rushed little talk with Roger McCrae, the department head, which always seemed to end with him patting her shoulder in a fatherly way.

She was small, fair-haired and pretty in a disorganised style, trailing scarves and weighed down by an immense leather bag under which her frail little shoulder sagged pathetically. She had small white hands that she used a lot, fluttering them as she spoke, patting at her mouth, tossing back her wispy hair. She appeared vulnerable and, well, David had to admit, ineffective. In fact, when it came to withholding her further funding there had been no dissent whatever, as far as he could remember. The sooner Julia gave up her academic pretensions the better, was the general consensus.

She had not gone quietly. There had been some sort of unpleasantness, he remembered now – some sort of threat of a university inquiry, some allegations of sex discrimination – but it had come to nothing as far as he knew.

He had felt sorry for her, in a way. He had seen her sitting in her car in the car park on a wet afternoon towards the end of term. He had been too embarrassed to look in her direction because his first glance told him that she was crying. He scuttled past, head down, but she opened her car door and called to him and he had no option but to turn and go back to talk to her. She got out of the car wearing a long waxed coat that flapped round her ankles and a leather cowboy hat. She looked as if she had been engaged in something to do with cattle or horses, but her face was distorted by tears and streaked with eye make-up.

David had felt at a complete loss, and looking distractedly from side to side but finding no source of help in either direction had suggested that they go and have a cup of coffee.

'Okay, but not in the refectory,' sniffed Julia. 'I don't want to see anyone I know.' So they had trailed into town and sat at a table in a steamy café, where David tried to take control of the situation and went to the counter and ordered two cappuccinos and substantial slabs of flapjack, the sort of thing that sustained hearty fell walkers on twenty-mile hikes. When he took them back, he found Julia staring tragically at the plastic daisies stuck in a jug that was sitting on the table.

'Oh dear, I don't do dairy!' she cried, fluttering her hands, as David put the cups down, and he had to go back to the counter and get her a herbal tea. He couldn't remember now what they had talked about – mainly Julia's problems, he would guess. He had eaten both the flapjacks in the end, while she sipped at her tea, which smelled of grass cuttings. But he did remember how he enjoyed seeing her large pale eyes fill with tears and how he had felt moved to reach out and hold one of the little white fluttering hands, like rescuing a butterfly from batting against a window pane.

He couldn't have been much comfort to her, but afterwards, when they went back to their cars, she had reached up and put her arms round him and laid her head against his chest and thanked him fervently for being such a friend. He had no option but to place a large hand on the back of the waxed coat and pat it up and down as he might have done to a dog.

That was the last time he had seen her, and to be honest, he hadn't thought about her since, until the e-mail that had come out of the blue and disturbed his peace of mind. Anyway, he thought as he prepared to switch off the laptop, it was late now, and she hadn't responded, so he would just have to hang on and wait for her reply.

He would have one more trawl before he switched off and went down to Alice. With a start, he saw a new message jumping on to the screen. The sight of the little closed envelope made his heart leap. It was from Julia, and when he opened it he saw that it was very long and that it began, *'dear david i cant tell you what it meant to me . . .'*

Later, as he stood at the top of the stairs listening to the muffled sound of the television from below, he knew without any doubt that he was being foolish, and that he disapproved strongly of the excitement and arousal that he was experiencing, but he also knew that he was set on a path from which he did not have the will to turn. For the moment, anyway. For the first time for many months he felt vigorous and alive.

Thankfully, Annie signed off her last piece of work and touched the key to send it on its way. Part of her job was to ghost-write the managing director's quarterly message to the staff, and she had tried to make it jaunty and encouraging in the face of poor company figures and the threat of job losses. Goodness only knew whether it would be accepted by him – a particularly soulless and unattractive man, in her view. He was apt to butcher what she wrote when she attempted to sound human or sympathetic. She had become quite a friend of his PA – a cheerful woman called Jennifer – and had run the gist of what she intended to write past her that morning. They had both laughed when Jennifer said, 'Well, if you asked me who wrote *that*, his would be the last name to spring to mind! I don't think he's ever wished anyone a happy anything in his life. *Profitable*, maybe, or *productive*, but not *happy*. Happy would be a waste of time.'

Frankly, Annie thought, she couldn't care less what happened to what she had written. It could end up in the shredder for all she cared as long as she got a cheque at the end of the month.

Downstairs she could hear Charlie putting the boys to bed. He got them overexcited by chasing them from room to room as if he were a boy-eating bear, but it was unusual for him to be back from school in time to do any of the evening routine and she was grateful for the time to finish off her work after supper.

She could hear Rory's screams becoming hysterical. He would never go to sleep now. Annie felt a wave of irritation. Charlie, blast him, just couldn't do anything right. He behaved as if he was a visitor to the family when he came home early – like a specially indulgent uncle. He disregarded her routine and just did things his way. He read the paper while the boys messed about with their supper and then shovelled the remains in the bin without insisting that they ate at least three spoons of vegetable. When he bathed them he left the floor swimming in water and the towels sopping wet and then played boisterous games just when they should be calming down for going to bed. They loved playing with him – she admitted that – but his main achievement was making life more difficult for her when he wasn't there, which was most of the bloody time.

She switched off the computer and sat swivelling on her office chair. As usual when she felt like this, a dialogue began in her head. A more sensible, balanced version of herself pointed out that in the long school holidays Charlie did more than his fair share of childcare and that she was better off than many of the school-gate mothers as far as that was concerned. Quite a lot of the fathers worked in London – an hour away by train – and were always unavailable except at weekends. All out-of-school activities, and even emergencies, had to be dealt with by their wives alone. Annie often overheard the sort of ad hoc arrangements that had to be made to cover hospital appointments or some other problematical situation. 'If you collect Oliver from football on Tuesday, I'll have Sean on Monday after swimming.' Heaven and hell days, they called them, when they were either with or without children.

Her bitter alter ego answered back that at least these absent men were well paid and came with all the advantages of a high standard of living: holidays abroad and help at home and money to spend on the sort of things that had been Annie's meat and drink when she was single. Four years ago Charlie had given up a good job in the City to retrain as a teacher, and although he was always pointing out the many advantages of his new, downsized career, and claimed that seeing more of his children was one of them, Annie often asked herself who it was who benefited most.

In her resentful moments it seemed to her that Charlie had effectively given up nothing. He loved teaching and bounced out of the door each morning with an eager smile on his face. The long hours he put in were taken for granted at the boys' independent grammar school where he worked. When he had applied for the post it had been spelled out that he would be expected to offer extracurricular activities, and the fact that he was a gifted club rugby player in his earlier days swung his appointment in the face of stiff competition. For two terms of the school year he coached the Junior Colts, and there was rugby practice or matches most Saturday mornings. In the summer he umpired interminable cricket matches on Saturday afternoons. He had made a lot of friends on the young staff and there was considerable camaraderie, and beer-drinking sessions out of school.

Oh yes, it was all very well for Charlie, whined the voice in Annie's head, because it was Annie who had given up her whole life to come and live in a dead-end village full of smug middle-class families. It was Annie who had given up her work, her identity, her friends, everything. It was she who had sacrificed herself to bearing and rearing children and Charlie seemed to have simply transmogrified into a family man with no accompanying pain. In fact he had got bigger, wider, louder, more confident, more sure of the rightness of his opinions, and above all he wore the mantle of self-righteousness because, after all, teaching was a worthy profession whereas the world of magazines and fashion was shallow, worthless, narcissistic.

She, by contrast, had grown smaller, greyer and shadowy. Her hair needed a proper cut but she hadn't found a decent salon in the nearest town, and she hadn't bought anything new to wear since the boys were born. Her remaining designer clothes hung unworn in the wardrobe, because what use was Galliano to her now?

There were a number of staff social events organised at Charlie's school and those that Annie had agreed to attend had been a hideous realisation of what she had become – a lesser, insignificant person. Nobody asked her what she did and the other wives were cheerful, uncomplaining types who stood alertly at their husbands' sides and listened, smiling, to their conversations. Their eager expressions reminded Annie of dogs grateful not to have been left at home.

'Your husband's great!' she was told by the head of sport, a man she instantly disliked for his shaved head and nose pushed to one side from prolonged scrummaging, she imagined, and his bully's swagger. She felt a rush of sympathy for all the small, timid boys who were no good at games. 'He gets stuck right in there. The boys love him, and although he's new to this teaching game, he has no discipline problems, unlike some.' He glanced contemptuously at a weedy young man with long fair hair, holding the hand of an equally insipid-looking wife, dressed as a sort of milkmaid in a long floral frock and flat Sarah Jane shoes. Annie later found out from Charlie that Jeremy taught Classics and had a first-class degree from Oxford. He did not deserve the scorn of a man whose specialist subject was the ruck and second-phase possession.

Mr Sports Bully was right, too. Charlie was great. Everyone said so, and called him a born schoolmaster. He was funny and clever and good company and widely popular. After the staff Christmas party Annie could imagine his colleagues saying, 'Did you meet his wife? Not what I expected at all. Silent and dull and resentful, I thought.'

The headmaster had been particularly patronising. When he sought her out and refilled her glass with hangover-inducing mulled wine, Annie felt he was interviewing her on her suitability for the post of wife of rising star. He talked of Charlie being fast-tracked into a promoted post, of how important it was that she and Charlie pulled together as a team, of how he would need her support if he took on more responsibility. 'Singing from the same hymn sheet' was the expression he used, and Annie looked back at him coldly, refusing to collude in this view of their marriage.

Even now, months later, a residue of that resentment rekindled in her heart. She turned out the light and went downstairs to the boys' bedrooms, which were made magical in the glow of the mushroom-shaped nightlights.

Annie knelt beside each bed in turn and gathered the drowsy child in her arms. How she loved them like this, their warm weight, the hair that smelled faintly of biscuits, the drooping, long-lashed eyelids, the tender skin, in Rory's case the skin of his arms roughened with eczema. She ran her lips over each raised patch. It was overwhelming, how she felt. Love rushed like a wave to fill her heart and drive out her demons.

When she went down to join Charlie he had already poured her a glass of wine and lit the fire in the sitting room. He was standing in the kitchen reading a textbook with his glasses on the end of his nose. He looked large and handsome and dependable. She went up behind him and put her arms round his middle.

'Hey!' he said, catching hold of her hands. 'What's all this about?'

'Nothing,' said Annie, rubbing her face against the back of his sweater. 'Sorry, that's all.'

'Sorry for what?' She could tell from his voice that he had continued reading.

'Just sorry.'

'Silly girl. Did you find your drink?'

He's completely unaware of what goes on in my head, Annie thought as she collected her glass of wine and went to look for some crisps. It's hardly his fault if I don't tell him. On the other hand, why doesn't he even want to know what I'm sorry about? It's not because he doesn't love me. Or at least I don't think so. I think it's because he's just not interested enough.

In retrospect, Sadie could see that it wasn't the best timing. Kyle had been up half the previous night with a difficult calving and in the end the calf had died. Its little collapsed black and white body had lain in the corner of the yard all morning. Kyle had been taciturn all day, but there was something perverse about her that made her choose the worst moment to talk about the baby.

Tamzin and Georgie were upstairs watching television before they went to bed and Kyle was sitting at the table in the cramped sitting room doing something on the computer. He was still wearing a T-shirt and his work dungarees, folded down at the waist. Sadie stood in the kitchen door wearing her Global Warming apron. The whole of the tiny cottage smelled of the fried onions that she had cooked Kyle to cheer up the home-made burgers she had produced for supper, and Sadie felt decidedly sick. She hadn't had a moment's nausea with the girls and it occurred to her that it must be a boy that she was carrying. It might have been better to keep this news for another day, but she couldn't wait.

'Guess what,' she said. 'I feel different this time. You know, not like I did when I was expecting the girls. I reckon this one's a boy, Kyle.'

Kyle didn't look up. His dark head seemed to glower over the keyboard.

Sadie waited. 'Aren't you going to say anything?' she said finally.

Kyle mumbled angrily at the screen.

'I can't hear you!' said Sadie loudly, sensing a fight and coming into the room.

'I've told you what I think. I've not changed my mind.'

'It's your baby too, you know.'

'Yeah, well, you can get rid of it then. I don't want it. I told you.'

'And I told you I'm not getting rid of it. It's a life, Kyle. I don't believe in murder. Anyway, I want our baby. You will too, when you get used to the idea,' she added rashly.

Kyle stood up, tall and lanky, his head nearly brushing the low ceiling. His face was contorted with anger. 'I've told you, you stupid bitch! I don't want this baby and that's that. If you have it, you're on your own. Do you get that? You can clear out. I never wanted you here anyway. It was you that pushed your way in. Well, I can tell you, I'm beginning to feel sorry for that husband of yours, the poor fucker!'

Sadie hit him then, a full punch that landed on the side of his face as he bent to pull up his dungarees, and for a moment he looked as if he might punch her back. Instead he pushed her hard so she took a step back and fell on to the shabby old sofa.

'You've done this on purpose, haven't you? You're a fucking witch, you are! It's your fault this has happened,' and he slammed out into the dark yard.

Chapter Four

THE NEXT WEEK Alice started telephoning caterers and comparing price lists. She had managed to book a small marquee and made an appointment with the well-spoken young man from TentsForTheMemory.com for him to come and take measurements of the garden. His name was Toby and he sounded like an eager fourteen-year-old public schoolboy. He commended her on her early booking and told her that had she left it any later he probably wouldn't have been able to help her. 'Our smaller-size marquees are very popular, you see,' he explained, 'for private garden celebrations throughout the summer months, especially landmark birthday parties. Our marquees come with the silk-effect lining you request and various options regarding window styles and column decorations and integral flooring and lighting systems. Is this by any chance a surprise or themed party?'

'Well, it's a surprise in the sense that we're having a party at all,' said Alice. 'I hadn't thought about a theme.'

'Theme parties are very successful,' went on Toby brightly, 'and if you do settle on a theme we can organise various fantasy effects to tie in.'

Alice began to feel that she was losing her way. 'What sort of themes?' she asked.

'Our most popular is a 007 or James Bond party. It gives masses of scope for glamorous costumes, you see.' By now Alice knew that she must take a grip on things.

'This party is a family thing, Toby, and apart from it all being lovely, with delicious food and so on, and, I hope, stress free, I don't think any theme is necessary. It will be a major achievement getting everyone here as it is, without asking them to dress up.'

'In that case we can discuss seating arrangements, back-drops and table decorations when I come round to view the site. May I recommend a chill-out zone? This is proving very successful with our customers where there is a wide age range among the guests.'

'No, that won't be necessary,' she said, realising that Toby was going to have to be kept on a tight rein or he would canter off with a very large cheque indeed. 'If anyone wants to sit down or have a little rest, they can use the house. As I said, we are all family, really.'

'The last things I should mention then, at this point, are toilet facilities, security, car parking, catering and waiting staff.'

'No. No, thank you,' said Alice. 'None of those will be necessary. Guests can use the house and the catering is taken care of, and people can park here or in the road. Really, Toby, it's just the tent that I need from you.'

'Very well, but I have to draw your attention to these important aspects of party planning, which can be very easily overlooked by the non-professional.'

'Well, I value your advice and naturally I want the party to be stress free. We can discuss everything when you come here, can't we?'

'All right then,' Toby conceded huffily. Alice felt he wanted to say, 'Anyway it sounds like a rubbish party,' as Rory or Archie might have done if their ideas had been similarly rebuffed. Never mind, his tent sounded perfect.

She had discussed the lunch itself at length with Margaret at work and they had pored over sample menus. Margaret surprised Alice by her grasp of what would work and what would be unsuitable. It turned out that for some years she had been undermanager in a four-star seafront hotel in Bournemouth.

'Allow five canapés per head,' she said, 'and choose the more substantial ones – they're better value because then you don't have to provide an entrée. You could have a lot of little cocktail sausages for the children – you could do those at home with no trouble.'

'That's a good idea, because I want to have champagne to start – I don't care what David says – and we can have the canapés then, before we move on to wine at lunch. Now, what about the main course – chicken supreme seems to be popular with the caterers, but I think it's very dull, don't you?'

'Why not have a more Mediterranean theme, since it's a spring party? Look, they do cold rare beef with a salsa. You could have that with warm new potatoes and a selection of salads and some of these special wood-oven pizzas for the children and vegetarians. The bitter chocolate roasted hazelnut torte sounds lovely for afterwards. You could have that with rasberries and cream, couldn't you? Ice cream for the children.'

'The beef would be terribly expensive, wouldn't it, but look, it's all locally sourced, which will keep Sadie quiet –

she's a food warrior and always up in arms about something or other, especially supermarkets.'

Margaret sighed and patted Alice's arm. 'It's your day. Stop worrying about what your children want for once.'

It's all very well to say that, thought Alice, remembering the fuss Sadie had made not long ago about some fish fingers she had cooked for the girls. They were one hundred per cent cod, Alice had made sure of that when she bought them, because she felt strongly about children eating proper food, but Sadie approached it more from the point of view of the fish, and there was something wrong with the way it had been caught.

She thought about Sadie now. She had been on the telephone last night sounding a bit low – she said she was tired – and asking if Alice could have the girls for the weekend. Of course she said yes. She loved having them to stay. If the weather was nice, she and David might take them down to the sea for a walk on Saturday afternoon. They could have fish and chips for supper on the way home – with their mother out of the way.

'When are you going to start looking for something to wear?' asked Margaret. 'I'll come with you, if you like. We could go to London. Do Oxford Street. Selfridges has all the designers on one floor.'

Alice shuddered. 'Thank you, Margaret, but that would be my idea of hell. I'd rather get something out of a catalogue that I can try on at home and send back if I don't like it.'

Margaret sighed. Alice was a lost cause. She couldn't imagine how any woman could fail to enjoy a day's shopping.

'Anyway, I'm not going to buy anything until I've lost at least half a stone. I'm really determined this time,' said Alice, thinking of that dream target weight that she and most of the other women she knew were seeking to attain, in her case without any success at all.

'You've got a lovely womanly figure. You just need to show it off. Shorten your skirts, nip in that waist!' Margaret laughed and clasped her own hands round her middle and pouted provocatively. 'Sex it up, girl!'

'God forbid.'

'Give your hubby a surprise. Get a makeover, like on the television.'

'No thanks, Margaret. I don't think David would survive a shock like that.'

But David was not thinking about the party at all. Instead he was waiting anxiously for the days to pass before he was due to meet Julia for lunch. Half the time he told himself that he was being a fool and that no good could possibly come of it for either of them. This was the part of him that remained rational and sensible and asked severely what Julia could possibly want from him.

He knew that professionally he couldn't help her in any useful way. A reference from a retired senior lecturer from a second-rate university department carried no clout and he knew that she knew that. He could offer her advice, he supposed, but he would have to be honest and point her away from an academic career. He could help her with her CV. He had plenty of experience at enhancing the profiles of rather weak graduates, and when he challenged himself on what exactly he thought he was doing with Julia Fairfield, that was what he told himself – that he was helping her with job applications, as a friend and former colleague.

The rest of the time he seemed to take leave of his sensible self and get carried on a wave of excitement. He knew in his heart that this lunch was nothing whatever to do with a professional relationship. It was all about what Julia had said in her e-mail, that her personal life was in pieces, that she was in a bad place after her marriage had broken up, that her husband had treated her very brutally, that she was alone and broke and unemployed and that she really, really needed someone to talk to, a friend whom she could trust.

He also knew that the feelings that this news aroused in him were not fatherly or avuncular – Christ knows, he had had too many crises of a similar nature with Sadie to want to take on board another off-the-rails female. How he felt now had a quite different origin.

An attractive young woman said that she wanted and needed to see him, had sought him out in fact. Of all the men in the department, past and present, it was he whom she had got in touch with. The exchange of e-mails seemed to have taken on an emotionally charged and intense character that took David back to the rainy afternoon in the car park, when, he saw now, he had been pretty useless.

Of course he had found other women attractive in the past and had experienced, in fact, a few minor extramarital skirmishes when the children were growing up and Alice, well, Alice had lost her initial allure. But the fact that Julia had contacted him; the whole internet thing, which made communication so easy; the exchange of mobile telephone numbers; and Alice being at work and he alone so much:

all these things altered everything and widened the range of possibilities in a way that threatened to get out of control.

He had made up his mind to tell Alice an edited version of the truth. In the past he had never lied to her — there was no need when he had a busy working life that provided plenty of opportunities for small flirtations. There had been conferences and so on, where after too much to drink in a hotel bar he had behaved a bit recklessly, although he had never been technically unfaithful. In the morning there would be a slight embarrassment and he would feel guilty when later he opened his own front door and was confronted by everything that his family meant — Alice in the kitchen, children doing homework, the sound of some quarrel going on upstairs, the television news playing unwatched in the sitting room. After a while the guilt would drop away. After all, there was no harm done and David felt relieved of any unpleasant consequences.

How he felt now was quite different, although there was no need, at this stage, to feel guilty about anything — other than, like Jimmy Carter, having lust in his heart. However there was something deliberate about his suggestion to Julia that they met at a wine bar in a cathedral city at some distance from them both. An hour's car drive would help him shake off his home persona and work himself up to impersonating the man that Julia apparently saw him as.

Oh God, what am I doing? David clutched his head. It was madness. Life was perfectly fine in the backwater he had drifted into after he had retired. There was Alice planning this bloody party, shoving menus under his nose and wanting to talk about some prat who was bringing round the marquee, and he couldn't give a toss about any of it. All he could think about was Julia and her little white hands and brimming grey eyes and the extraordinarily unsettling news that she had always found him attractive.

Sadie did not give up easily. Anyway, this was not a battle she was prepared to lose. She loved Kyle and she was going to have his baby. It was as simple as that. His reaction was just a temporary glitch and she was confident that, handled right, he could be brought round. One of the things she loved about him was that he disliked confrontations. He couldn't bear to argue. He would rather go out of the room than pick a fight, and the only reason he had reacted so angrily, Sadie knew, was because she had driven him into a corner. Well, she wouldn't do that again. She would be sweet and kind and non-confrontational and wind him gently round her little finger. That was why she was sending the girls to Alice for the weekend. She wanted time alone with Kyle.

The main reason for his violent reaction, she knew, was financial. They were only just managing as it was, and a baby would make it hard for her to work, for a while at least, and they would sink into even worse debt. Sadie didn't like to think of what they owed three or four credit card companies, but they had both cut up their cards and were now paying back – just a little each month, although it hardly seemed to cover the interest.

There was an alternative. We can just default on payments, she thought. We can stop paying and declare ourselves bank-rupt because that's what we are anyway. What did it matter if the credit card companies had to write off a few thousand pounds when banks went bust owing millions and millions? She and Kyle were just victims of the financial system. It was hardly their fault that they couldn't pay back loans at extortionate interest rates and when the credit card companies had been clamouring to lend them more than they could afford.

They would still have a roof over their heads because the cottage came with Kyle's job and they didn't own anything that could be repossessed, and with the baby, their baby, their future as a family would be secure. Eventually they would make some money somehow or other. Maybe, like Charlie, she could retrain as a teacher, and work in a nice village primary school that grew its own vegetables. Sadie felt optimistic about the future even though at the moment it seemed a bit precarious.

There was also an alternative plan. They could borrow the money to pay off their debts. She could ask Marina for a loan. The flat her sister had bought two years ago had cost half a million, so she could surely spare a few thousand to help them out. Conveniently Sadie forgot that at the time she had shouted that bankers' bonuses were morally indefensible. Any loan would be on a proper basis, of course, paid back with interest. She wouldn't ask her otherwise.

Anyway, somehow or other they would manage. All she had got to do was convince Kyle. He didn't understand about families, having such a crap one himself, kicked out of home at sixteen when his mother took a violent man as her lover. He had often told Sadie that he had never felt he belonged anywhere until she and the girls moved in and she put up curtains and painted furniture found in charity shops and always had a jug of flowers on the kitchen table.

If Sadie had stopped to think, she might have realised that in her relationships with men – to date, all disastrous – she always assumed the role of an indulgent mother, until eventually the man in question began to behave more and more like a child.

Now she was convinced that if Kyle could be coaxed into believing that everything would be all right, he would come round and start being nice again. She would kiss the sore place and make it better. What she didn't want to think about was the indigestible fact that Kyle already had a seven-year-old child, a boy called Tyrone, born to a sixteen-year-old girlfriend he had met in a hostel, with whom he had no contact.

Sadie felt badly about Tyrone. Not only had the poor kid been given the name of a pit bull terrier, but when Kyle first told her about him, a few weeks into their affair, she had felt more than a pang of jealousy. She didn't want Kyle to be anything but hers, and another woman's child, and a son at that, weakened her exclusive hold on him. She was relieved to learn that Leanna, the mother, was a drug addict living somewhere in Newcastle, that Tyrone was in foster care and that Kyle had never seen him. It was easy to forget his existence, which Sadie promptly did, though not entirely.

Sometimes when she saw Kyle playing with the girls, hoisting one of them on to his shoulders or holding their hands as they walked across the field to look for a new calf, she had a disturbing sense of the little boy who was missing from the picture, who had a rightful place beside his father.

She once suggested as much to Kyle, but he looked at her fiercely and said, 'Just leave it, will you? Don't go meddling in any of that. I don't want nothing to do with it. I didn't even know she was pregnant and I don't know for sure the kid is mine. She was a slapper, was Leanna. She'd sleep with anyone for a joint.'

'Yeah, well that's all about her, or how she was then, but what about the kid? He's the innocent party here. Doesn't he need a father?'

'He might do, but then so did I, and I managed without one. We can't all have what we want. I don't have anything to do with him. I never have and that's how it is.'

Sadie had to accept this as bald fact, but it nagged away at her, this thought of Tyrone growing up knowing nothing about his father. He was the same age as Georgie, who, granted, wasn't living with her own father but at least she knew who he was and had sporadic contact with him when he remembered she existed. The Tyrone business was a bad thing, a discreditable thing, and it made Sadie uneasy. It made her feel uncomfortable enough not to want to tell anybody else in her family because she knew it reflected badly on the man she loved. This shadowy child, now seven years old, haunted her by his absence.

Maybe, she thought, when she had had this baby that she was carrying, Kyle would be so converted to fatherhood that he might agree to find Tyrone and bring him to live with them. It would be another mouth to feed, but Sadie was sure they could manage, and it would be a good thing, a noble and unselfish thing on her part. She liked to think of Ty, as she would call him, recovering from his terrible start and benefiting from a proper family life and a wholefood organic diet. The baby would bring them together. The baby was a blessing for them all.

Meanwhile she would treat the row with Kyle as if it had never happened. Although he was glowering and silent, she behaved quite normally. At the weekend when the girls were away she would win him round, and then she would break the news about the baby to the family. Impatient to tell somebody, she posted her dilemma on Mumsnet and was so engrossed by reading all the supportive comments that flooded in from other mothers across the country that she forgot the time and was late to meet the school bus at the top of the quarter-mile farm drive, not that the girls weren't old enough to make their own way home by now.

'Have you spoken to your mother about the party?' said Lisa to Ollie at supper. 'She rang last week when you were out, and before that, she sent us an e-mail. You were supposed to ring her back. I said we'd go, of course, but she'd like to hear it from you, I expect.'

Ollie, who had done two surgeries and a string of home visits followed by a practice meeting and was dark-eyed with exhaustion, looked up from his plate of pasta and shook his head guiltily. With two of his partners off sick, he had barely had a moment to himself all week.

'Remind me about it, will you? What sort of party was it?'

'She's planning a big family do in the spring to celebrate lots of stuff: her sixtieth birthday and a wedding anniversary. You should know. It's *your* family. She talked about a real event — marquee, caterers, a brass band for all I know.'

'It all sounds a bit out of character. Has she won the lottery or something?'

'She said that she and your father have never had a proper party to celebrate anything and she thinks it's time they did.'

'I can't see Dad taking that line. He doesn't like parties.'

'She's evidently changed his mind somehow.' There was something in Lisa's tone that suggested a trace of hostility or resentment when she spoke of Alice and David. She had never quite accepted that her new husband's tribe was so important to him and that loyalty and affection towards the family was paramount. She knew, when she checked herself, that it was her experience in France that made her so wary. However hard she tried, Jean-Louis's large family had treated her as an unfortunate outsider, and later, when things went wrong and she discovered he had been conducting an affair with Jacqui, they closed ranks and showed her no understanding or sympathy.

'It sounds great, Mum,' said Sabine, who sensed the undercurrent and recognised her mother's tone. 'I think a party's a great idea. I really like your family, Ollie, especially your mum and dad. They're cool.'

'She said that to me the other day,' said Lisa, amused. 'I told her, they're hardly *cool*! Old-fogeyish I'd have thought was nearer the mark.'

'They *are* cool, Mum! They're not like hip or anything, but they're cool about things. They give us a really nice time when we stay there, don't they, Agnes? They let us do loads of stuff.'

Agnes hesitated, realising that there was some division of loyalty and not knowing who to please. 'I like the dog. Roger's cool.'

Ollie laughed. 'I can tell you they weren't cool when we

were growing up. We all had to do jobs in the house and garden – and not for pocket money – and we had to eat what was on our plates, all that sort of stuff.'

'Yeah, and got sent up chimneys,' said Agnes cheekily. 'You're just like Papa. He's always telling us about his cruel childhood and how the teacher hit them with a stick and having to go to Mass twenty times a day or something!'

Lisa laughed, and Sabine knew that she liked it when they talked like that about their father. 'That's a load of rubbish. Jean-Louis was spoiled rotten,' she said. 'He was fussed over by his mother and grandmother and doting sisters from the moment he was born. That's why he has never grown up. He is still basically a spoiled child.'

'Have you still got the e-mail? I'd better reply to it.' Sabine was grateful that Ollie's question curtailed a discussion of Papa's shortcomings. It didn't seem fair to talk about him like this in England, where he couldn't ever be seen in a good light and had no one to stand up for him. She and Agnes should have spoken on his behalf, but it would upset their mother too much if they did.

'Yes. Sabine can show you after supper. There's only one response allowed anyway, which is "Yes, we'll be there!"'

'There won't be a problem with that, will there? It's far enough ahead to keep the day free. I'm just wondering what the anniversary would be. God, I think it must be forty years they've been married! And Mum is sixty this year and Dad is sixty-two, I think.'

Lisa hummed 'When I'm Sixty-Four' as she cleared away the plates.

'I will still need you, if you go on cooking like that!' said Ollie. 'That was delicious, sweetheart.'

Sabine looked from one to the other. When Ollie called her mother 'sweetheart', it made a little tight place in her chest relax. 'Sweetheart' was the best you could call anyone, she thought, if it was said in the way Ollie said it. It made her mother smile and pass a hand over his head as she leaned across him to reach a plate. Please let it make you happy, thought Sabine, because this is what you wanted, isn't it? She remembered the terrible banging of doors and shrieking, her mother's face congested with anger and tears. This was a better place to be, this warm, untidy kitchen in a square house in a Wiltshire village.

Ollie was a safer sort of man than her father. Sabine looked across at him. He was big and tall, with almost black curly hair and a crumpled sort of face that creased when he smiled. His movements were slow and deliberate and he had large square hands with clean pink fingernails. His moods didn't seem to change that much, and although he was sometimes a bit quiet when he got back from work because he was tired, she supposed, he wasn't moody or grumpy or anything. Slowly she had learned to relax with him, and most of all trust him with her mother's happiness.

Agnes had been naughty from the start, making scenes and wanting to be the centre of attention, but Ollie had been great. He just hadn't got involved. He took a newspaper and went into the sitting room and turned on the news. Sometimes he said something like 'Hey! We don't shout at one another in this house, okay?' but he never got heavy or pretended that he was, like, the boss of them. Somehow he calmed things down and you sort of knew not to push things. Eventually Agnes recognised that you wouldn't want Ollie to be angry with you and behaved better when he was around.

Papa was so different. He was always laughing or shouting and life with him was either fun or terrible. He covered her and Agnes with kisses and enveloped them in hugs but on the other hand he sometimes hit them or banged the table when he was angry. He didn't beat them or anything, but struck out when he was in a temper. All you had to do was dodge out of the way. There were loads of times when you didn't dare go near him, and they had learned to read the signs and keep clear until his mood had improved.

Jacqui was good with him. She took no notice when he shouted and he didn't make her cry like he had Mum. Jacqui bossed him about, in fact, and always made him do what she wanted. When she was angry with him she was really scary. She went icy quiet and sometimes got in her car and drove off, and Papa spent the rest of the day trying to get her on her mobile, pleading and saying he was sorry. Now she was pregnant he was always telling her not to lift things or get tired, and stroking her short black hair, which was cut like a boy's, and kissing her neck.

It made Sabine really sad to think that when Mum had been so unhappy and had cried a lot of the time, Papa hadn't wanted to stroke *her* lovely long hair or kiss *her* neck. Why had it been like that? How could it be that people who loved one another enough to get married and have children could then end up being horrible to one another?

The only good thing was that they both seemed happy now – at least Papa did, but she was still worried about her mum. There was something not right, Sabine knew, but she didn't know what it was. Ollie was cool – it wasn't anything to do with him, she didn't think – but there was something else that made her mum unhappy a lot of the time. There was a new little frown line creasing the space between her eyebrows, and when she wasn't smiling her mouth turned downwards as though she was thinking about something sad.

All the time Sabine felt anxious about her. She loved her mum so much, but her love felt like a useless burden, because it wasn't enough to make her happy. She hung around her, trying to please her and make her smile, and she thought a lot about what was wrong in bed at night, and at school. The worst thing was that in her heart she knew that it must be her fault, because by going to their dad's for part of every holiday and at half-terms, she and Agnes made their mum unhappy.

When she talked to Agnes about it, all she said was 'It's that bitch Jacqui. It's because of her. There's nothing we can do. It isn't our fault!' But Sabine knew that Agnes liked Jacqui really, and that it was much better being with Papa now that she was there. Agnes seemed to be able to switch sides so easily, moving smoothly between their parents, settling in wherever she was and not worrying about what she was powerless to change. She didn't seem to think much about Papa while she was in England, or worry about their mother when she was happy back in France. Sabine had to make her keep in touch with the absent parent, otherwise she was sure she wouldn't have bothered.

'Sabine! Show Ollie the e-mail. He can send a reply from your computer,' said Lisa, starting to collect the plates. 'Go on. Agnes and I'll clear up down here.'

Sabine led the way upstairs with Ollie plodding obediently behind her and sat down at her desk.

'Here,' she said, finding the message from Alice and opening it up for him to read.

'Goodness!' he said. 'Whatever's got into her? Still, a party would be fun, don't you think? Could you and Agnes bear to meet all the crazy members of my family in one go? Although I suppose you are used to enormous families, what with your dad's crowd. How is he, by the way?'

Sabine blushed. 'He's okay,' she said, twisting her hair round her finger and looking away from Ollie's face.

'You keep in touch with him, don't you? I mean, it's important that you do.'

'Yeah, well, sort of. I send him e-mails and stuff. He's busy a lot of the time. Or away. Jacqui sometimes replies for him.' She blushed again. Just saying Jacqui's name in the small space between her and Ollie made her feel uncomfortable. Her mother would never say her name. Jacqui was always 'she' or 'her', spat out with a bitter expression.

'This old computer is pants, though, isn't it? Does it have a webcam? I didn't think so. You use Skype? If we got you a webcam, you could see one another. Tell you what, I'll give you a new laptop for your birthday. This one's a dinosaur. It's so slow, too. You do homework on it, don't you? Okay, kiddo, a new one it is. We'll go and choose one on Saturday, if you like.'

Sabine hesitated. 'Mum doesn't really like it . . .' she said. 'I mean, she doesn't really want us to just . . .' She didn't know how to finish.

Ollie looked up at her, his eyes searching her face, and

she turned away again, anxiously rubbing her nose with her hand.

'What do you mean? What doesn't Mum like? Do you mean she worries about what you might get into online? That's easily sorted. There are all sorts of blockers we can have fitted.'

'No, it's more that she gets a bit upset about us . . . you know, Agnes and me, and Papa,' she finished weakly.

'No! You mean being in contact? Surely not?' Ollie looked genuinely shocked. He leaned back in Sabine's wobbly desk chair with all the old embarrassing pink Barbie stickers on the back and she worried that he might break it.

'She likes to . . . well, see what we say, I suppose. I don't think she likes us to . . .'

'Well that's ridiculous. Of course you must have easy and private access to your father. Look, Sabine, leave this with me, okay? You know your mum; how she gets a bit upset about things. Unnecessarily, really. Just at the moment she's finding things a bit hard.' He looked at Sabine for a long moment and she felt herself blushing. Finally he said, 'Has she said anything to you about the baby?'

'What baby?' Sabine felt as if she was being dragged from a safe shore on to an expanse of very thin ice and that any moment she would fall through into icy black water.

'Well, she obviously hasn't told you.' Ollie stretched out his hand and caught at Sabine's wrist. 'I'm telling you now because I think you are old enough to deal with it. Your mum and I are trying for a baby. We have been for a while but no luck as yet.'

Sabine wished that she could snatch her wrist away. Trying

for a baby! How embarrassing was that. Sex, fucking, shagging. It was all grown-ups seemed to think about.

'She's a bit stressed about it, to be truthful. You know, she wants it so badly and when it doesn't happen it gets her down. It's worse because of your dad's baby with Jacqui. It makes it harder for her, see.'

Sabine shrugged and chewed at her thumbnail. She didn't know what sort of face she was supposed to make.

'It's nothing to do with her not being satisfied with you and Agnes – of course it's not that. It's just that we feel we would like our own baby. It seems right somehow, and would join us all into a proper family. You would be such a great big sister. There would be quite an age gap, I know, but you would be around for a few years while it grows up, before you go off to university or whatever.'

'Yeah. Cool,' said Sabine in a flat voice. The prospect of this hypothetical baby left her feeling confused.

'Hey! Are you okay about it? I know it's quite something to get your head round. It won't change anything in some ways. Not us, or how we feel about each other, or how much your mum loves you. I mean, in some ways a baby is a bloody nuisance to have around, but we'd get used to that, I guess; all the mewling and puking and so on. Despite all of that, people do seem to love them. Or at least, they love their own and tolerate other people's.'

Sabine shrugged again. 'Yeah. Cool. I'm cool about it.' In fact she didn't know what to do with this knowledge that her mother and stepfather were having sex with procreation in mind. She couldn't work out why Ollie had told her. Why hadn't he waited until this baby was a reality – or at least definitely on its way? Her father hadn't said anything until they went to stay last Christmas and it was obvious that Jacqui was pregnant, and he'd made it easy by not making it a big deal. He didn't go in for all this talking about what it would *mean*.

Anyway, she didn't buy all this hype about babies holding things together. If that was true, then why had her papa not been satisfied with her and Agnes and their mum? They had been a family, hadn't they? A proper family, but it hadn't meant anything in the end. There was other stuff that mattered more.

'So you see,' went on Ollie, 'it's all been a bit stressful for your mum recently, and that's why, Sabine, I think she's being a bit unreasonable about contact with your father. It's not logical, I know, but I think because she really minds about Jacqui being pregnant it's made her a bit jealous of your relationship with your dad. If he's getting a baby, why should he have you too? That sort of thing.'

'Okay,' said Sabine, wishing all this would end. 'It's okay. Really, it's fine.'

'No, it's not. Not *absolutely* fine, it's not. I'm going to get you a new laptop, that's a promise, and set you up with webcam so that you can keep properly in touch with everything at Pompignac. I'll speak to your mum about it and I promise she'll be okay with it. When is the baby due, anyway?'

'In June sometime, and it's a boy. They know that already.'

A pained look passed over Ollie's good-natured face before he managed a smile. 'I see. Nice for them. Nice for your dad. Nice for you too, you and Agnes, to have a little brother. A half-brother.'

'Yeah. It's cool. We won't get to see him until the summer holidays, though.'

'I suppose not. It's a bit far to go for a weekend.'

Accidentally Sabine caught Ollie's eye and they exchanged a look that was more eloquent than anything they had managed to say. Ollie recognised Sabine's discomfort and she saw the tender longing in his face.

'You're a great girl, Sabine, you know that? It hasn't been easy for you and Agnes, but you've done so well, and you really care for your mum, and I really, really appreciate that.'

Sabine felt a sudden, hot threat of tears. She didn't want to be thanked or to be asked how she felt about things she didn't even want to know about. She wished that her life could be simple, unremarkable, just home and boring school and friends and stuff, and not muddled and confused with grown-ups and their angst — some of which she felt she was responsible for but which she could do nothing to make better.

'So,' said Ollie, turning back to the screen. 'What about this party? Could you send my mother a reply from us all? Tell her we'd love to come.'

Chapter Five

SOMETIMES ALICE WISHED that she could step off her life for a while, as if it were a bus that would trundle on without her and which she could pick up again at a later stop en route. She felt she would like to sit in a calm, quiet place where nobody knew her and where she didn't have to smile. She would like to feel the muscles of her face fall into whatever expression came naturally in repose and let her shoulders droop wearily.

Granted, life wasn't nearly as exhausting as when the children were small, but then there hadn't been any time in which to worry, apart from about unalterable things like not having enough money, or the depletion of the rainforest. These days it seemed she had the luxury of enough time to worry about everything, and if there was nothing to worry about then she worried that calm days could not last and that there must be some ominous storm gathering on the horizon.

For instance, Alice knew there was something wrong with Sadie. When she dropped the girls off at the weekend she sat slumped at the kitchen table, her face pale and her eyes tired. She was wearing black leggings with two small holes in the right knee and the sort of short fur boots that lent her sturdy legs the look of a hairy-heeled horse. Her top half was encased in an unflattering hooded fleece jacket and her hair was scraped back in an untidy knot.

It didn't taken Alice long to wonder if she was pregnant. She had that pale, turned-inward look that she observed in the women attending the prenatal clinic at the surgery, as if the process of growing a baby took some inner concentration. Well, she hoped to God she wasn't. As far as Alice was concerned, another baby would be a total disaster. Of course she didn't ask her outright, just said, 'You look a bit washed out, Sade. Are you all right?'

'Yeah, I'm okay, thanks, Mum. Just knackered. That's why it's so good to have the girls off my hands this weekend.'

At the other side of the table Georgie and Tamzin regarded their mother solemnly.

'Well, it's a treat for *us*!' said Alice in a bright voice, smiling across at them. 'I thought we might go to the sea tomorrow.'

'Great. That's great, isn't it, girlies? Well, I'd better go. No thanks, I really don't want coffee.' Sadie stood up and went round the table to kiss her daughters. 'Be good. No quarrelling. Do as Granny tells you.' She turned back to Alice. 'Georgie's eczema cream is in her wash bag. They needn't have a bath tonight. They had one last night – and a hair-wash – ready for inspection! Thanks, Mum. Is it really okay for you to bring them back on Sunday?'

'Of course it is. It will be a pleasure.'

'How is the party going? The plans, I mean.'

'Good. Margaret at work has been very helpful about menus and so on. She used to work at a hotel.'

Sadie made a face. 'Ugh! Hotel food!'

'Stop before you start!' said Alice, raising her hands. 'Even you, Sade, will be pleased with what I've chosen.'

'Sorry. Am I that much of a pain in the arse? Don't answer that. It's my principles, you see. I have to live by what I believe.'

'Yes, dear,' said Alice lightly. 'Very commendable, but this is my party, not yours.'

'Well, Mum, I said I'd help, so you've only got to ask. I'll do anything – fetching, carrying, cleaning, flowers. Nearer the time we should sit down and think it through. Make lists and everything. After all, you won't get any help from the others. You say Dad has been okay about it all? Does he know how much it will cost?'

'Yes, he's been fine, and no, he doesn't know – nor do I for that matter, but for once I don't care. It will be money well spent. And thanks for the offer of help. I'll definitely need you, but I don't want it to be a big deal. I want you here as a guest, wearing something pretty and drinking champagne, not slaving away in the background.'

'Wearing something pretty, huh?' Sadie pulled a face. 'That might be a problem, unless it's an artfully reconstructed organic mixed corn sack. I never go anywhere where there's a shop these days.'

'In that case we'll go shopping together and I'll buy you something – the girls, too.'

Sadie slipped her arm round her mother's waist and kissed her cheek. 'You're great, Mum! Isn't she, girls?' They nodded obediently.

'So what are you planning to do this weekend?' asked Alice, still unclear why she had been asked to have the children as if there was an emergency.

'Kyle has got Sunday off, which doesn't happen very often. I thought we could go out somewhere tonight – the cinema or the pub. It makes a difference knowing that you're not up at four thirty the next morning to do the milking.'

'Yes, of course it does. Well, have a lovely time. How is Kyle, anyway?'

'He's all right, thanks.' Sadie's eyes slid away from her mother's face. 'He's fine, in fact,' she said, kissing her daughters' heads and picking up her mobile telephone and keys from the table. 'I'll be off, then.'

Alice watched from the window as her daughter reversed Kyle's pickup out of the drive, knowing that all was not well. She turned back to Georgie and Tamzin. It was tempting to question them, but instead she said, 'What shall we do, then, darlings? Let's take your bag upstairs, and then how about making some cupcakes for tea? We could do pink vanilla icing.'

The weekend went well despite horrible wind and rain on Saturday afternoon, when Alice lit the fire and got out all the old videotapes her own children had loved. David helped them to do a puzzle of the Grand National and then they sat on the floor glued to *Black Beauty* while he read the paper and dozed and answered their interminable, urgent questions about the plot.

He was a good grandfather, Alice thought as she tidied the kitchen and made a cup of tea – kind and patient and forbearing, unlike grandfathers when she was a child, who were generally aloof and stern and ancient-seeming. When the film was over she would get their coats on and they could all walk up the lane with Roger to where some shaggy ponies were turned out in a field. David would come too, holding Tamzin's hand on the way out and Georgie's on the way back. He was an important figure in their lives – the only man whose presence they could rely on.

How much Alice had regretted Sadie's choice of father for her children, and she was now convinced there was something wrong, and that led her to speculate on the subject of Kyle as a father figure. Whichever way she looked at it, and however much she liked him, she couldn't see that he was suitable – far too young, for one thing. Oh dear! Her heart felt so full of dread and anxiety that she could hardly lift the kettle to pour hot water into the mugs.

How she loved them, the two sturdy little girls she could see through the open sitting-room door, lying on the floor on cushions, in their ragbag rainbow clothes. How she wished she had it in her power to make things safe and secure for them. She looked sadly at the tray of blotchily iced cupcakes generously decorated with hundreds and thousands that they had spent the morning making. How much did children take in, pick up, absorb of adult fears, or could a day be made happy by a cake-baking session and a pony's nose to stroke?

She felt a small movement by her side and a little hand slid into hers. It was Georgie. 'Granny,' she whispered, 'can you come and watch the film with us? I want to sit on your lap. It's got to a sad bit.'

'Darling, of course I can. I'm coming right away. Look, you can carry the plate with the cakes on it.'

Later, with Georgie's head resting comfortably on her chest, Alice stroked her granddaughter's very fine hair, the colour of dark chocolate threaded with gold, and thought, this is all I can do. David was leaning forward to explain something to Tamzin, who had turned her wide-eyed little round face up to his. Just be here, she thought. That's all we can do.

It wasn't any more reassuring when she and David drove the children back on Sunday afternoon. It had been a bright morning and they had spent a happy time at the beach, throwing sticks for Roger, who obligingly trotted off and brought them back to lay at the girls' feet for a repeat performance. The waves sighed in and out over the silvery shingle and the sky was high and blue and the sun strong enough for Alice to lean against an upturned dinghy and turn her face, with closed eyes, to receive its warmth.

A few other families joined them on the strand, well wrapped up, with dogs and kites and footballs and frisbees, and above the sound of the waves Alice could hear the chorus of happy shouts and calls as children ran to and fro and an excited collie tried to round them up.

She watched what appeared to be a perfect family, the father tall and good-looking in a woollen cap with a baby in a backpack, and the mother nearly as tall, and slim and blonde, in a pink coat. They both wore the sort of rubber boots that were designed for striding across grouse moors, and called to their children in carrying voices. The two older children, two girls about the same age as Georgie and Tamzin, had some sort of spinning toy that the father was trying to teach them how to use. Not many minutes passed before she learned that their names were Flora and Flavia. She watched as they galloped about, pulling at their father's arms, shrieking with laughter, and how he chased them with wide-open arms and when he caught them lifted them both off the ground in a bear hug, despite the baby bobbing about on his back, its Peruvian-looking woollen bonnet fallen over its eyes.

They had the sort of attractiveness that drew the eye, and Alice noticed that Georgie and Tamzin, tumbling about with David and Roger, had also stopped to look. David, impervious, walked on, but it touched Alice to see her two little granddaughters pause and stand watching, their faces rapt, as if they knew they were witnessing something special. Suddenly, and irrationally, Alice disliked the attention-provoking family, parading their success in life, their happiness and good genes and wise choices and good taste. Go on, rub our noses in it, she thought crossly. Where does it leave the rest of us, the also-rans, the less than perfect? Where does it leave Tamzin and Georgie, with all that they have to put up with?

She felt reproved when later, in the beach car park, the smiling woman, who was loading her own children into child seats in the back of a huge 4x4 with a hitch on the back – for *the pony trailer*, thought Alice, still irritated – looked across and waved cheerfully and said, 'Lovely day!' Alice had to smile back. She's a nice person, she thought, with a happy family. I'm just envious, that's all. Not for me – for them – and she glanced at her granddaughters' faces, but they looked fine, pink from the fresh air and running about, laughing and happy, and looking forward to the promised fish and chips.

Children accept what life deals out of them, she thought. They don't know any different. But that didn't stop her feeling anxious on their behalf, and even more so when she and David drove them home on Sunday evening.

The farm cottage looked welcoming enough and there was a fire lit in the sitting room, where Sadie was lying on the sofa watching a video. She looked better. Her hair was loose and fell prettily on to her shoulders and she was wearing some eye make-up and lip gloss. Her daughters fell on her with open arms and smothering kisses while Alice unpacked the basket of things she had brought back with them on to the kitchen counter. Ribena, apple juice, yoghurts, and the leftovers that would make another meal.

David sat down in the armchair and became engrossed in the film, while Alice asked Sadie about her night out and knew instantly that something was wrong, simply from her daughter's tone of voice and the fact that she wouldn't meet her eye. She couldn't quiz her if she didn't want to tell, and not in front of the girls, but later, as she and David were leaving and returning to where their car was parked in the dark yard, she had the opportunity to take Sadie's arm and say, 'Sade – is everything okay? You would tell me, wouldn't you?'

Hidden by the darkness, Sadie's face gave nothing away, but she hung on to her mother's hand for a moment and said in a breaking voice, 'Oh Mum . . . I can't talk about it now.'

'That was a terrible film, you know, that Sadie was watching,' said David later, settling into the driver's seat and fastening his seat belt. 'Historically inaccurate and ridiculously fanciful . . . in actual fact, the occupation of France wasn't a . . .' But Alice wasn't listening.

'David, there's something up with Sadie. She told me as much when we were leaving.'

'What do you mean? What's up?'

'I don't know. She didn't tell me. But there is. I thought so on Saturday morning when she dropped the girls off. Didn't you notice it tonight?'

David sighed. He was sick of agonising about Sadie. He had worried about her for years. If she wanted to live in a damp cottage with a Neanderthal boyfriend, frankly, that was her choice. Sadie was a grown-up.

'No, I didn't,' he said. 'She seemed all right to me. That's the trouble with you, Alice. You're always looking for something to worry about.'

When Annie next switched on her computer, she found an e-mail informing her that her contract with the DIY chain was being terminated. The in-store magazine was being folded. It no longer met the needs of the streamlined management and the style failed to reflect the company's updated profile. She was thanked for her services and that was that.

Her first reaction was deep dismay. It was crap work that she hated, but at least it was a job. When people asked, it was what she could say that she *did*, as if it defined her as a person and justified her existence. She had hung on to it because it was work she would chuck the moment that something better came along. She saw it as a tiny foothold that she would eventually use to climb back into her old life. Now, even that had been knocked away from her.

There was a time when the first person she would have turned to would have been Charlie, but now, unfair though she knew it was, she blamed him for what had happened. It felt as if it was his fault that she was stuck in a ghastly job she hated, but which she was now very upset to have lost. She didn't want to hear him telling her that it wasn't worth having anyway. She resented deeply that while he was happy and fulfilled, it was easy for him to tell her to be positive and point out that now she would have more time with the boys.

With the loss of the job went her excuse to retreat to the attic to work. With it went the pretence that she had other things to do. Now she would be totally at the mercy of the family. There would be no escape.

Quickly she typed a farewell message to Jennifer, a person whom she had never met but who was more real to her than any of the mothers at the school gate, and then she turned off the computer and sat looking at its blank screen. So that was that. She checked her watch. She had time to go downstairs and take a very long and hot bath with some nice bath oil before she had to go and collect Archie. Although it was only half past eleven, she would pour a large glass of white wine and take it with her. If she didn't feel like speaking to Charlie she would wait to tell him when he got home in the evening. He was impossible to get hold of when he was in school with his mobile tele-phone switched off anyway. There was no one else she felt like speaking to, but all the same she took the telephone into the bathroom with her and when it rang she picked it up and answered.

It was Alice.

'Hi, Alice.'

'I'm sorry to interrupt you if you are working, but I just wanted to run this menu by you – for the boys, I mean. At the party.'

The goddamn party, thought Annie. 'Oh, right,' she said.

'Are Rory and Archie okay with rather special pizza followed by ice cream? I have to give numbers to the caterers, you see. Tomato and cheese and pepperoni? Then strawberry, vanilla or chocolate. What do you think?'

'Sounds perfect. They don't actually like tomato, but they can pick it off. Honestly, Alice, you know children. One day they'll eat something, the next day they won't.'

'Yes, of course, you're right. But in principle pizzas are a good idea, do you think? For all the children?'

'Perfect.'

'Are you okay, Annie? I *have* interrupted you, haven't I? I'm so sorry.'

'No, you haven't. I'm in the bath, to be perfectly honest.'

'The bath? Oh, I see. Well, I hope you didn't have to get out to answer the telephone. Have you been to the gym or something?'

'No. I'm having a bath in the middle of the day because I'm fed up. I've just been sacked from my miserable job with no nice redundancy pay-off and no notice.'

'Oh, Annie. I'm so sorry. Really I am.' Annie could sense Alice searching in her mind for something to say. Something buoying, no doubt, to make her feel better. 'I know how much you need to have something to do, and even though the job wasn't anything like as exciting and demanding as you were used to, I can quite see why you feel dejected.'

Well, thought Annie. That was a surprise.

'Is it going to be easy to find something else? That fits in with the boys and so on.'

'No, I shouldn't think so.'

'Well, Archie goes to school next year, doesn't he? Why don't you think about getting some sort of help and going back to work properly? Full time, I mean. If that's what you want to do.'

Annie was surprised. 'That's not what I expect my mother-in-law, of all people, to suggest,' she said. 'It sounds a bit too much like abandoning my children.'

'You wouldn't be abandoning them, would you? Perhaps you could do a bit of work from home. Journalists do, don't they? All those women who write endless columns about their home lives must have some sort of arrangement – as if we don't have enough problems of our own, I always feel. You could get an au pair or some sort of nanny for the rest of the time.'

'Well, maybe. It wouldn't be easy, though, with Charlie being so full on at that school of his.'

'But he has very long holidays when he could take over at home.'

'Well, thank you, Alice. The power of positive thinking!' Annie meant it, too. She didn't actually believe for one moment that full-time work was a possibility, but it was kind of her mother-in-law not to deliver a homily on how her place was by the hearth or in the kitchen or blacking the grate or scrubbing the front step, or tell her that she should be glad that losing her job meant that she could have more time with the children. She felt grateful for that.

'What does Charlie say?'

'I haven't told him yet. I haven't told anyone. You're the first.'

'Will he be sympathetic? I mean, does he understand how important your work is to you?'

'Hmm. Well, I suppose he saw the stuff I've been doing recently as a rubbish waste of my time. He is rather evangelical about teaching, you see. As a new convert, he thinks that doing something worthwhile – making a differ- ence, he calls it – is the important thing.'

'Oh dear! Has he got pompous?'

Annie laughed. 'No, not really. He's just tremendously committed to teaching and that particular school. The head- master is one of those scary, messianic men who demand nothing less.'

'I see.' There was a pause, and then Alice said, 'I'll have to go. I'm on my coffee break. I'm sorry to have disturbed your bath, Annie, and I am really sorry about the job. Don't give up hope that something better will come along. Love to the boys, and Charlie, too. Come and see us soon!'

'Yes, we will. Thank you, Alice. Pizzas are fine. Goodbye.'

After she had rung off, Annie lay back in the cooling water and considered the conversation she had just had with her mother-in-law. Despite herself, she felt marginally more cheerful. She had twenty minutes before she was due to collect Archie. She had better get a move on.

Later, standing at the nursery school gate with her hair still wet, but for once wearing some make-up, Annie nodded and smiled at other mothers and thought, this is it. I'm now exactly the same as any of these stay-at-home types. I'd better get used to it. She caught the eye of a tall, untidy woman hovering outside the railings with a large, muddy, heavy-coated dog. She was wearing a multicoloured coat of the Navajo Indian variety. In fact she looked as if she might have rolled out of some sort of eco house with grass growing on its roof. Annie vaguely knew who she was: the mother of a 'difficult' child although she could have passed for his grandmother. The boy, Damon, was in the same class as Archie, and Annie had guessed that he must fall into some sort of special category because he sometimes seemed out of control, kicking and screaming on the street or running wildly across the park with uncoordinated limbs, ignoring his mother's yells to come back.

He had behavioural problems in school, too. Last term Annie had had a telephone call from the head teacher to say that Archie had bumped his head, but when she questioned him she discovered he had been pushed out of the Wendy house by Damon. Then she was called to go and collect him early because he had suffered a black eye – again Damon was the cause. During outdoor play, said Archie's teacher, he had been a little rough and hurled Archie across the playground and into collision with the wooden picnic table. Archie didn't complain. He said that Damon was a bad boy sometimes but he was his friend. He said he made him laugh.

Since then, Annie had noticed that Damon's mother was something of a pariah. She was always standing alone, gazing into the middle distance. She had a large, bony-nosed face, with strong, almost masculine features, and a shapeless mass of hennaed hair, in colour and texture not unlike that of her woolly-coated dog.

On an impulse Annie walked over to her and said, 'Hi! I'm Annie Baxter, Archie's mother.'

'Oh, God!' said the woman, grimacing. 'What's he done now?'

'Who? Damon? Nothing. No! Don't worry!'

'Thank God for that. That's why other mothers usually talk to me. To complain.'

'I see. Oh dear. Actually, all I was going to do was to introduce myself and say hello.'

'Well, in that case, hello!' The woman had a clipped way of speaking and a curiously old-fashioned, educated accent. She sounded like Miss Fox, who had taught Latin at Annie's girls' school twenty years ago. Her face remained unsmiling, but there was relief in her voice. 'I'm Fiona. Fiona Thompson.'

'Do you live in the village?'

'Yes. The other side of the park. Hampton Road. I've lived there for four years. I moved from Oxford when Damon was born. I felt a baby needed somewhere with a garden. And you?'

'Yes. We have a house on The Lees. We moved from London about the same time as you.'

'How do you find it?'

'The village? Well, lovely, of course. Pretty country, and great for the kids. Good schools and so on.'

'Oh, really? I think it's ghastly. Pat likes it, though.' She indicated the dog.

Annie laughed nervously, wondering if she had misunderstood, but a glance at Fiona's face told her that she had not.

'Surely not? Why is it so awful?'

'You must have noticed that Damon has some problems. He's borderline autistic and very demanding. I wonder now whether it would have been better to have stayed in Oxford and managed somehow in the flat. At least I had some support there and people were less clannish.'

'I see.' She's on her own, thought Annie – no mention of a partner or husband.

'To be fair, it's much better for Damon here, in a small village school. Oxford nurseries are pretty cut-throat and I don't think he would have managed nearly so well. It's on behalf of myself that I'm moaning. His behaviour doesn't endear him to other parents so I am generally *persona non grata*, and apart from that I miss having what I think of as a proper, adult life.'

'I know the feeling!'

'You do? You appear pretty well adapted. Part of the scene. As an obvious outsider, I have become rather observant.'

'As a matter of fact, I'm not at all "well adapted", as you put it. Today I was sacked from the very low-grade editing job I have been doing for the past three years. I feel fairly gutted, to be truthful.'

Fiona considered this piece of information. 'It's never good to be sacked,' she said, 'but sometimes it can lead to other things. Did you enjoy the work?'

'No.'

'Then I should be glad if I were you.'

Their conversation came to an end when there was a sudden surge towards the door of the nursery school. Fiona tied Pat to the fence and she and Annie joined the other mothers. By the time Annie had collected Archie and his school bag, Fiona and Damon had disappeared. She and Archie walked home slowly, holding hands. His class were exploring spring and he wanted to sing her a song they were learning about rabbits and lambs, undeterred by a sketchy grasp of the words and little idea of the tune. There was something very endearing about his enthusiasm and his upturned, eager face, and for some reason Annie didn't feel as bad as she had done earlier.

It was a bright spring day with patches of clear sunshine sparkling through the grey winter trees beside the footpath, and tiny green spears had suddenly appeared on the bushes on either side. There were birds singing and bustling about in the piles of dead leaves. Spring, to Annie, used to mean the bumper edition of the magazine with 'What to Wear This Summer' blazoned across the front. 'Twenty Pages of Key Fashion Ideas!' 'The Ten Essential Pieces for Your Whole New Look!' She had never taken much interest in what it meant to the natural world. Archie, apparently, knew more than she did.

As they walked, she thought about Fiona Thompson. She tried to imagine what it would be like to be her. What kind of lost adult life was she referring to when she had expressed dissatisfaction with the village? Annie couldn't imagine it was a social circle that she was missing. She did not give the impression that she was a woman who would care much for coffee mornings or lunches or that sort of thing. When she got home, she would Google her and see if anything came up.

'You're brave,' remarked Margaret as Alice finished her telephone call. 'Giving your daughter-in-law advice like that.'

'It wasn't advice!' protested Alice. 'Not really. I wasn't *telling* her what to do. I was just suggesting that she might think about going back to work when Archie starts proper school.'

'Doesn't she like being at home?'

'Not much, I don't think. She's not like Sadie, who is never happier than messing about with her children but has never really settled down to doing anything serious. It makes

David despair when he thinks of all the education we supported her through and yet she has never had what he thinks of as a proper job.'

'Parents are never satisfied. Mine never were. My mum liked it when I was in the hotel business, but she would have preferred me to marry a well-off man and not have to work at all. Then when she realised I wasn't going to give her a grandchild, she began to say how disappointed she was. That really took the biscuit considering she never lost an opportunity to tell me and my brother she didn't want us when we were kids.'

'Oh! But, Margaret! I wasn't criticising Annie or anything like that. I only said—'

Margaret gave a snort of laughter. 'You don't have to listen to me. I'm the last person to give anyone advice. Look at the mess I've made of things. Here I am, fifty-two years old, no kids, not on speaking terms with my only brother and not a man in sight!'

But when they rinsed their coffee mugs and returned to work, Alice wondered at what Margaret had said. She was sure that Annie had sounded pleased by her suggestion, but perhaps she should have kept quiet and just been sympathetic. And to be really truthful, if it came to it, she would be dismayed if she took her advice. She would be very concerned at the thought of her two little grandsons being cared for by some disenchanted East European eighteen-year-old, but it was no good thinking things like that. No good at all.

She wondered what David would say. They are grown up, they must make their own decisions, she imagined, remembering the conversation they had had about Sadie.

He seemed to find it easier to keep a safe distance from the lives of their children and their families. He didn't take it all on board like she did, which was sensible really. He had found it easier to let them go as they grew up and ran their own affairs.

Today he was going in to Salisbury to have lunch with an ex-colleague who had fallen on hard times. That was typical of him too. If asked directly for help, he would be there, doing whatever he could. He was a man you could rely on for sensible, practical support in a crisis. She imagined David and his new haircut tootling along in his old car in the spring sunshine. It was a pretty drive, the back way to Salisbury, winding between open sweeps of downland and through villages with inviting pubs. She would have liked to be there with him, making a day of it. It would be nice when she eventually retired to be able to do things together.

David, in fact, was anything but tootling along. He was driving fast and erratically, feeling alternate dread and eager anticipation. He was oblivious to the passing countryside or the sun moving across the hills, whose flanks were still clothed with silvery-brown winter grass. He ground his teeth with impatience when held up behind a slow-moving car driven by an elderly woman whose head was barely visible over the steering wheel, and raced ahead when she signalled to turn left and negotiated the manoeuvre as if driving a Sherman tank. Then there was a hold-up in Wilton, and despite the fact that he had masses of time to spare, he drummed his fingers impatiently on the steering wheel.

He had worked out exactly where he would park, but he had forgotten that it was market day and the centre of the city was jammed with cars, so he had to change his plans and use a multistorey car park that disgorged him into an unfamiliar shopping precinct. When he reached ground level, he thought he had forgotten his mobile telephone and stood frantically patting his pockets while posses of very young women pushing strollers steered round him. He found his telephone safely in an inside pocket and took it out to check if he had a message. He half thought Julia might get cold feet and cancel – but there was nothing. He still had plenty of time, but he couldn't dawdle, and strode through the shopping precinct as if he was in a hurry, past the coffee shops and chain stores, whose windows were sprouting plastic daffodils and pyramids of Easter eggs and where the models wore tiny, bright summer clothes.

Out of the sun the wind was cold and sent eddies of litter into corners of the mall, but the girls who sat on the line of benches with their babies and toddlers were wearing skimpy tops with bare arms and legs. They all seemed to be fat, David noticed. They put him in mind of a colony of blubbery sea mammals and pups, lolling about on a rocky shore. Why weren't they back in school, these child mothers? he wondered as he strode past. Was their education really over, sunk without trace in a sea of prams?

When he reached the appointed wine bar he hesitated outside, reading the menu, which was chalked on a board propped against the wall. He was twenty minutes early and through the window he could see that only a few tables were occupied, but he would go in anyway. There was a rack of newspapers for customers' use and he could get himself a glass of wine while he waited for Julia. If her past form was anything to go by, she would be late.

Of course there was nobody he knew inside, but he was glad that the waitress showed him to a table tucked away behind a sort of screen on which various posters and notices were pinned. He sat down, with a thumping heart, feeling absurdly self-conscious. It was annoying to react like this when he was a man in his sixties. He felt he was letting himself down. He got his mobile telephone from his pocket and laid it on the table and fussed about checking for glasses and wallet.

The waitress had disappeared without asking him if she could get him a drink and he saw that the newspaper rack was right inside the door, which meant he would have to emerge from behind the screen if he wished to get one. No, he would stay put where he was and study the notices displayed above his head. Art courses, wine clubs, gardens open to the public, organic vegetable box schemes, a creative writing workshop, a performance of the *Messiah* – it was all there, the preoccupations of a middle-class cathedral city, as far removed from the lives of the teenage mothers in the shopping precinct as it was possible to be.

Five minutes later he caught the eye of the waitress and asked for a glass of red wine. 'Do you want to order, sir?' she asked. 'Today's specials are on the blackboard by the bar.' She was a tall, dark-haired girl, so thin that her hip bones jutted through her black trousers, a few inches from David's face. She seemed far too young to be at work. It occurred to David that every girl seemed too young today. It's because I am old, he thought. It's a sign of my age.

'No, no. I'm waiting for someone. We'll order together. When she comes.'

Twenty-five minutes later he had finished his wine, the restaurant had filled up and there was still no Julia. Where the hell was she? He tried her mobile telephone, which appeared to be switched off. The waitress had started to look pointedly in his direction every time she passed the table. After forty minutes he decided that he could sit there no longer and got up. He didn't want to eat on his own and Julia was evidently not going to come.

He felt annoyed – with himself and her – and his irritation made him feel more like his normal self. 'I'm sorry, but there's evidently been some mistake,' he said to the waitress. 'I won't take the table any longer.' He paid for his wine, gave her a small tip, struggled into his coat and left. If this was some bloody silly film, he thought, Julia would come running towards him at the last moment and all would be well, but there was no sign of her, and he walked back along the busy streets on which almost everyone seemed to be eating or suckling at a bottle. Pies and sausage rolls and baguettes were jammed into open mouths – all within sight and sound of the great medieval cathedral spire that rose above the rooftops to point its finger into the pale spring sky.

So that was that, then. He felt, on the whole, greatly relieved. He took a wrong turning somewhere and found himself amongst the market stalls, and stopped to buy some good-looking sausages from a stout, rosy-cheeked woman who had pictures of pigs displayed on the stall. The pigs were very large and spotted black and white and were snout down in grass under apple trees. On an impulse he stopped again and bought a plastic bowl planted with white hyacinths.

Bearing gifts, he drove sedately back home to Alice. Not

far out of Salisbury, and without knowing it, he passed Julia driving fast in the opposite direction.

Sadie felt down, but not out. What didn't help was that she was sick every morning and hardly able to drag herself out of bed to see the girls off to school. By ten o'clock she was better and able to eat some toast and tidy the cottage and later go across the yard to the packing shed. Her job had to be done, however she felt, and there was no question of asking Kyle to help her out.

The weekend had not gone as she had planned. Kyle remained resistant to the idea of her keeping the baby and for the moment she was not sure what she was going to do. The one thing that was non-negotiable from her point of view was her refusal to have an abortion, and so she had to pin her hopes on Kyle changing his mind. At least they were talking to each other again and they had enjoyed good and urgent sex on Saturday night, but when they had finished and were lying side by side in bed, Kyle had remarked, 'You'll not get round me like this, you know. You'll not get me to change my mind. It's your choice, babe. If you want to stay with me, then go and get seen to. Simple as that.'

Sadie began to cry and he had reached out and put his arms round her, but he didn't retract the threat and she was wise enough not to choose this moment to say that there was no way she was changing her mind either.

The trouble was, she no longer felt confident that all would be well if she just let things go for a while, or that Kyle would eventually be persuaded to accept the baby. There was a steeliness in his attitude that frightened her.

What if? she couldn't prevent herself from asking. What happens to us then? He couldn't do it to us, she told herself. He couldn't do it to the girls. He loves Georgie and Tamzin, and he loves me. He couldn't turn us out. He's always saying that having us here is the best thing that's ever happened to him.

It had been so hard not to tell her mother on Sunday evening, but she was glad that she hadn't. It wouldn't help to have her parents' opinions thrown into the ring. It was nothing to do with them and they couldn't influence the outcome. She had longed, though, to have her mother's arms round her and receive her uncritical sympathy and support. There was no one like one's mother. Her father was a different matter. Just at the moment she wasn't keen to hear what *he* would have to say about the corner she was in.

The packing shed was cold, much colder than outside on this sunny morning. She propped the door open and let the brightness flood across the step on to the concrete floor. Tiny motes of dust danced in the thick shaft of light. Outside, the hens were busy in the yard, scratching at the weeds and taking dirt baths. They had started to lay again after their winter rest.

It was therapeutic, mindless work, counting mushrooms into brown bags, weighing spring greens and rainbow chard, lifting cold, round swedes from their nets. She liked handling the vegetables, with their cool smoothness and earthy smell. She was careful with them, respectful almost, arranging them in each box like a still life, standing back every now and then to survey the effect.

When she had finished, she had time to go back to the

cottage and get on the computer and check Mumsnet. Her dilemma had created a huge response – almost all very supportive of her and her viewpoint. Only one or two were critical, saying stuff like every baby needed two parents or that conception should not be a random act of God. But that's exactly what it is, thought Sadie. That's why it's so wonderful.

She typed in a new message, giving the latest update, ending 'So what do I do now? I'm feeling pretty desperate.' When she had finished, she went on to the girls' primary school website. She checked the weekly newsletter and realised that she had forgotten to send Georgie with rubber boots and a packed lunch for a trip to a plant nursery. Damn. All this other stuff going on was taking her mind off her daughters, and she felt guilty and ashamed.

Getting out the mixing bowl, she started making a batch of oat biscuits from one of Alice's recipes, and while they were cooking she e-mailed the head teacher with an offer to come into school and give a little talk about organic vegetables. Last week Tamzin's class had been addressed by a father who worked for Western Water, who Sadie considered little better than legalised terrorists. Being busy helped her to feel more positive, and when she heard Kyle whistling in the yard as the cows trooped into the dairy for afternoon milking, she had more or less convinced herself that everything would be all right.

However, that evening, after the girls had gone to bed and she was finishing clearing up in the kitchen and putting extra-special packed lunches together for the next day, Kyle turned from what he was doing on the computer and said,

'It says here you have to get it done by twenty-four weeks, and no probs. So get yourself booked in, babe. Get an appointment tomorrow, okay? Don't let it go any longer.'

Sadie stood, open-mouthed, with dishcloth in hand.

'I'm not doing it, Kyle,' she said finally. 'I'm not killing our baby, whatever you say.'

'In that case, I want you out of here. I don't like doing it to you, or the girls, but it's your decision. You'd better tell your mum you'll be staying with her for the foreseeable future, unless you've got other plans.'

'Kyle! Don't do this to me. Don't do it to Tamzin and Georgie.'

'*I'm* not doing it. You are. You got yourself pregnant. You were supposed to be on the bloody pill, weren't you? It's your choice, like I said.'

'You can't kill your own baby, Kyle.'

'Don't give me that! It's not my *baby*. It's a blob of jelly. It's just a dot. It's a nothing. All they do is give you an injection and that's it. A termination. It's not even an abortion if you get it done quick.'

'Kyle, it's already a life! A precious life.'

'It won't be a precious life if I don't want it. I'm not ready to be a dad. I don't want the responsibility.'

'You'll want it when you see it, hold it in your arms. I'm sure it's a boy, because I wasn't sick with the girls. You'll want him then, Kyle.'

'Yeah, and what sort of dad will I be? We've got debts, Sade. We live in a tied cottage. This job could go any day. Don't you ever read the papers? Dairy farms are folding every week, especially small units like this.'

'You'd find another job. There are other farms.'

'Look, I'll not change my mind. You get it done next week or that's it. We can't afford a baby and that's final. If you go on with this, you're on your own. I can't say clearer than that.'

Chapter Six

'I'VE DECIDED TO get proper invitations printed,' said Alice at supper, 'and I thought that maybe you could look out some old photographs for me. There are all those boxes of family photos in the cupboard in the sitting room. I want to find the ones that show the special times – like that one we've got framed of us all on the beach in Cornwall. It was someone's birthday – Marina's I suppose, because it must have been August. That's the sort of thing I want – special events down the years – and then I'll organise them into a sort of collage and get it put on the front of the invitation with the printed part on the back – like those Christmas cards people send showing what their families got up to in the past year.'

'One of those ghastly exercises in seasonal boastfulness, you mean?' said David. 'The ones that are designed to make the receiver feel an envious failure, with ugly and untalented children and boring lives?'

Alice laughed. 'No! Not a bit like that!'

'Can you remember the card we got one year with a picture of the sender's *house* on the front and inside a list of all that they had had done to it in the past year? New bathrooms and underfloor heating, I seem to remember.

Not entirely in keeping with the spirit of Christmas – not much about the lowly stable there.' His voice was heavy with sarcasm.

'David! Stop it! Don't get on to one of your pet hates while I'm trying to tell you something.'

'I don't want photographs of me on the front of anything.'

'Don't be silly. It won't be *you*, as such, just you in relation to the rest of us; you as part of the family, although I was thinking we could use that photograph we've got somewhere of us at that college ball when we were first engaged.' David grunted. 'I thought about twelve photos should do it. Us, the children, the grandchildren . . .'

'Have we got photographs of the grandchildren? All of them, I mean? The new ones too?'

'Well we've got hundreds of Mo on the computer. Marina has sent a whole dossier from intrauterine onwards. Oh goodness! Have we got Sabine and Agnes? Because Ollie and Lisa went off on their own to get married, we missed out on wedding photographs when the girls were bridesmaids. We must have some somewhere from last summer but I don't know that they are particularly good. Would you look them out? If not, I'll ask Lisa to send me some.'

David was only half listening because every few moments his thoughts returned to Julia and he ran through various versions of what could have happened to her. A misunderstanding could be ruled out, because the exchange of e-mails had made the arrangements quite specific. A change of heart was possible, but then the failure to contact him and cancel the lunch was rude and unforgivable. A terrible accident was possible but unlikely. Instead, David remembered Julia's late entrances to department meetings, the flustered explanations, the special considerations that had to be made. It's her style, he thought. She doesn't behave in accordance with the rules and obligations that govern other people's lives.

It was a relief to be at home, eating the sausages in the kitchen with the bowl of hyacinths on the table. Alice had been touchingly pleased by his gesture and hadn't asked him many questions about his lunch. It was too complicated to tell her that his ex-colleague hadn't turned up and the whole thing had been an exercise in wasting time. It was easier to pretend that it had taken place and was totally unremarkable.

Alice wasn't interested anyway. She had been on the telephone to Marina for about half an hour, discussing the whys and wherefores of taking baby Mo to Syria to meet Ahmed's family. He guessed that Marina was working herself up about flying and then the risks once in Syria. She had always loved a drama. Having a partner like Ahmed − a dissident journalist who was out of favour in his own country − was typical of her. An ordinary, run-of-the-mill Englishman would not have been nearly controversial enough. Ahmed's family were well-to-do, apparently, and had a large house in the suburbs of Damascus − in the same neighbourhood as the British Embassy, he had been told, which he supposed might be useful if Ahmed should be arrested and thrown into jail, which was the outcome that Marina appeared to be anticipating.

Alice had been sensible and reassuring. They both agreed that Ahmed would not ask her to do anything that was dangerous or could put Mo at risk, and she promised to ask the paediatrician at the surgery about small babies and flying.

What a lot of fuss parents made about babies these days, thought David. When Charlie was a few months old he and Alice had spent two months touring France and Spain in a clapped-out old Citroën Deux Chevaux, camping where they could, with Charlie sleeping in a little wicker basket thing. The last time Marina and Ahmed had ventured out of London, they arrived in what was referred to as a people carrier, as if on a military exercise, with the back of the tank-like vehicle loaded with equipment.

'Poor Annie,' sighed Alice suddenly, and then, in an altered tone, 'These sausages are delicious. I wonder if one can buy them anywhere other than the market. I was thinking of doing some sausages for the party.'

'Why poor Annie?' David couldn't remember if he was supposed to know about something that made Annie eligible for Alice's sympathy.

'I told you! She has lost her job. That editing thing she does online. She sounded very down about it today. I told her that she could always go back to proper work when Archie starts school next year.'

'Could she? How?'

'Well, I don't know. But people do, don't they? Obviously they have to arrange childcare, but it is perfectly possible.'

'I should have thought she would have preferred to look after her children while they are so young.'

'David! You can't say that sort of thing. Mothers have the right to choose whether they work or not.'

'I should have thought the choice was whether to have children in the first place, and not whether you want to look after them.'

'*You should have thought!*' cried Alice. 'You are so judge-mental and reactionary! Don't you dare say that to her.'

'In my experience, women who go back to work when they have small children are a nightmare. They always want time off, and to go home early, and facilities to breastfeed, and they spend most of their time whining about how tired they are and wanting to do less than anyone else.'

'Of course they do! Although I am sure you are being unfair. How else can you juggle a job and small children? The responsibility for the home and everything still seems to fall on the mother, doesn't it? You can't imagine Charlie telling his headmaster that he can't teach the afternoon lessons because Archie is at home ill, can you? It just wouldn't happen.'

'I should have thought that if Archie was at home ill, Annie would *want* to be at home with him. *You* would have wanted to be at home with any of ours, wouldn't you?'

'Well of course I would, and so would Annie. She's a very devoted mother, but that doesn't mean she should lose the opportunity to work, does it? The system should be flex-ible enough to accommodate emergencies like that.'

'Isn't raising children a series of emergencies, large and small, that one parent or another ought to be around for?'

'You're impossible to argue with,' said Alice quite crossly, but as she got up to collect their plates, she thought of Sadie and Marina and Annie, and wondered how it was that none of them seemed to have found a satisfactory solu-tion. Really, it had been easier in her day, when she had stayed at home with the children until Sadie started secondary school and nobody expected her to be anything other than a full-time mother.

But then I haven't really achieved anything, she thought. I haven't had a career. Not in the eyes of any modern young woman. I have had a series of jobs that fitted round the family. I have enjoyed work and earned enough to feel independent, but that's all. Considering I have a good degree in English, I might have expected to do more. But to be fair, all I ever wanted was to be a wife and mother. To me, it was always the most important thing. Alice tried to imagine herself in some other sort of role – as a solicitor, specialising in divorce, or a female vicar in a surplice, shaking hands with her parishioners at the church door after Sunday morning Matins. I couldn't have done it, she thought. I would never have wanted to devote myself to anything outside the family.

David escaped from the table and went upstairs to turn on his computer. He was not really surprised to see that three messages had arrived from Julia, each heralded by a little exclamation mark in the margin.

dear david, he read, *i'm so so sorry i was staying with my sister as i told you and i had no idea salisbury was so far i thought it would only take me twenty mins or so and it was more like an hour and i started a bit late because my sister wanted me to go and see a cottage she is thinking of buying and then i found I had left my mobile behind and by the time I missed it it was too late to go back and get it and I didn't have your mobile number it was on my phone what will you think of me I am just so so sorry.*

The second was exactly the same, sent in error, he supposed, but the third read, '*I still really need to see you but i guess you wont want to be bothered with me again.*'

David wasn't at all sure that he did, but nevertheless spent several minutes tapping out a reply.

Dear Julia,
Of course, I did wonder what had happened to you, and am relieved that no accident was involved. I waited for an hour or so and then guessed that you weren't coming. If you really want to try and arrange another meeting, I leave it to you to suggest time and place. Best wishes, David.

What did she want with him anyway? He was an old man to someone of her age. He was past it; 'it' being anything useful. As Alice had just told him, he was reactionary and judgemental, although really, he couldn't see anything wrong with that.

He thought fondly of Alice. She had been so easy to deflect. It had only taken two pounds of organic sausages and a bit of an exchange about the role of women to get her off the trail of what he had been up to. He had been tempted to tell her the truth about the abortive meeting with Julia, but really it was less complicated to invent a story. He didn't think of it as a lie. It was more an expediency.

The door opened suddenly behind him and he jumped guiltily.

'What are you doing up here?' asked Alice. 'Why don't you come down and keep me company?'

David hastily tried to clear the computer screen. 'Just checking on something,' he mumbled, trying to block her view. 'I'll be down in a sec.'

Alice came to stand by his shoulder. 'You know,' she said

in a thoughtful voice, 'all this stuff going on with the girls . . . Sadie, Annie, and then Marina tonight . . . it makes me think how lucky we were, David.'

'What do you mean, lucky?' The bloody thing wouldn't switch off and Alice must have a clear view of his e-mail in-box, but she didn't seem to notice. She was too intent on making a pronouncement.

'Life was more simple for us when we were their age. There was less choice, I know, and we had lower expectations, perhaps, but really, I had all I ever wanted as a young woman: you, and four happy, healthy children. I don't regret any of it.'

At last, with maddening slowness, David's computer screen faded and he was able, with relief, to pat the hand that Alice had laid on his shoulder.

'I'm glad to hear it!' He felt on the point of calling her 'old girl', but managed to swallow the words.

'And that's the main reason I want this party,' she went on. 'Because we have never celebrated any of it. We have never celebrated our family life. We may have made mistakes and done some things wrong, with hindsight, and worried about the wrong things, maybe, but I think we did our best, David, I really do, and here we are, still a happy, united family. It's an achievement, it really is!'

David looked up at his wife. Her face was rather pink and he could see that she was speaking with great earnestness. He didn't know what had inspired this outbreak of feeling. As far as he could judge, their life as a family was as chaotic and problematic as ever, but then Alice seemed to be going through a strange stage – this insistence on having a party, for one thing. He wondered if it could be put down to post-menopause or some other mysterious female malfunction.

'It's you, though, Alice,' he said, meaning it. 'It's you at the heart of it all.' He stood up. 'Come on. We'll open a bottle of wine. We could both do with a drink.'

As he led the way down the stairs, thankful that he had escaped from a tight corner, Alice put her arms round his waist. 'I do like the haircut!' she said in a playful voice. 'You're still a sexy man, you know.' David thought of what it had been like when they were young and he had loved it when Alice took the initiative with sex. Now he wasn't so sure that he was up to it, especially this evening, when he felt rather wrung out.

After two glasses of wine, Alice dropped off to sleep on the sofa with her mouth open. David extricated himself and spent the rest of the evening finishing the bottle and watching a crime drama on the television in which a desperate husband murdered his wife on their wedding anniversary in order to run away with her sister.

Seen from the man's point of view, it was all an exhausting waste of time and effort. Disposing of the body in Windermere was a tactical error for a start. David tried to imagine the task of wrapping the whole of Alice in black plastic and parcel tape. These days it would be very hard to manhandle her into a car boot and then on board a small and flimsy boat that looked in danger of capsizing.

He was glad that he had never felt like murdering her, and he certainly wouldn't want to run off with her sister, Rachel. He had always been grateful that Alice and Rachel were so different and he had chosen the sweet-natured, easy-going sister and not the bossy one who had grown fat and career-orientated as she had got older. If Alice had not been asleep he would have told her as much. He might even have told her he loved her, which would have been true, because he did. She was the foundation of his life, was Alice.

However, when she woke and went off to make a cup of decaffeinated tea, the drama was over and a football match begun and David forgot what he had intended to say and Alice seemed to have got over her romantic in-clinations. Instead she filled a hot-water bottle, ate a few biscuits out of the tin, and went off to bed, yawning, on her own.

Annie deliberately waited until the boys were in bed and Charlie had sat down with a pile of sixth-form essays to mark before she told him that she had been made redun-dant. 'By the way,' she said, in a rehearsed voice, standing in front of the table and throwing a shadow over the sheaf of papers, 'I have lost my job. I heard today.'

Charlie put down his pen and looked up at her in concern. 'Oh darling! Why? Why on earth?'

'They're scrapping the mag. Economy drive, I guess, and apparently it no longer fits the company profile. I can't say that I'm surprised. According to Jennifer, store managers are laying off staff by text, with no warning – so my little informative articles about how to use a stepladder are hardly what employees are interested in. They aren't stupid – they know that the true message from the management is "you'll be bloody lucky to hang on to your jobs and we'll make sure you don't find out until the last moment".'

'Bastards! Well, to be honest, I shall be glad you're not part of it any more.'

'Oh, really?' Annie was immediately defensive. 'At least it was a job.'

'But we've been through this before,' said Charlie with laboured patience, as if he were talking to one of his fourth form. 'You don't need to have a job – especially one like that. We can manage without the pathetic money it paid.'

Annie crossed her arms and glared at him. 'Oh, can we? At least it was *my* money.'

'You are always saying that – but what does it matter whose money it is? Why do you always make out that it does? I don't get it. When do I ever treat the money I earn as exclusively mine?'

'Okay, you don't do that – but that's how I feel about it. That's how it seems to me. Look, I've been independent since I left school – more or less – and at least my "pathetic" job meant that I had an income of my own, however small.'

'So this is all about money, is it?'

'You know that's not what it's about. It's what that crap job represented.'

Charlie got up and went into the kitchen, looking for a beer. 'I don't understand,' he said, opening the drawer to reach for the bottle opener. 'What did it represent? It didn't represent your true worth as a professional journalist – no way!'

Annie followed him through and leaning against the counter said, 'I know it didn't. It was a horrible job, but it was something that I *did* outside of the boys and the house. It was a link to the grown-up world.'

Charlie sighed. He had started to dress like a schoolmaster, in corduroy trousers and a check shirt and woolly jumper. He ran his hands through his hair. His face was tired. He works too hard, thought Annie. She imagined how the few women on the staff would find him attractive. She imagined him having an affair and explaining to some woman as they lay in bed that his wife was a dissatisfied shrew.

'You're just never happy, are you?' he said. 'After Rory was born you hated it in London. You hated going back to work and leaving him with that childminder. You hated the job, the editor, the foreign assignments – you were always angry and exhausted. When we talked about moving out and starting a new life you were as keen as I was. Are you telling me that you regret it now?'

'I regret *some* of it!' cried Annie, throwing up her arms. 'Of course I do. Why do you treat it as a crime for me to admit it? You say I was always complaining about work, but that's *so* not fair. I was sick of some aspects of it but I had just had a baby, for God's sake, and you were working flat out and it wasn't a good time for either of us.'

'I'm not going back, you know,' said Charlie quietly. 'Nothing would make me go back to working in the City.'

'This isn't about *you*! It's obvious *you're* all right. It's obvious you love your job and that ghastly headmaster at whose feet you all worship, and that whole bloody school!' She followed Charlie back through to the sitting room. He turned to search her face, looking puzzled and hurt.

'Why are you being so unpleasant? Is it me that you're fed up with, because that's what it sounds like. You seem to be turning this into a personal attack on me.'

'It's not about *you*, I keep telling you that. Or if it is, it's because of the extent to which you don't sympathise with how I feel. You don't understand what all this is doing to me.' Annie heard her voice rising with a tremor of self-pity that she couldn't help.

'All this?' said Charlie, looking about him with a puzzled expression, as if the answer was to be found in the comfortable sitting room in which they stood. 'Nice house – twice the size of where we were in London – garden, countryside, two happy, healthy kids, enough money! What more do you want, Annie? You know, I sometimes worry about you. I worry that there is something missing, an inability to be grateful for what we've got, or else the judgement to see how fortunate we are. You want to talk everything down, don't you? The village, the school, my job, everything. I tell you, I'm getting sick of it, and I worry about the effect you have on the kids with all this negativity. You never used to be like this.'

Annie felt herself trembling as her anger with him suddenly turned back on herself. He was right, of course. Everything he said about her, she thought herself on an almost daily basis. She crumpled on to the sofa in despair.

'Well what can I do?' she cried. 'What am I to do? I can't help how I feel!'

'Get a grip, for a start,' advised Charlie sternly. 'Pull yourself together.'

The remark made her anger rise again. 'How dare you talk to me as if I'm one of your bloody school kids having a strop?'

Charlie sighed and came to sit beside her and took her hand. 'All right. I'm sorry. Let's take this step by step. Let's start with how you resent the fact that I love teaching.' He held up his hand to silence her as she began to speak. 'Don't deny it, Annie, because you know it's true.'

'Here we go again – every discussion we have always starts and ends with *you*! What I resent is that you go off every morning to do something you love with people you like in an environment you find stimulating and rewarding, and I'm stuck here day after day. You might want me to say that being a little homemaker and baking cupcakes and having everything lemon fresh and shiny for when you come home is a satisfying life, but too fucking bad. It isn't. It's driving me insane. I'm lonely and depressed and if you were less wrapped up in your own cocoon of sanctimonious happiness you would have taken the trouble to notice what's happening to me.'

'You think that I haven't noticed? This is where we started this conversation. I just don't know what to do to make it better for you. I thought we had everything we wanted. You wanted children more than I did. You made sure you got pregnant both times. I can remember how happy you were, smug almost, that you got pregnant so easily while some of your friends were having to go for IVF. The consequence of having children is that your life has to change. It has changed for both of us. Look where we are now compared to five years ago.'

'Stop talking to me as if I am a retard!' Annie snatched her hand back. 'You don't have to say stuff like this as if I need reminding about wanting children or the changes they bring. You make it sound as if I don't love them.'

'You're always moaning about having to look after them, as if it was some sort of penance.'

'How dare you! How dare you say that!' Annie jumped

up. Although she was furious with him, half of her anger was because she knew there was truth in what he said and half that she did not want to be forced to admit it. Once it was spoken, it was out – and then what? It terrified her to even look over the edge of that abyss. If she admitted that for the majority of the time she didn't enjoy her children or their company, her life would unravel. All the careful knots she had tied to hold it together would slip and she would slide into a place she did not want to consider.

'Look,' said Charlie in his understanding voice, 'do you think you need some help? Do you think you should see the doctor? If you say you are depressed, that is.' It seemed to Annie that he made being depressed sound like a terrible personal failing.

'I don't know. I need to have some time to think, but I resent you saying I moan about looking after the boys. I have them day after day, whereas you just come home and—'

'You're doing it now. Listen to yourself.'

'I'm pointing out that I have the lion's share of childcare, and therefore—'

'Because I have a job, Annie. I go out to work!'

'Exactly!'

'And I must point out that I do my bit when I get home in time, which I do whenever I can, and in the school holidays.'

'Yeah, yeah, but why should it be like this? Why shouldn't it be me going out to work? Why shouldn't it, now that Archie is at nursery four mornings a week and starts school in September?'

'How could that possibly work? There has to be someone at home. He does mornings only for half a term, and even after that when he goes full time, he and Rory get out at three thirty. What sort of job would accommodate that? And what about holidays and half-terms and inset days and days when one of them isn't well? We *agreed*, Annie, that the quality of their childhood was what mattered most. We *agreed* we didn't want to put them in childcare or have some disenchanted au pair looking after them. Are you suggesting we go back on all of that?'

'Please, Charlie, stop pushing me! I'm not suggesting anything. I'm just saying that I would like to consider alternatives without you telling me I need to see the doctor. Perhaps I do, but that's for me to decide. Look, what I am is thoroughly pissed off that I've lost my job. All right? Can you accept that? I know it was a job that you despised and considered unworthy, but it was important to me. Perhaps now I've lost it, it's time for me to consider what else is out there, and that's what I intend to do.'

Charlie sighed heavily. 'That's up to you, I suppose. Look, by all means, but you know that I can't compromise *my* job, don't you? There's no question of that. I'm confident that I'll be in a promoted post by the end of the year and probably head of department when Geoff Rivers retires.'

'Here we are again,' said Annie stonily. 'Back with you.' She stood up, hating him. It felt as if her unhappiness was an inconvenience to him, nothing more. 'I'm going out,' she said. 'I need a break.'

Charlie shrugged and went to sit at the table. He took up the first essay in the pile. 'As you like,' he said. 'Some of us have work to do. Quite a lot of it.'

In the kitchen she grabbed her leather biker jacket from the back of the chair – her very, very expensive statement jacket of ten years ago – and angrily pushed her arms into the sleeves. She picked up her purse and keys and slammed out of the front door. Outside it was a clear, cold night with quite bright stars piercing the darkness. A dramatic-looking moon sailed high above.

Not knowing where she was going, she set off. As she walked, she reflected on their quarrel. It was hopeless and childish to bicker like that. Why couldn't they discuss the whole thing rationally, listening to each other's point of view? She knew that her attack on Charlie was unfair, but she felt so angry with him. What's going on between us, she thought, that we can't even talk about things any more? There seems to be this great store of resentment that surfaces the moment we talk about anything that really matters. No wonder I feel stifled. I suppose at the bottom of it is that Charlie won't cut me any slack. My job is here, looking after the boys, and that's that.

She crossed the main road and went into the deserted park, where the empty children's swings moved very slightly to and fro, casting eerie swaying shadows on the ground. How many hours had she spent pushing the boys backwards and forwards until they were old enough to propel themselves? Archie had only recently got the knack. She gave the wooden roundabout a hefty shove and set it creaking into motion before she walked on and out into Hampton Road. She had already looked up the number of Fiona's house on the school website, and a few minutes later she opened a rickety garden gate and stood outside a red-bricked terraced house. The curtains in the downstairs room were open and she could see Fiona sitting on a sofa in a knocked-through sitting room reading a newspaper – much of which lay about her feet. She looked large and solid and was wearing some sort of checked lumberjack shirt and jeans. Without hesitating, Annie knocked on the door.

Hours later, when Annie turned her key in the lock of her own front door, the house was in darkness. Charlie hadn't thought to leave the outside light burning or even the hall light on. It was late – past two o'clock – but she felt very wide awake and disinclined to go upstairs and sleep. She would have liked to go into the sitting room and play music or watch the television, but she didn't dare disturb the children, so instead she felt for the kitchen light switch in the darkness and put the kettle on to make a hot drink.

She had had an extraordinary evening. Fiona had proved to be funny, clever and entertaining, and for the first time for ages Annie felt more interested in someone else's life than her own.

Over very strong cider she had learned that Damon was conceived with donated sperm, that Fiona had never had a serious relationship with a man, indeed was not certain of her sexuality, but knew that she wanted to be a mother and set about making it happen, much to the dismay of everyone who knew her, especially her immediate family. At the time she had a coveted teaching post at Oxford University in the Department of Theology and Oriental Studies, but after Damon was born, he cried non-stop more or less for two years and was plagued by colic, insomnia and ear infections. As he got older his difficulties grew and behavioural problems began. His nursery school could not cope with his manic surges of activity and unpredictable rages, and Fiona, exhausted and terrified for his future, was at her wits' end. She thoroughly researched what her GP had diagnosed as borderline ADD – he had wanted to prescribe Ritalin to control Damon's behaviour – and decided to resign from her job. On her own she discovered that her son had a whole range of food sensitivities and suffered from low blood sugar. Modifying his diet corrected many of the behavioural problems, and taking him out of the city nursery and moving to the village provided a more gentle pace of life that seemed to suit his needs. Fiona now worked part time as an online tutor for the university.

Annie had sat listening to all of this, feeling ashamed of her own despairing nature. Why, she had nothing to complain about. Her life was perfect, a bed of roses, in comparison. Most of all she was impressed by Fiona's dedication and selflessness. She was also a good listener, and when Annie provided the reason for knocking on her door at night and asking to come in, Fiona followed her halting explanation without interrupting.

'I know how you must feel,' she said. 'My online tutoring is my lifeline even though it's mostly tedious and eats into the very brief time I have to do things for myself.'

'But the thing is that Charlie is quite right when he says that I was fed up with my proper editorial job – I was, but only because trying to do it well and cope with a baby was just too much. I so wanted to be a good mother – a much better mother than mine had been – and I just found it all so stressful. Up until then I was confident that I could handle most situations, and suddenly I couldn't any more. Then I was pregnant again and it coincided with Charlie wanting a career change, and here we are.'

'Yeah. Feeling isolated, inadequate and misunderstood!'

'You've got it,' said Annie. 'But where do I go from here? I feel as if I have run into a brick wall.' She was already aware of a weighty assurance about Fiona. It wasn't just that she was physically big; she felt she was also a woman of substance. She was clearly extremely bright.

'I'm not a suitable person to give advice. Most of my life decisions have been considered eccentric, or mistaken, by my family. You'll have to work out your own solution.'

'Yes, I realise that. But talking to you makes me feel I should stop whining and put the boys first — exactly what Charlie says, in fact.'

'Why should it be whining to express your own needs? If they are reasonable, that is. It strikes me that you have been denying your true feelings. Why should every woman be cut out for motherhood and caring for young children? You've done it for five or so years. Maybe it's time to consider another arrangement. I don't believe that full-time mothers are morally superior, do you?'

Annie considered. 'Well, yes, I do, in a way. It's definitely what I feel I should be and what everyone who counts in my life expects of me. I am just completely shit at it.'

Fiona pulled a face and refilled their glasses. 'That's some guilt trip you're on.'

'Yes. Endorsed by Charlie.'

'Does he know how unhappy you are?'

'He thinks I'm hideously hard to please. He thinks I should pull myself together and appreciate how lucky I am.

Which I agree with. I wish I could. Especially after hearing your story, which is humbling, by the way.'

'It wasn't my choice and none of it was easy. Quite a lot of it was done with bad grace. I just happen to want the best possible chance at life for Damon, which is selfish in a way, because, after all, he is an extension of me. I wouldn't have done it for anyone else's child.'

'Yes, I can see that. All parents are the same. They can be utterly ruthless to further the interests of their own children. Think of the extent to which perfectly honest people will lie to get their offspring into good schools. I'd be the same. I don't lack dedication in that way. I just hate being at home with them. There, I've said it now. I HATE BEING AT HOME WITH MY CHILDREN!'

'What would a man do in your circumstances? I've often found it helps to consider that question. It helped me when I was fighting to stay on the college teaching staff and coming up against a hierarchy of white middle-class misogynistic males. It kept me tough and focused.'

'Well, in my case, a man would outsource the boys. He'd find an arrangement that freed him up to do what he wanted or needed to do and he would convince himself that it was also in their best interests.'

'Exactly. So what's stopping you?'

'Charlie would be horrified, and I would be frightened of the condemnation of everyone else and desperately concerned that the boys were not being looked after properly.'

'Would a man feel like that?'

'No, not in Charlie's case. He wouldn't care what anyone thought, but to be fair, he would be very concerned about the quality of childcare and the impact on the boys.'

'So approach it from that angle but don't let it stop you from pursuing what you want to do. Get the childcare sorted. It's perfectly possible. Then have a reassessment, as I had to do. Damon's needs were not being satisfactorily met by anyone else but me, and therefore I gave up my job. Your kids are much more straightforward.'

'Oh God! The thought of actually doing it makes me sick. I don't know what job I would be offered, for starters. I am desperately out of the loop now. My sort of journalism depends on having an ability to see ahead of the trend, and I am five years out of date.'

'Then move to a different type of publication – as I had to do with teaching. You've had time out and you've now got children – perhaps the sort of journalism you were doing before isn't possible. Some sacrifices have to be made, but remember, a man would make sure that any compromise was acceptable to achieve his main objective.'

Annie sat in silence for a moment. She was feeling distinctly drunk on the cider that Fiona had produced. Tomorrow she would have a hangover, but for now her mind was racing and she felt an optimism that had deserted her for years.

'Thank you so much, Fiona,' she said, looking at her watch. 'Really, it's been great just to talk to you. I knew that you were different from the Mummy Mafia at nursery, but you always looked so aloof that I backed off talking to you. I'm so glad that I knocked on your door tonight. If there's anything I can do to help *you*, please say.'

'What I would really appreciate is if you could bear to ask Damon back to play after school. No one else does, you see, because he can be very over the top and some children are scared, or get fed up with him. I'd have to come too, if you didn't mind. At least to begin with.'

'Of course I'll do that. Actually Archie really likes Damon. He counts him as a friend. When can you come?'

Now, waiting for the kettle to boil in her own kitchen Annie felt the afterglow of sisterly camaraderie. In Fiona's company she had felt able to be herself and her confession had lifted a great load from her shoulders. Think like a man! she reminded herself. Shed the guilt. Tell Charlie she had had enough, and that from now on her own needs had to be considered as well.

Upstairs, Charlie turned over and stirred in his sleep. As he came back to consciousness he was aware that Annie wasn't lying beside him. He strained his ears to hear any sound from downstairs and caught the merest whisper of the kettle boiling and a tiny clink of china. He felt an instant reminder of the resentment he had felt earlier. How dare she flounce off into the night in that childish way and then disturb his sleep when he had a full day of teaching and then an after-school hockey match? God, she was selfish and thoughtless. It was all very well for her to be still awake at half past two in the morning. She had sod-all to do all day while the boys were at school, even less now her so-called job had folded. She was making a point about being awake and suffering because of the row they had had. She was turning into her mother, a neurotic, bitter woman who had driven her husband away and now lived in the rancorous belief that life had treated her unfairly. Frankly, he was getting tired of it. His patience was wearing thin. They couldn't go on like this.

Sadie considered that her next move should be to go and see the doctor. It gave her time, for one thing, and got Kyle off her back. She made an appointment with the female doctor in the practice, an attractive young woman to whom she had taken Georgie when she had an ear infection. Sitting in a Scandinavian type of blond wood chair across from Dr Sangster's desk, she guessed they were about the same age. She saw a thin gold band on the doctor's wedding finger, but there were no telltale family photographs on her desk. She was dressed simply in a short grey skirt and an expensive-looking cashmere sweater. She was tall and slim, with short blond hair tucked behind her ears. Her long legs encased in black tights were entwined round each other like a teenager's. Sadie felt large and unkempt by comparison. She pulled her sleeves down over her chapped red hands and dirt-rimmed fingernails.

If I had made other choices, she thought, this could be me, sitting here at this streamlined desk, writing out prescriptions in nice clothes. If I had listened to Dad. She was glad that she hadn't on the whole. The sky outside the window was an enamel blue with racing fluffy white clouds. Quite hot March sun streamed in. I'd hate to be stuck in here, she thought, dealing with sick people and unhappy people and people like me, who have fucked things up. One after another we troop through this room and nice, pretty Dr Sangster deals with us with a special sympathetic smile and then goes home and dismisses us all from her mind. Professional distance, it was called, Sadie believed, and she would be hopeless at it.

'How can I help you?' asked the doctor, consulting her

computer screen and then turning to smile at Sadie. 'It's Sadie, isn't it?'

'Yes,' said Sadie. She felt suddenly weary and did not know exactly where to begin. 'To start with, I think I am pregnant. Well, I know I am. I've done the test twice.'

'When was your last period?' asked Dr Sangster with an especially radiant smile, although Sadie noticed that her eyes slid to look at Sadie's hands, searching for a ring on her finger.

'No, I'm not married. I live with my partner. I've got two other kids. Not his. I've been married before.'

'Do we have your records here?'

'Probably not. I've only recently registered.'

'You want this baby, do you? I mean – this is a planned pregnancy?'

'Not planned, but yes, I want to keep it. Of course I do!'

'Good. So we need to check you over and discuss your dates and book you into the antenatal clinic. There are a few forms to fill in about your own health and so on, and then I will make you an appointment for you to see the midwifery team.'

'My partner doesn't want it,' said Sadie. 'He doesn't want the baby.' She watched for a reaction on Dr Sangster's pretty face. There was none.

'Are you in a long-term, stable relationship?'

'We've been together nearly two years. I thought it was long term. Kyle is a bit younger than me. He's finding it hard to think of himself as a father.'

'Are there other pressures? Unemployment? Money?'

'Well, we're skint, but that's nothing new.'

'So how are you going to deal with this?'

'Well, I'm going to have the baby.'

'Hmm. I see. What will you do if he doesn't come to terms with the pregnancy?'

'I'll have to find somewhere else to go. We live in a tied cottage, you see.' Sadie imagined the house that Dr Sangster drove home to every evening; a country cottage, probably, with a Cath Kidston ironing board cover and maybe an Aga in the kitchen, and a husband opening a bottle of wine, his suit jacket over the back of a chair.

'I'll apply for council housing, I suppose. I've no alternative.'

'I see. Well, let's have a look at you. Can you hop up here for me?'

Ten minutes later Sadie was back sitting in the blond wood chair.

'So you say your partner thinks you have come today to arrange a termination?'

'Yes.'

Dr Sangster sighed and turned back to the computer and typed a note. Sadie eyed her suspiciously. She knew that doctors and social workers worked hand in glove and she didn't want any interference other than financial support.

'What are you writing?'

'I'm just making you your appointment with the ante-natal team,' said Dr Sangster, smiling again. 'You are a healthy young woman and there should be no complications with your pregnancy. At your next appointment you will be given our pregnancy pack and have the chance to discuss various preferences for the birth. Do you have any questions?'

'No, I don't think so. October the first, you said, for my

due date? That's a good day for a birthday. It sounds like the beginning of something, a new season.'

'Yes! A very good day,' smiled Dr Sangster. She got up to conduct Sadie from the consulting room.

Driving home in Kyle's truck, Sadie felt both excited at the prospect of the birth of her baby and worried about the future. 'I want you and love you,' she told her tummy. 'Don't you worry about a thing, little bean.' She still couldn't really believe that Kyle meant what he said. She had got to decide what she was going to tell him. She was torn between lying and telling him that she had arranged for a termination to give herself a bit of time, and braving it out with the truth. If he really meant what he said, then she would have to think about what to do next, and her first priority must be the girls and their security and happiness. She had no money and so her options were limited. She would have to apply to the social services for housing and benefit, and maybe go to her mum's in the meantime. But that was her last resort.

What she couldn't really believe was that Kyle would throw her out after the times they had shared. They had enjoyed such spectacular lovemaking, and when he had rescued her and the girls when things were tough, he had been so supportive and sympathetic. She had felt safe lying in his strong brown arms. How could all that now mean nothing? She had power over him, she was sure, because she had given him as much as he had given her. When she had moved into the cottage it was dirty and damp and mean and she had turned it into a home to which he returned after a winter's morning milking to find hot bread in the oven, the woodburner glowing, the beds made, the kitchen swept, the girls' drawings pinned to the cupboard doors. She had given him what he had never had as a boy – a proper home where he was loved. He had once told her that he had never had a birthday cake made for him until the year she and Tamzin and Georgie had made him a chocolate sponge and iced it with buttercream and piped his name on the top.

Couldn't she make him see that with his baby as well, they were an even stronger unit? A family was the best place from which to go out and face the world and to come back to at night. It was what she wanted passionately for Georgie and Tamzin – that sense of belonging some-where that her parents had given her. It couldn't always have been easy for them, but she couldn't ever remember feeling insecure or anxious about anything at home. There were rows and stand-offs – particularly between her and her father – but her parents had been like rocks throughout her life, strong, predictable, loyal and together. Her father had despaired about some of the choices she had made, but he had never thrown her mistakes back in her face.

It wasn't that she wanted to be like them – their marriage worked because her mother was unselfish while her father was an old git in lots of ways, and Sadie wouldn't tolerate such a partnership – but she still believed that she and Kyle worked well enough together to provide this baby and her girls with a secure childhood.

And she didn't want to be alone again. She really didn't. She couldn't bear the thought, in fact, but she had to face up to that possibility if she couldn't get Kyle to change his mind. If he made them leave, she would have no home and no job. Christ, what a mess she had made of everything. She thought of cool, poised Dr Sangster, who had evidently done everything right.

It's the girls who matter here, she thought as she drove, and whatever happens I must try and make it okay for them. This baby is going to make things hard, but I can't do anything to alter that. I can't turn the clock back. She imagined having to go back to living in a rented flat in Yeovil, where she had to sleep in the sitting room on a lumpy sofa bed and the girls' room was little more than a passageway with bunk beds and there was no garden and nothing to do after school except sit on her bed and watch television. I can't do that to them again, she thought. I'll have to find something else. I'll have to find a way.

She still hadn't decided what to say to Kyle when she drove into the yard and saw him moving amongst the cows, which were standing in the yard in the sunshine, placing a hand here and there on a bony black and white rump. He heard the engine of the truck and looked over, raising a hand in greeting, his face breaking into a smile. Sadie waved back, but her spirits flagged. Optimist though she was, she did not feel confident. She got out of the truck and went over to talk to him. She had decided she was going to tell him the truth. She didn't feel up to playing games.

Ollie had been as good as his word and had taken Sabine out on Saturday morning and bought a neat little laptop in a sugar-pink colour with built-in webcam. He had spent a long time downloading various programmes including MSN and Skype and then left her to it, and apart from her mother saying that she was trusting her to use the internet responsibly and that she was too young to go on Facebook – although everybody knew that all her age group were already signed up – there had been no more suggestion of supervising her contact with her father; in fact, Ollie had said in front of Lisa that the reason he had updated the old family computer was so that Sabine could better keep in touch with France.

'What about me?' wailed Agnes.

'Well, you too, of course.'

Sabine had glanced anxiously at her mother, but she was sitting at the kitchen table with a mug of coffee and looking completely cool about it. It was hard to know what she was thinking, and Sabine wondered exactly what Ollie had said to her on the subject. She hoped that he had been tactful and hadn't made it sound as if she had been bitching behind her mother's back.

So here she was, up in her room pretending to be doing her homework before supper but really checking her e-mails again on her secret Hotmail account, and as usual there was nothing from her dad or Jacqui, despite the fact that she had sent several messages and some photographs she had downloaded from the camera she had been given for her birthday. She knew he spent a lot of time on the internet, so it couldn't be that he hadn't seen them in his in-box, but perhaps he was away on a business trip, or was just too busy to reply. She had typed his name into her new Skype contact list but he was never online and so she hadn't had the opportunity to use the webcam. In fact, she was no closer to keeping in touch with France than she had ever been.

What was worrying her now was that the Easter holidays were only two weeks away and there had been no talk about flights to Bordeaux and when she and Agnes would be going. She had also worked out that Jacqui would be nearly seven months pregnant and maybe she had to stay in bed or something and had said to Papa, 'This time I can't deal with your girls – not this time. They must wait until after the baby is born,' and then after he was born she would be too tired or it would be inconvenient and slowly she and Agnes would be eased out of the family.

This thought made her chest ache with sadness because she knew that Papa would miss them for a bit and then slowly, slowly he would get used to them not being there and then eventually he would forget them, and she couldn't bear for that to happen because she loved him so much. She knew that her mum would like her to think of Ollie as her dad – but he wasn't, and she didn't think that he would want her to. She liked him and everything, but she could never love him as she did Papa, who she *belonged* to. She had the same dark, shiny hair and olive skin; she was his flesh and blood.

So now, this afternoon, she had to decide what to do. She had already been online and found a flight on a budget carrier for the day after school finished for the holidays, and what she couldn't decide was whether to telephone her dad on her mobile and tell him when she would be coming as if it was all arranged and then take it to her mum as a fait accompli, or do it the other way round. There were disadvantages either way. Maybe Papa would say he had to discuss it with Jacqui or that that particular day would be inconvenient, and argue about whose turn it was to pay for the tickets. Her mum would be annoyed that Papa had gone ahead and arranged a flight and she might say that there was a reason why she couldn't go then – dentist appointments for instance – although there was nothing on the calendar in the kitchen.

If only her parents could just speak to one another and fix it between themselves, but if anything, communication had got worse while they were arguing about money. This was called 'maintenance' and Sabine knew that it meant money that Papa had to pay for her and Agnes and that, according to their mum, he didn't want to support them. It made her feel awful – as if she had a price label stuck on her forehead and Papa didn't think that she was worth what was written on it.

She picked up her mobile telephone and went to close her bedroom door. Agnes was at a friend's house, so she couldn't ask her advice, and anyway her sister didn't seem to feel the same way that she did about Papa. She didn't seem to understand that they needed to show him that although they now lived in England they still thought of him as their father and that he was as important to them as ever. Agnes wouldn't speak French any more, for instance, and she wanted to change her name because she didn't like how it sounded in English with a hard 'g'. When Sabine had talked to her about going to France at Easter, she had made a face and said that she didn't want to go because she had a new friend, Ruby, whose parents had asked her to go with them to Ibiza for a week at the start of the holidays. All their mum had to pay was her plane fare and pocket money. So even though Sabine had argued that they should go and see their father as a sort of duty, Agnes had screamed at her and said that she could go to France on her own if she felt like that.

Sabine didn't mind going on her own. She was used to the flight, and the regional airports at both ends were small and easy to navigate. So it was up to her to fix it up, and although she wasn't sure how it would work out, she found her father's number and pressed 'call'. He answered almost immediately.

'Sabine, *cherie*. How are you, darling? A good girl, I hope.'

'Yes, yes, but Papa, you never answer my e-mails.'

'Darling, it has been mad here. You know what it can be like. I don't have a moment to spare for the things I want to do, but I love to hear from you. You are a good girl to remember your papa, not like that naughty Agnes. I never hear a word from her!'

'Papa! What about the Easter holidays? You know we have two weeks off school. Can I tell Mum that I'm coming out to you? I don't think Agnes will be coming because she has been invited to go to Ibiza, but I want to come. I have found a cheap flight to Bordeaux. I can send you all the details.'

'Wait a minute, darling. Jacqui and I are going to be away – a little holiday before the baby is born. It is the only time available before it is too late for Jacqui to fly.'

'Well I could come too. I wouldn't be any bother.'

'Darling, we are going to the West Indies. It wouldn't be possible.'

Sabine's heart sank. Her voice started to tremble as tears threatened. 'But Papa, when can I see you? Christmas was the last time. I really, really want to see you. I miss you, Papa.'

'My darling girl! And I miss you too.'

'What dates are you away? Could I come just for a weekend or a few days?'

'Look, I'll speak to Jacqui. I'll send you an e-mail. I don't have the diary here before me.'

'Please, Papa!'

'What is the matter, Sabine? Is there something wrong? Are you unhappy in England? Is your mother—'

'No! No! I'm not unhappy, Papa. It's all fine. I just want to see you.'

'Okay, my darling. I'll talk to Jacqui and then I will be in touch. We'll see what we can do.'

Even as they exchanged loving greetings to end the call, Sabine knew that she didn't hold out much hope, because she no longer trusted her father to do what he promised. It wasn't just him, it was all grown-ups. One of the things the divorce had taught her was that adults got it wrong a lot of the time, and that very often they let people down even when they didn't mean to.

She sat back in her chair and thought. If Agnes was going to be away, then maybe her mum would want her out of the way too, so that she and Ollie could get on with their bonking programme. The more you did it, obviously, the more chance there was of the tadpole thing getting stuck on the egg – they had done human reproduction in Biology – and the better the chance of it turning into a baby. Since Ollie had talked to her about it, she'd noticed a thermometer on the bathroom shelf, and that was all part of the process – getting the right time in her mum's cycle. She didn't want to think about all this stuff but she couldn't help it. She had even wondered what it would be like to kiss Ollie on the lips, with tongues and everything, and do it with him. She hated herself for being so gross.

So the thing was, as soon as she got the dates from her dad – and she would have to ring Jacqui if he didn't get on and send them to her in an e-mail – she would book herself a flight on the internet. She could use her mum's credit card and get the money off her dad later. Then she would just turn up in Pompignac and she would be helpful and no bother and her dad would remember what it was like to have her as a daughter and they would all be happy together.

They would be able to say later, 'Can you remember the time, just before Etienne' – or Luc, or Alexandre, or whatever his name was going to be – 'was born and we did such and such?' She would be part of Papa's life again and not just a reminder of the unhappy past. She remembered the awful time when she had run screaming to cling to her mother when her parents were having a fight and Papa had seized a chair and held it above his head as if he wanted to throw it at her. 'Stop it!' she had shrieked. 'Don't, Papa! Don't!' and her mother had goaded him, shouting, 'Go on! Throw it, you bastard!'

She knew her parents would never get back together and really she didn't want them to. Ollie was a better husband for her mother, she could see that, her happiness was safer with him; and Jacqui had tamed her father into a less difficult, calmer man. She could see things were better as they were, apart from the fighting over money and the bitterness left behind. It was so hard to believe that her father wouldn't pay the money for her and Agnes. He was always so generous to them – buying them loads of stuff that their mother tutted over when they came home. Why would he try to get out of paying for their food and bus fares and school uniforms? Why would he refuse to pay for Sabine to learn the clarinet when it was him who had made her love Mozart's clarinet concerto by playing it all the time in his car? Her mother had shouted at him on the telephone about that, while Sabine sat on the stairs and begged, 'Don't! It doesn't matter! Please don't!' In the end Ollie had offered to pay for her lessons, but then she didn't really want to learn any more and had given up after a term.

She felt better now that she had a plan. If she hadn't heard from Papa by tomorrow after school, she would telephone Jacqui to find out the dates of their holiday, and then she would go ahead and book her flight and tell her mother that her father had fixed up for her to go to Pompignac and that would be that. She would go on her own, get the shuttle from the airport, a bus from town and walk from the main road. She wouldn't care if Jacqui had turned her bedroom into a nursery, which she suspected she had. She would sleep in Agnes' little room; she would sleep anywhere.

The rest of the holiday she didn't know what she would do. It would be nice to go to see Ollie's parents. She liked Alice and David and she liked being at their house. She had Alice's e-mail address. Maybe she would send her a message, ask how they were, and Roger, say she was looking forward to the party, tell her that she was going to see Papa in the Easter holidays. David was always interested in their life in France and said what a wonderful country it was. One day, he said, he would like Sabine to take him to her home and show him Bordeaux, which he had heard was a very fine city. She liked to think that she could do that. She imagined him at Pompignac talking to Papa about wine. It would be like bringing both sides of her life together.

Chapter Seven

WHEN ALICE HAD a day off, she looked forward to it
in a way that made her wonder whether it was time
that she gave up work altogether. She enjoyed pottering
about in the kitchen getting breakfast without the need to
watch the clock and hurry, and she enjoyed the prospect
of the whole day stretching ahead to be filled as she wished.
Since David had retired she liked to plan to do something
with him – a walk on the Dorset downs and lunch in a
pub, or a drive to the sea, or else a day devoted to doing
something in the garden or the house, maybe just a trip to
the dump with a load of recycling.

It was a time when she felt closest to him, talking when
they felt like it, sharing a bottle of wine at lunch, sometimes remembering the past, discussing the children or the
grandchildren, occasionally wondering about the future –
should they stay in the too-large house, should they move
to somewhere better suited to old age, what sort of retirement was facing them? They certainly wouldn't be well off
– Alice, thanks to her part-time jobs, had very little pension,
and their savings were looking more and more precarious
as the country plunged into financial crisis. The house was
their security in uncertain times.

It was hard to get David to talk about the future. He had a gloomy dread of a long old age and failing health and he doubted that modern medicine would allow him to die neatly and quietly and without fuss as his parents had done within a year of each other. And Alice sometimes wondered, especially after leafing through the money section of the Sunday paper, whether he had got a proper grip on their finances. She had always left it entirely to him to move their savings about if necessary and had never asked to see any sort of financial projection for the future or even a balance sheet for their joint finances. She managed their current account, and the small inheritance left to her by her father remained in the building society in which he had invested it. She was vaguely aware that she was being lazily complacent, but one of the advantages of marriage was long-term security and allowing her husband to take care of things that she felt were in his domain. She didn't pretend to know anything about SIPs and ISAs or share portfolios.

Today, she thought, looking out of the kitchen window at the garden, where the spring sunshine was lingering on the grass littered with the debris of winter and the matted flower beds, she and David could do a bit of tidying up. They could rake the lawn and turn over the beds and plan some planting for the party. Perhaps they would go to the garden centre and do that couples thing of pushing round a trolley and discussing plants together.

She made a pot of coffee and put some croissants in the oven to warm and then went to the foot of the stairs to call David to come down. She heard a muffled reply and then the door of his bedroom opened and he crossed the landing to the bathroom. Alice went back to the kitchen and sat down to look at the newspaper.

A few minutes later there was a knock at the front door, followed by a ring on the bell, which surprised Alice because she thought it was broken. It was on David's list of things to do and like everything else on the list was not making much progress towards completion. Roger began to bark and followed her into the hallway.

Standing on the doorstep was a small young woman with fair hair scooped up somewhere behind her head and loose tendrils round her face, which was smooth and pale. She was dressed in a wrap coat with a trailing, uneven hem, a long black skirt and the sort of sheepskin boots that Sadie wore. She was hung about with bracelets and beads and hoop earrings, and over her shoulder carried a fortress-like bag, strapped with buckles and chains. She appeared to be greatly surprised to see Alice.

'Hello,' said Alice. 'Can I help you?' The girl must have come to the wrong door.

'I was looking for David, Dr David Baxter, but maybe . . .' Roger stepped forward to inspect her skirt, wagging his tail.

'No, no. You've come to the right house. He's my husband.' The two women looked at one another, Alice smiling politely and the young woman still registering surprise.

'Oh, I see. Well, I just . . .'

Where was the clipboard? thought Alice. The girl was some sort of market researcher, she supposed, although she didn't seem very professional.

'I used to work with him. We were colleagues at the university. He offered to help me with, well, a few things . . .' Her voice trailed off and she glanced down the street as if she was looking for someone, or seeking an escape route.

'Oh, I see. Well, do come in. I've just made some coffee. He'll be down in a moment. David!' Alice called up the stairs. 'David! There's someone to see you! Did he know you were coming, because he didn't mention it . . . but then he is incredibly forgetful. He seems to be quite busy with university stuff at the moment. He met an ex-colleague yesterday for lunch . . . I can't remember exactly who.' By now they had reached the kitchen and Alice turned and said, 'I'm Alice, and you are?'

'Julia. Julia Fairfield. It was two years ago that I worked with David. I haven't seen him since. Actually, I had quite a traumatic time in the department . . . sexual discrimination, that sort of thing, and David was very kind.' She spoke in nervous little rushes and her hands fluttered round her mouth, which Alice noticed was shiny with lip gloss. 'I won't have coffee, thank you very much. Do you have any green tea? If not, I'll just have hot water and a slice of lemon.'

'Yes, he would have been kind,' said Alice, searching in the cupboard for some alternative tea bags left behind by Sadie. 'His students always said that about him. He took a lot of trouble over them. So what are you doing now?'

'I'm staying with my sister. I . . .' and at that moment David walked in. Alice had her back turned, getting another mug out of the cupboard, and she did not see the expression of pure horror on his face.

'Oh!' he said, swallowing hard and giving a small nervous cough. 'My goodness! Julia! I suppose you've brought your CV for me.' He turned to address Alice. 'I promised to help Julia with . . . um . . .'

Alice turned back and filled their mugs and poured milk into a jug and found teaspoons in a drawer and brown sugar from the cupboard. 'There!' she said. 'I'll leave the tea bag in and you can fish it out when it looks right for you.' At the moment the liquid in the mug was the colour of pond water.

'Oh, thank you,' murmured Julia.

'Shall I leave you to it?' said Alice. 'Take your mugs through to the sitting room, why don't you? The heating's not on but it'll be quite warm, I think. Would you like a biscuit?' and she turned back to the cupboard to reach for the stack of tins.

David took the opportunity to make frantic gestures in Julia's direction, mouthing, 'Don't say anything about yesterday!' Julia stared at him uncomprehendingly.

'Not very exciting, I'm afraid,' said Alice, peering into the tin she had selected. She had decided against offering a croissant – too much of a performance, with jam and butter and plates and all the crumbs. 'Here, David, take the tray. Julia, why don't you follow him through?'

They both did as they were told, trailed by Roger, who was interested in the biscuits, and Alice heard the door shut behind them. Well, she thought, as she settled down again with her coffee and a warm croissant and the newspaper, *that* was unexpected. She would tease David later that he had forgotten all about a visit from rather a pretty young woman, presuming, of course, that it was prearranged. The girl, Julia, or whatever her name was, seemed a nervous little creature, but one of those who didn't mind putting other people out on her account. All that business with green tea was a giveaway. She couldn't remember David ever having mentioned her as a colleague. He seemed rather awkward in her company and Alice guessed that he probably had a low opinion of her professionally. It was typical of him to agree to help her now. He was always particularly kind to no-hopers, like the man he had had lunch with yesterday.

David closed the door behind him and then carefully put the tray on the coffee table. He straightened up and looked at Julia, trying to work out what the visit was all about, what exactly he had got himself into. It was the first time he had seen her in two years and she looked exactly the same – no older, anyway. Maybe her hair was a bit different, bunched up behind her head; there seemed to be more of it than before and he imagined it loose down her back. His mind was full of questions – of course she could easily get hold of his address, but what on earth had induced her to come knocking on his door? What was she thinking of?

Julia had screwed herself up very small on a corner of the sofa. Her long coat and skirt trailed on the floor and her bangles jingled as she smoothed the material over her knees. 'I'm so sorry,' she began in her little-girl voice. 'I'm so sorry if this is awkward. I thought your wife worked. I didn't know she would be here. I just came to apologise for yesterday. I'm on my way down to Cornwall, you see. A friend has lent me a cottage for a week or two, and I saw where you lived on the map and I thought I could call in and apologise, and see you in person . . .'

David felt a sense of relief, as if the situation, which had looked bizarre and unwelcome, had shrunk to something manageable.

'Oh, don't give it a second thought!' he said brightly. 'But I hadn't actually told Alice and she might have thought it was strange . . . that's why I was making those ridiculous faces at you in the kitchen.'

'Oh, I see,' said Julia. 'Oh dear, have I made things difficult?'

'Not at all. Anyway, this really is a good opportunity to show me your CV.' He looked at the bag that was sitting, chained, at Julia's feet. 'I expect you have got it with you?'

'No, no, I haven't. I didn't think to bring it.' She looked upset at the idea.

'Well, I suppose we can sketch something out in rough for you to work on. You can e-mail me a draft, can't you? Would that be helpful?' He got up to search about for paper and a pen.

'Yes, it would, but the thing is, I can't really think about anything much – not professionally anyway – when everything else in my life is in such turmoil.'

David sat back down again. 'Oh dear,' he said lamely. 'You mentioned your marriage was over. Are you divorced now?'

'Not yet. We are still at loggerheads, with solicitors and everything. I've had to sell the house. It's all been horrible. Declan, my husband, won't pay for anything. I've been saddled with his debts. In the middle of it all, I lost my job. I was teaching at a private business school and the whole thing folded overnight and none of us were paid.' Julia paused to tuck her hair behind her ears and swallow hard, raising her filling eyes to the ceiling.

'Oh dear,' said David again, panic beginning to rise. If it went on like this he was going to have to call for Alice.

'I'm really sorry to have come here. I shouldn't have

done, but you know, when you have really been through the mill, it's amazing how many people you think of as friends just melt away, and I kept remembering how kind you were to me and I felt that I had to see you. There, I've said it now. You can throw me out if you like. I wouldn't have come if I had known your wife would be here.'

'Oh, Alice won't mind,' said David, not quite sure what Julia was getting at.

'You know, that day in the café,' she went on, 'I've never been able to forget the strength of that *connection* between us. I know it's impulsive of me, but if ever I get that sense of being drawn to someone – karma, you could call it – I can't deny the truth of the feeling. I have to be guided by it.'

David was completely lost by now. What was she on about?

'I only—' he began, but Julia interrupted him.

'No,' she said, 'it wasn't "only" anything, except that you were the only one who expressed any regret for how I was treated. Afterwards, when I thought back over the time I was working in that department, and with the help of my spiritual teacher, I was able to see how much you supported me, and I began to realise what your feelings really were. I *allowed* myself to accept them for what they were when I was made aware of the positive effect of remote energy transference. I realised, in fact, how strongly you felt for me.'

David stood up and looked at her in alarmed confusion, but before he could say anything in his defence, she had jumped up and pressed herself against him where he stood with a mug in his hand, so hard that he could feel her little breasts and the firmness of her thighs against his legs.

'Hey!' he said, reaching behind him with the mug, searching for somewhere to put it down. 'Hey! What's all this?' With his hands free he tried to extricate himself, but she clung like a limpet and soon he was patting her hair in a soothing way, while trying to remove himself from her grasp.

She was really very pretty, he had forgotten how pretty she was, and when she lifted her little soft hands to draw down his face so that he could not avoid looking into her eyes, he gave up trying to push her away and allowed her to kiss him on the mouth. He even found himself returning her kiss before recovering and saying, 'No, no, Julia, really. My wife . . .'

'Don't say this is wrong. It's not wrong. It's something beautiful and rare. Just feel the good energy flowing between us.'

David thought it unlikely that Alice would see it quite like that and he was uncomfortably conscious of her presence a few yards away in the kitchen with her cup of coffee. Any moment the door to the sitting room could open and she would appear.

'Not here!' he said, extricating himself and realising that his words suggested that it would be all right somewhere else, which was not what he meant. He couldn't go around kissing girls half his age.

'Where then? Come to Cornwall with me. I've been lent a cottage for two weeks.'

'I can't possibly do that. I am a married man, Julia.'

'But not happily! I always knew that there was something repressed and unfulfilled about you. I realised later that your subtle energy system was blocked. Your chakra cannot breathe.' She shot a critical glance round the room in all its shabby homeliness. 'David – I am offering you a chance to experience love and passion again, to remove the negativity in your situation. I respect your marriage, I really do, and I'm sure Alice is wonderful, but this needn't threaten anything. It's just a small, impulsive chance to be alive again. Don't you want to take it?'

'Julia! If you think I could go off to Cornwall with you without threatening my marriage, you are off your head!' At the same time David was thinking, I probably could, in fact. I could tell Alice that I was going for a few days, walking the coastal path. I've often talked about doing it. But the thought of going with Julia was quite out of the question. She was clearly mad or suffering some sort of breakdown. And all the stuff about him having been in love with her . . . where had that come from? On the other hand, he did feel sorry for her. She seemed to have had a horrible, an undeservedly, horrible time.

'But,' he went on, 'it's very touching that you have suggested it, and it makes me feel, well, grateful in a way that you could even think of me like that.'

Julia sat down again, nursing her mug of tea and staring distractedly at Roger, who had inched himself very close to the plate of biscuits, on which he was concentrating his steadfast attention.

'But I must keep in touch,' she pleaded, looking up at him. 'I can't lose you again. We have so much positive energy between us.'

'Of course,' he said kindly, 'and if there's anything I can do . . . I really mean that.'

'I shouldn't have come,' she said pathetically. 'I might have guessed that you wouldn't have the balls . . .'

David felt offended. 'It's not exactly a question of balls. You can't expect—'

'No, no. I'm sorry. I understand, I really do.' In a surge of activity, she scrabbled about in the handbag and pulled out some folded sheets of paper. 'I'm going to give you my address in Cornwall, and if you change your mind, then come. I'll be there for two weeks. I need the space to sort out my head and I want to do some writing. I'll be alone. Just come.'

She found a pen and wrote down an address in large, round, childish handwriting. She passed him the sheet of paper.

'You haven't got children, have you?' he asked, it suddenly occurring to him that she might have, by now.

'No. No, thank goodness. Declan always wanted them but I couldn't, it wasn't possible . . .' She looked down, her lip trembling, and David very much wanted to take her in his arms. The poor little thing, he thought. The dice certainly seemed to have been weighted against her.

'So you lost your job? Where was it you were teaching?'

'In Brighton. I did a TEFL course so that I could teach English as a foreign language at this business college – well, that's what it called itself. I was teaching Russian teenagers who were unspeakably abusive and unpleasant, so I didn't mind so much about the job, but I minded not being paid for two months.'

'Oh dear. Well, I wish I could help in some way, but you know, now I'm retired, I don't have much influence anywhere.'

'David – that's not why I'm here. I mean, I do need help, but not in that way. I am seeing a counsellor who is guiding me through a self-healing process. My aura has been so badly damaged that it will take time to repair. But I will get there. I can promise you that!' She looked up with a sudden smile that melted his heart. She talked a complete load of bullshit, he thought, but that was nothing new. She was still enchanting.

'I had better go,' she said, standing again, and while she kissed him for a second time, Roger, seeing his opportunity, cleared the plate.

'So what was all that about?' said Alice when David went back into the kitchen, having seen Julia, via another embrace, out of the front door and into her car.

Where did he start to explain? How could he begin? The whole thing seemed to be travelling very fast out of control. He didn't even know how his voice would come out when he spoke in reply. His breathing was too fast and his hands were shaking.

'She didn't bother to say goodbye to me, I notice. She's obviously madly in love with you, David!' Alice spoke lightly, but David's heart pounded and his throat felt tight.

'Don't be silly. She was in a state about everything. Her life has basically gone pear-shaped.' He began to load the mugs into the sink.

'Put them in the dishwasher!' commanded Alice, and then the telephone rang and she moved to answer it. David complied and then, seeing the croissants on a plate, began to butter one for himself. It was better to be doing something other than making eye contact with Alice while she interrogated him. What on earth had prompted that remark about Julia being in love with him?

'Oh, no! Sadie! Wait a minute. Tell me again. What exactly has happened? You're not? When did you find out? Oh Sadie, darling!'

Oh God! thought David, looking across at his wife. Her face was etched with concern. Whatever had happened now?

Chapter Eight

'So?' asked David when Alice finally put down the telephone.

'Oh, David! It's terrible. Sadie's pregnant. I told you I thought there was something wrong when she was here. Kyle wants her to have a termination but she won't hear of it. He says she has got to choose between him and the baby!'

'What do you mean, choose between him and the baby? It's *his* baby, isn't it? Fatherhood isn't a *choice.*'

'Well, it is to the extent that he says he doesn't want it, and if she chooses to go ahead with the pregnancy, he insists that they separate. He doesn't want anything to do with it. He says that he'll give up his job and the cottage, and go back to tarmacking roads or whatever it was he did before. I suppose he'll have to pay maintenance, but basically that's it. Sadie is absolutely distraught.'

'God almighty!' said David with great emphasis. 'How has she got in this mess?' He thumped the table with both hands.

'That's not the hard bit! Think of us — Sadie herself was an accident, remember.'

'But we were married! And I took responsibility for my child. How can Kyle just walk out?'

172

'He blames Sadie, I suppose. I imagine she was in charge of birth control. He says he told her from the start he didn't want children. She, apparently, thought he would change his mind if it actually happened.'

'So it was planned on her part?'

'I don't know. I didn't ask her that directly. She told me she was happy when she found out. She wanted to have Kyle's baby. She thought it would make them into a family.'

David threw his hands up in despair. 'How can they afford a baby? I thought they could only just manage as it is.'

'You know that having no money has never stopped Sadie doing anything, but Kyle thinks otherwise. Not being able to afford it seems to be his main objection. And he's so young too – only in his early twenties.'

'You say that, but we were the same age when we had Charlie. We considered ourselves quite grown-up enough. This modern extended childhood hadn't been invented then.'

'*David!* Don't shout like that. It's not me you need to argue with!'

'I can't believe how she can behave so irresponsibly. What is she intending to do now?'

'She says that she'll stay on the farm until the Easter holidays and then she asked if she and the girls could come here. As I said, she seems to think that Kyle will give up the job and move away. He doesn't want to be anywhere near her and the girls, apparently.'

'She won't consider an abortion?'

'You know Sadie. Not in a million years.'

'Jesus Christ! What a mess. I have to agree with her that you can't terminate a life just because it is inconvenient, but why did she allow herself to get pregnant in the first place when Kyle had made it clear that he didn't want a child? That's what I find unforgivable. I mean she's not sixteen, is she? She's not been brought up on a sink estate with a mother on the game and a succession of "uncles", and a pit bull terrier on a chain in the garden.'

Alice ran her hands through her hair. 'What's the point of arguing about the whys and wherefores? It's too late now. We've got to work out how we can support her – or, more importantly, the girls.'

'Well, coming to live with us doesn't solve anything.'

'It's a temporary measure until she sorts something out. We've plenty of room, so of course they can come. I said so just now.'

'What about school?'

'They have two weeks off for Easter.'

'And after that? When term starts again?'

'Sadie will have to get them there somehow.'

'She has no car and it's a forty-minute drive – at least.'

'Then we'll have to help. David! Stop making it worse! I don't know all the answers.'

'I'm only pointing out the obvious difficulties. I agree we must help her, but we have to be realistic.'

There was a silence while they both looked at each other in despair.

'I can't bear to think about Tamzin and Georgie facing another upheaval in their lives. They have only just settled down on the farm and now they are going to have to leave it all behind and start again.' Alice wiped at the tears that were wetting her cheeks. 'And another man walks out on them! How can they be stable and secure in their own lives when this has been the pattern of their childhood? How can

Sadie do it to them? I know she didn't intend this to happen, but how can she be so *careless* about their lives? She loves them, but she doesn't seem to understand the consequences of what she does and the impact it will have on them.'

'Well we'll just have to pick up the pieces as best we can,' said David stoutly. He got up to put an arm round Alice's shoulders. 'As you say, it appears to be too late to change anything, but I can lend her my car for a start, so that she can ferry the girls to and fro, or I can do it for her. We can help her to find somewhere to live. I suppose the girls may have to move to another school. There's unlikely to be much available housing where they are now.'

'If she leaves the farm, she'll lose her job too. It wasn't much, but it kept her going. She'll lose everything.'

'She was only working there because of him.' David couldn't bring himself to say Kyle's name. 'She has a degree, for goodness' sake! She could get a better job than hoeing vegetables – even if they are organic.'

'She enjoys it and it fits in with the girls. It was her choice and she was happy, David. I've never seen Sadie so happy – and now this!'

'It's a disaster! And she has a good brain! I blame that bloody stupid university course for the direction her life has taken. It filled her head with nonsense and left her with a vast student loan to repay and no job prospects. This is the result.'

'What could we have done? We had to let her make her own choices.'

They lapsed into miserable silence, remembering the past. David recalled the stormy scenes when he had tried to influence his daughter in some way and Alice thought of Sadie as a dimpled, plump child, sweet-natured and always laughing. She also thought of Georgie and Tamzin. Perhaps I should look after them, she thought. I could give up work and look after them. It suddenly seemed an obvious solution, and David could help. But there would be a baby, too. She felt dismayed at the thought. Was she still up to looking after a baby – the endless feeding and changing and sleepless nights? And where was Sadie in this scheme? Out at work doing some David-approved type of job? It seemed unlikely.

'So what happens next?' asked David. 'You say that Sadie is staying on for the moment? Doesn't Kyle have to work out his notice? Or is he going to walk out on his cows as well as his unborn child?'

'I don't know. I didn't ask about him. He's very upset, according to Sadie. She sounds sorry for him, if you can believe it.' When she thought about it, Alice felt sorry for him too, although at the moment she couldn't work out quite where the moral high ground lay. If he was so dead set against becoming a father, perhaps he should have done something about preventing a pregnancy. However, she knew enough from her work in the surgery to be aware that a termination was often regarded as a form of contraception. Young men in particular seemed to take this view.

'He wants me to get rid of it,' a miserable teenage girl would sob over the telephone, and Alice could hear in her voice the longing for a shawl-wrapped bundle of her very own to love and push round in a new pram.

'I suppose nothing will happen until the girls break up and then they'll all come here. Thank goodness we never moved. Sadie can have her old room and I'll put Georgie and Tamzin in Marina's.'

David had no difficulty in imagining the house taken over by them all and his peaceful, solitary days disrupted. His life would be wrenched away from him again. Much as he loved his granddaughters, he felt the whole thing was a disaster – for everybody.

'In that case,' he heard himself say, 'I may go away for a few days before they come. I've been thinking of going to Cornwall and walking part of the coastal path.'

'What? With Edwin?' Edwin was a long-standing walking partner, an ex-university colleague who had moved down to live in a bleak cottage on Bodmin Moor. Alice seemed to remember that his wife was Cornish.

'Yes,' said David. How easy Alice made it for him. If she wasn't so distracted by Sadie, she might have questioned him more closely. As it was, his lie slipped past in the winking of an eye.

Alice's day brightened after lunch when she telephoned about the bouncy castles and her booking was confirmed for the party. Then when she checked her e-mails in the evening she found a message from Sabine. She called David to read it. She had always made an effort to be warm and welcoming to Ollie's stepdaughters and it was a pleasant reward that Sabine was responsive and seemed to like her new family in return. 'She says she would like to come and stay with us in the holidays, David! Isn't that lovely? It will be fun for Tamzin and Georgie too. I am going to write back and say she is welcome any time. She's such a funny, reserved little thing. Imagine her going out to Bordeaux on her own at Easter. According to Lisa, their father hardly takes any notice of the girls, but Sabine always wants to go.

I think it's a sense of loyalty, don't you? It must be hard for her when Lisa runs him down all the time. Marrying Ollie doesn't seem to have healed the wounds. She still seems very bitter. She hasn't "moved on", as they say.'

Re-reading the message herself, she decided that when Sabine came to stay in the holidays she would involve her in the party plans to make her feel really embraced by her new family. She could help work out the seating, or make place cards or something, or maybe a big family tree, with photographs of each person, that could be pinned up on the day to show how the family was like an oak tree – sturdy and broad with far-spreading roots.

David made an acquiescent noise in response. After lunch he had taken Roger for a walk and sent a text message to Julia and could think of little else. He remembered her slim body pressed against his and the white nape of her neck where her hair was drawn up in a straggling bun affair. He had suggested that he drive down to Bay Cottage next week for a couple of days. At first he had put 'nights' but hastily altered the text. Who knows – he might very well call in on Edwin anyway. He had no idea how the trip would pan out, he told himself. It might all be completely innocent and above board. The only problem was that Alice had said how nice it would be for Roger, and so he was lumbered with him and his dog bowls and smelly blankets and tins of meaty chunks.

Once Sadie had told her parents, she experienced a sense of relief and gratitude even though it made her feel about fourteen again. At least now, if the worst came to the worst, she and the girls had somewhere to go for the time being, and just confessing to them the extent of the mess she was in made her feel better. Meanwhile the atmosphere between her and Kyle had become solemn and sad but they were no longer arguing or angry. They seemed curiously drawn to each other's company, so that once the girls were at school Sadie put on her rubber boots and went into the milking parlour and helped hose down. She watched Kyle working, admiring his athletic build and his strong brown forearms, and when the last cow trooped out into the yard, he came over and took the brush from her and put his hands on her shoulders.

'Why, babe? Why have you done this?' he said sadly. 'Didn't we have enough? Weren't we happy as we were?' She slipped her arms round his waist and laid her head on his chest.

'I can't change it now,' she said. 'I can't turn back the clock.'

At lunchtime they went upstairs to the room that Sadie had painted in buttercup yellow so that the sloping ceiling glowed with light. Even their lovemaking seemed sad and nostalgic.

'Why is it, Kyle?' Sadie asked in a little voice. 'Why do you feel like you do? Why can't you see things differently?'

'You'll never understand,' he said, tracing his fingers across her breast. 'Not coming from a family like yours, where everything's all nice and you're all there for each other.' This remark was a breakthrough, thought Sadie. It was the first time he had managed to articulate anything regarding his feelings.

'What's wrong with that? It's what families should be about. You're part of it too. They care for you as well.'

179

'That's bollocks for a start. It doesn't work like that. They'd kick me in the teeth if it suited. It's only you they care about. And your kids.'

'Why are you so anti-family? We've been happy, haven't we? We've lived like a family.'

'Yeah, but I never thought it would last. Why should it? Life is shite and something would have come along and you'd have left me, or I'd have lost this job or some other shit. It's being real, what I think, and I don't want a kid of mine to go through it. I don't want to put a kid through what I had when I was growing up.'

'But it wouldn't be like that. We would be great parents, you and me. This baby will have all the love in the world!'

'Yeah, you say that now. How do you know how things will turn out? I've already got a boy out there who doesn't know his dad. I don't want another one fucked up.'

Sadie didn't answer. She thought of Georgie and Tamzin. Were they fucked up? Of course she regretted some of the stuff that had happened in their short lives, but she had done her best to provide them with some stability and they knew they were loved. Kyle walking out on them now was just about the worst thing and it seemed she could do nothing to stop him bar sacrificing the life of the baby she was carrying. Just say she agreed to a termination, could she, hand on heart, swear that she and Kyle were going to be together in ten years' time? No, she couldn't, and she would have the rest of her life to live as a murderess.

The sadness of her situation overwhelmed her again and tears slid down her cheeks. For the moment she loved this man in whose arms she lay, but the future remained a blank. If she was really honest, this cottage, this farm could not be the backdrop for her whole life – she would want something more, she knew that.

'Will we see you? Will you keep in touch with us?' she asked.

'No,' said Kyle, turning away to lie with his back to her. 'What's the point? I don't ever want to see the baby. I don't want nothing to do with it. Tell it I'm dead for all I care. It won't be any different than with the girls. They never see their dad. It will keep things tidy. They'll all know where they are, like.'

Sadie thought of her own father. They had had their ups and downs, and she more than any of them had crossed swords with him as a teenager, but secretly she thought it was because he loved her most. She had been the spoiled baby, the one he spent most time with as a child. She remembered the walks and the nature stuff, the bird-spotting, the telescope he had bought her when she had shown an interest in astronomy. Even when she had telephoned yesterday and her mother answered the telephone, she had wanted it to be her dad. He had rung her back in the evening to tell her that he would do anything he could to help and that he would lend her his car and share the school run. His support – without any criticism – had made her cry.

Kyle had never had any of that. He didn't know what it was to be loved and supported by a father. It was no wonder he didn't feel up to the role.

Kyle got out of bed and started to pull on the clothes that lay scattered on the floor. 'I don't want to do this,' he said, looking down at Sadie. 'You're making it happen, babe. It's you that's breaking it all up. Just remember that.'

As if I could forget it, thought Sadie, climbing out after him. She had been sick this morning in the polytunnel when she had been cutting courgettes. In ten days she would have to pack up the cottage and move out. All her efforts to turn it into a home would be dismantled. At some point she would have to ask the farm manager if she could store stuff in a disused packing shed until she found somewhere to live, but she couldn't do that until Kyle had handed in his notice, which, as yet, she wasn't sure he had. She hadn't pressed the point because she was hanging on to the frailest hope that he might change his mind.

There wasn't much at the moment that she didn't feel responsible for. Soon she would have to tell the girls. The only good thing was that they were going to stay with their grandparents for the holidays. That would soften the blow of leaving the farm.

She sat on the bed to reach for her jeans and caught sight of her image in the glass on the wall. Jesus, she thought, staring at her swollen, tired face, all of a sudden I look old. Where's the girl disappeared to? Soon I'll be the mother of three children. A feeling of great anxiety weighed down on her. God knows, she thought, God only knows how I'll manage.

The atmosphere between Charlie and Annie was also strained. She had crept into bed in the early hours and could tell just from the way that Charlie lay over on his side that he was angry. In the morning he was curt and uncommunicative and left the house especially early. Annie had intended to be positive and generous and to apologise for walking out in what she now felt was an unhelpful way, but there had been no opportunity. She felt as if she had been put on the naughty step and was being punished by a withdrawal of attention as recommended by child behaviourists. This was reinforced when she later found an answerphone message telling her that he would be home late because of an after-school hockey match. There was no reference made as to whether this would fit in with any plans that she might have.

After she had taken the boys to school, Annie went up to her attic and drafted an e-mail to her former editor, herself no longer at the helm of the magazine but now heading up a de luxe monthly colour supplement for a top financial newspaper. She was a childless woman in her fifties, married to a Labour politician, who initially terrorised her young staff, but in the end Annie had grown to respect and admire her. She asked if they could meet for lunch sometime in the next few weeks. She then made a list of anyone else she could contact as a first tentative step in getting herself back into the frame.

The second prong of her attack was to explore the subject of childcare. If she held fire with work – and goodness, assuming she was lucky enough to find anything – until September when Rory began school proper or from November when he started doing a full day, she reckoned she could reasonably aim to work three full days and two from home. She would need a childminding arrangement for before and after school, and if Charlie couldn't commit to doing his share – and realistically she couldn't see how he could – it would be expensive. During the holidays he would have to take over or make some other arrangements. She knew that sounded uncompromising and as if she was landing responsibility on him, but why not? Think like a man! Of course she would have to take it gently, because she didn't intend to antagonise him any more than was inevitable. She wanted to take him with her, to convince him that it would work.

But the boys . . . the boys. Annie got up from the computer and paced the small space of the attic in agitation. She went to stare out of the window. She could just see the roof of the primary school, the old bell tower of the original grey stone building, the flash of the brightly coloured Portakabins that lined the old playground. She still felt agonised about hiving them off to some woman to look after, but she would get the best possible person, she really would. She owed them that, and then the time she *did* spend with them, she promised, she would be so patient and cheerful, she would be such fun. She would be the sort of mother she wanted to be. The sort of mother they deserved.

On an impulse she picked up the telephone and rang Alice's mobile number. There was no answer and she did not leave a message. She didn't really know what she was going to say anyway, except she wanted to thank her mother-in-law for making her feel that going back to work was an acceptable proposition.

A few moments later the telephone rang and it was Alice with a breathless explanation that she couldn't find her mobile but she could hear it ringing from afar, and that when she eventually located it in the bottom of her bag, it was too late.

'Is everything all right?' she asked anxiously.

'Yes, yes, everything is fine. The boys are well. Archie was class Star of the Week. He's terribly pleased with himself.'

'I'm sure he is! How did he earn that distinction?'

'It's here on the newsletter from school . . . wait for it! "Ash Class Star of the Week is Archie Baxter for excellent animal sorting" . . . whatever that means.'

'Excellent animal sorting! It sounds somehow biblical, doesn't it? Sheep from goats decision-making. Haven't you asked him?' Alice's tone was light but Annie felt an instant pang of guilt. Yes, of course she had, but she hadn't listened properly to his answer and now couldn't remember what he had said.

'Actually,' she said, 'I've rung to thank you for your support the other day – you know, when you said I sounded a bit down about losing my job. You made me feel a whole lot better when you suggested it would be perfectly possible for me to consider going back to work – proper work.'

'Oh!' said Alice. 'And have you?' She remembered what David had said and felt slightly alarmed. She hadn't intended to influence Annie. She was only trying to cheer her up.

'Yes, I have. A lot. In fact it's caused a bit of trouble with Charlie, who is dead against it. He feels that we made a decision when we moved out of London that I would give up work and look after the boys. He doesn't see that it's negotiable.'

'That's so typically him. He always was dogmatic and stubborn. He could never be in the wrong when he was a little boy. You'll have to find a way of making him think any change is his idea.'

'Easier said than done. To begin with I am going to have to go ahead without his support, I'm afraid. If I manage to get a job and sort out the boys I'll have a horrible time convincing him I'm not letting everyone down and reneging on my duties as wife and mother.'

'Oh dear!' said Alice. 'As bad as that?' Her heart sank. There didn't seem to be much compromise in the air at the moment. There must be some adverse planetary alignment that was causing friction in the Baxter family.

'Yup!'

'I don't know what to say. Obviously it's something you have to sort out between you. I feel that I shouldn't have expressed an opinion at all . . .'

'Oh! Don't backpedal now! I can't tell you how you encouraged me.' Annie heard the uncertainty in Alice's voice. She knew she would hate to feel that she had stirred up trouble in her son's marriage, but hell, maybe she should understand how things really were.

'Anyway, I've met a really interesting woman – the mother of a child at Archie's nursery school. She more or less told me to get off my arse and look for a job if that's what I want. Behave like a man, she said!'

'Oh! I see,' Alice said, imagining some rabid feminist with a proselytising mission. 'Does she work herself?'

'Very part-time. She's an extremely clever woman who used to lecture at Oxford, but her little boy has some problems and she prefers to look after him full time. She's a fantastically dedicated mother.'

'It sounds as if there is no father involved.'

'You're right. Damon was conceived by donor sperm.'

'Goodness!' Alice's mind raced. She thought of Sadie and her unborn baby, and Tamzin and Georgie – effectively fatherless – and this woman deciding to have an unknown man's baby. How fragile all these arrangements seemed without the solid rock of a family. What a struggle for a woman on her own to provide everything a child needed. She remembered how David had been at the centre of everything – maybe not a nappy-changing father in the modern idiom, but a permanent and loving fixture in the children's lives.

'Anyway,' said Annie, 'Fiona might even be able to do some of the childminding. Archie will be in the same class as her son. It could work very nicely.'

'I see. Well, good luck with it all. I mean, I suppose it's early days and you will have to find a job first.' Perhaps none of it will happen, Alice thought but didn't say. Why couldn't Annie be content with things as they were? She had a nice home in a pretty village, and surely Charlie was a good, reliable husband? The boys were past the difficult years, and with Archie about to start school she would have more time to do her own things. Couldn't she just take an art class or join a book club or something?

Even as she allowed these thoughts to enter her head, Alice knew they were treacherous. Why *should* Annie pretened to be content with that sort of life if she wanted something different? *Think like a man!* Charlie wouldn't be a house husband even if you shackled him to the kitchen, so why should Annie stay at home if she hated it? They would have to compromise somehow, because they owed it to the boys to make the best possible arrangements for them. It wasn't good enough for Charlie to dig his heels in and pontificate.

'No, really, good luck, Annie,' she said with more confidence. 'If there's anything I can do . . .' She couldn't say 'we can do' because she knew that David would be disapproving.

'And I do support you, you know. I realise that you need a proper job, a rewarding job, and you've given Rory and Archie the best possible start.'

'Thank you. I think I'll be a better mother in the long run.'

'In your case, I think you will . . . happier, anyway.'

'I hope it will be a better arrangement for all of us. Anyway, enough about me. How are the plans for the party?'

'Coming along,' replied Alice, thinking, shall I tell her about Sadie? and deciding that perhaps this wasn't the time. 'We've got Georgie and Tamzin here for the Easter holidays, and Sabine too, so we can have a big garden clear-up and get the invitations written and the tables planned.'

'Oh, lovely!' said Annie, but Alice could tell she wasn't really listening. She couldn't blame her. She had enough going on in her own life. 'I must go. Time to collect Archie. I've got Damon coming to tea so I mustn't be late.'

'No, you go. Goodbye, Annie, and good luck with it all. Your plans, I mean. Love to Charlie and the boys.'

Alice came off the telephone and sat for a moment, thinking. However much David might say that the best possible way to bring up children was to have a stay-at-home mother, she was convinced that Annie should go ahead with her plans. The boys will be *fine*, she told herself. Charlie and Annie were devoted parents and that should be enough. Their love and some common sense should guide them. It would need a change of attitude on Charlie's part – but for goodness' sake, he married a bright career girl, what did he expect?

She didn't agree with all the agonising about how to bring children up. It was a modern preoccupation that made parents feel inadequate and guilty. In the past it seemed people just got on with it. Children used to grow up in slums, malnourished and living on the streets, and at the other end of the spectrum were sent away to boarding school at seven years old. What could be more cruel or unnatural than that? Yet parents believed that they were doing the right thing and children *survived*.

She thought of poor Marina fretting about Mo from her City desk, while Ahmed pushed him round the supermarket, changed his nappies and took him to job interviews. How did his Syrian grandparents from a traditional family feel about this arrangement? she wondered. Of course they would be deeply concerned, just as she and David were, because although it was a practical solution to the situation, it was not the system of child-rearing that they were familiar with.

Sadie was much more of a worry because of the lack of money and security and the absence of a father figure in her children's life, and yet she was the most natural and loving parent of the lot – if she could swap places with Annie and be a provided-for stay-at-home mum, she would be in heaven. Everything that Annie hated, Sadie loved – the time to mess about cooking, and making stuff out of cardboard, and helping with reading at school – and yet she had managed her personal life so disastrously that it seemed she would never achieve what would make her happiest.

Alice sighed. At least she and David were in a position to help. They had David's pension and her small salary and some savings. It was their job to be the safe haven for Tamzin and Georgie, and if Annie went back to work, to help out at half-terms and so on with the boys. She felt a pleasant sense of purpose and she knew that David would agree with her. That was the strength of a proper family – that you pulled together when it was required. He might deplore Sadie's judgement and disapprove of Annie's need to go back to work, but he would do whatever was required for the grandchildren.

She glanced round the kitchen, which was in a mess, with lunch plates still on the table. Like the rest of the house it was shabby and needed doing up. It still bore the marks of the family that had been reared there, the little piece of broken skirting board where one of the boys had skidded after a football, the cork message board made by Sadie, trimmed with seashells, some of which had fallen off over the years, the lumpy pottery ashtray on the windowsill. There was still a drawer full of novelty biscuit-cutters and pieces of toys and old-fashioned crayons and magnets and marbles and school badges and other childish clutter that had never been thrown away. The attic was full of cardboard boxes of A-level notes and outgrown football boots and broken kites. They should have cleared it all out, they really should.

We haven't moved on, David and I, she thought. We're still stuck where we were when we had the children at home. We've never taken the house back, or our lives, for that matter. She thought of her sister, Rachel, and how she and her husband had moved several times since their children left home and were now in a shiny modern house with a manicured garden and their children restricted to looking out from silver-framed photographs neatly arranged on a polished surface in the drawing room. They had a spare room with an empty chest of drawers and a fitted wardrobe containing nothing but Rachel's work suits hanging in dry-cleaner's plastic bags.

They had a clean new car and planned holidays and shopped together and had people round for dinner and owned proper patio furniture. They seemed to have regained something of what they were as a couple before children interrupted their lives, and we haven't done that, thought Alice. Really, David and I have never recovered, she thought, and didn't know whether she was glad or sorry but was conscious of being judged as something of a failure in terms of having a proper, mid-life lifestyle.

She hadn't given supper much thought and now wondered whether she would cook something special just for the two of them. The whole day seemed to have been taken up with angst over Sadie but she still had time to drive into the nearest small town and buy some steak and a better than usual bottle of wine. She could give David a surprise and cheer them both up. She wondered where he had got to and guessed he was in his room. Perhaps he was planning his trip to Cornwall. She was glad he was going. It would do him good to have a break, and maybe it was a sign that he was moving towards a generally more positive mood. She could, of course, ask for a few days off and go with him. Although he and Edwin had walked alone in the past, there was no reason why she should not be included. She imagined striding along a grassy clifftop with the sun on her face while seabirds wheeled overhead and waves broke in gentle white frills on a blue sea far below. David would lead the way down a narrow path fringed with spring flowers towards a thatched pub and a crab salad lunch, which they could eat at an outside table.

Later, after supper, while David drained the bottle of wine into their glasses, she brought up the subject.

'So have you planned your trip? Do you know when you'll be going?'

'What trip?'

'Oh, David! You always do that. Answer a question with a question. Your walking trip! You said you'd go away for a few days before Easter. Before Sadie and the girls come to stay.'

'Oh, that. No, I haven't thought any more about it. But if I go, it will be next week. Only for a few days. We've got maps somewhere, haven't we? I must look them out and give Edwin a ring.'

'Would you stay in pubs? You wouldn't camp, would you?'

'God, no. It could be cold and it's almost certain to be wet.'

'I thought maybe I'd come with you. It would be nice to have a little break.'

Later David congratulated himself on not missing a beat.

'Well that would be nice. Could you get time off?'

'I could try. So many of us are part-timers that it's some-times possible to swap things round.'

'Well, see what you can do.'

'I will. I'll have a look tomorrow. It would be nice, wouldn't it? To do something together.'

'Of course. If you really think you would enjoy it – the walking, I mean.'

'How far will you want to walk a day?'

'Ten to fifteen miles, I should think.'

It sounded a lot to Alice. The vision she had in her head changed to one of trudging up a hill in the rain, the view obscured by a grey mist. Her boots would probably rub and she would look fat in her waterproof trousers. Maybe it was better to let the men go off on their own.

David got up to look in the fridge for some cheese. If Alice decided to accompany him, then he would accept that the gods were intervening to save him from whatever this madness was that consumed him. She would save him from himself and he would accept his fate with grace. It was perfectly true what he had told her, that he hadn't begun to plan the walk. Instead he had been texting Julia suggesting that he call in on her on Monday, and she had texted back to say how happy that made her and then had sent another text to say, '*You'll stay of course*' and he had replied after a lot of thought, '*Let's see shall we?*'

So far he hadn't had to lie to Alice – not an out-and-out lie, anyway – but for almost the first time in his married life he felt shifty and on edge. Before he had come down to supper he had erased the messages from his mobile telephone and switched it off. He must be careful, he knew that, because he now had something to hide.

'That was delicious,' he said, sitting back down. 'Thank you. A bloody good bit of steak.'

'A good bit of bloody steak.' Alice smiled at her husband across the table.

'I'll clear up,' he said kindly. 'You go and sit down and I'll bring you a cup of coffee.'

'I never have coffee at night. Ever. Haven't you noticed?'

'Well I'll bring you a brandy, then.'

'That'll give me a headache.' Alice got up and began to collect dirty plates. David didn't stack the dishwasher to her satisfaction so she might as well do it herself. 'I'll have a cup of tea, though, if you'll put the kettle on. We could watch the second part of that detective thing on the television. It begins at nine.'

'You slept through the first part.'

'That doesn't matter. I can never follow the plot anyway.'

The next day at work she almost forgot to look at the rota for the following week. With a bit of juggling she could probably carve out the time to go with David, but when she told Margaret she gasped theatrically and said, 'You're off your rocker! Walking! At this time of the year! Get that man of yours to take you somewhere warm and sunny, where you can lie on a beach and snap your fingers for a young man to bring you a drink.'

'Margaret! It's only two or three days we're talking about here. We can't go to the Caribbean – not that we could afford it – and I don't like beaches anyway.'

'Then go to one of those boutique hotels in Cornwall. You must have seen them in the colour mags. I think one of them bans children – adults only. No one our age wants our holidays spoiled by snivelling brats.'

'We can't afford that. David would hate it anyway.'

'Well you wouldn't catch me letting a couple of men walk me off my feet across a lot of wet fields of sodding sheep.'

'You're doing a good job of putting me off.'

'I should hope so! Let him go on his own. You go shopping for that party outfit. Have a day in Bath if you won't go to Oxford Street.'

'You're sort of convincing me . . . I don't suppose it would be much fun. Now, I've got to tell you about Sadie.'

'What's she done now?'

When Alice had finished recounting the latest turn of events, Margaret fixed her with a stern look. 'Your Sadie should bloomin' well stand on her own feet. She'd be a bit more responsible then, and you should have your own life at your age, Alice. You shouldn't be always running after your kids.' She said this kindly, moving to the kettle with two mugs. 'Coffee?'

'Yes please. But Margaret, surely you understand why David and I must help her? We couldn't do anything else. David feels exactly the same as I do.'

'Yes, I know. I'm only winding you up. You've got a lovely family. You and David have done a good job. Talking about that, how are the party preparations?'

'We're getting there. The marquee is booked, and the caterers, and the bouncy castle, and I'm starting on the garden over Easter. I'll get the kids to help me.'

'Good. They should be giving you this party, not the other way round.'

'But it's me who wants to celebrate all of them. It is really.'

'If you say so. Anyway, I hope you're going to turn down that walking trip. Let the miserable old buggers do it on their own!'

Alice smiled weakly. Her conversation with Margaret had left her feeling rather flat. 'I expect you're right,' she said.

'What do you think of this top? I got it on eBay for a fiver and it's this year's stock too.' Margaret was wearing a brightly coloured stripy T-shirt with a slashed neck and a tie belt. 'Animal prints are in, big time.'

'You look great, as usual,' which she did, thought Alice. She admired Margaret's spirit in making an effort and caring about fashion, whereas she herself seemed to have completely run out of steam, and her diet efforts had so far been disastrous. Last night it was the anxiety over Sadie and the thing going on between Annie and Charlie that she blamed. Visits to the biscuit tin always made things seem less worrying – for a short time anyway.

Chapter Nine

THE FORECAST WAS good for the day that David set off for Cornwall. The old car in which he had trundled backwards and forwards to the university for years was loaded up with walking gear, and Roger sat on the back seat on a tartan rug, panting with excitement and smearing slobber on the window.

Far from feeling excited himself, David was filled with a sense of doom, and as he drove he willed a disaster that would impede his progress down the A303. Instead he sailed along in relatively light traffic. It was too early in the year for caravans and motorhomes heading west and there were, miraculously, no hold-ups in Yeovil.

He had said goodbye to Alice with unusual tenderness, but she, late to get off to work, hadn't noticed and had kissed his cheek briefly. 'Have you got sun cream?' she asked. She couldn't say goodbye to anyone without running through a list of what they might have forgotten. 'Mobile? Charger? Wallet? Keep in touch, won't you. Have a lovely time!'

It seemed incredible that she hadn't picked up on his altered state. He supposed the answer was that she wasn't much interested in him any more – not as a person in his own right. She was too preoccupied with the rest of the family. This thought made him feel hurt and resentful in equal measures. If she didn't care about him then she didn't much care what he was doing, and this was true – she had barely asked him what his plans were for the next few days. She had made it so easy for him that it seemed almost her fault that he was setting off on this particular adventure, or whatever it turned out to be. She should have stopped him, she really should. A little more interest and concern on her part would have made it impossible for him to even contemplate this wild goose chase.

Of course he knew this was being unfair. It fell into the 'my wife doesn't understand me' category of lame excuses. He knew it wasn't Alice's fault – more the state of their marriage, which had grown dull and unexciting. Was this escapade all to do with sex, then? He supposed it was. Sex with Alice was pretty limited due to a lack of desire on both sides – which was normal, he supposed, in a marriage as long as theirs. *Of course* it was normal, he reassured himself. If they felt like it, they did it, with varying degrees of success, but sex was no longer the be all and end all it once had been. Lust had been replaced by an easy sort of affection that was quite appropriate at their age.

Without even liking Julia very much he felt desire for her because she was young and pretty and for some reason seemed to fancy him, and this was the biggest aphrodisiac of all. She apparently didn't see him as a clapped-out old man but as a potential lover, while Alice appeared to completely discount what his children would call his 'pulling power'. She had mocked his new haircut, for instance. Little did she know that only a short time later a young woman would be running her hands through his barnet while she assaulted him with kisses.

So there you are, Alice, he thought. He wondered how, if the boot was on the other foot, Alice would appear to other men. She was still lovely to him. He suddenly thought of her laughing at something he said, her face lit with amusement, as she concentrated on stirring a pan or chopping onions. He thought of her as she was the other evening when she had shed tears for Sadie. Her face was red and blotchy and she pushed her hair behind her ears just as she had done as a young woman. That happened sometimes. He got a sudden glimpse of the girl she had been when they first met and started going out together, and the years rolled away and he remembered the old Alice.

He had read an article in the weekend paper about older women who behaved in a predatory way towards younger men, but the accompanying photographs showed grandmothers with perma-tans and bleached blond hair wearing miniskirts way above their wrinkled knees. Alice wasn't like that, obviously. She wasn't glamorous or dressed up as a teenager, but she was still beautiful because he could see the girl in her. He thought of the warmth of her smile that age had not altered and the prettiness of her soft blue eyes.

There had been times in the past when he had been jealous. She once had a terrific crush on a doctor in the practice. She couldn't stop talking about him and went off to work looking pretty and lit up. It had festered on the whole summer and ended with a terrific row during which she had admitted that she was a bit in love with him but that she would never, ever do anything, and anyway, he was a married man with children. David had known that what she said was true, because one thing about Alice, he thought, was that she was truthful.

He was past Taunton now and had joined the motorway. In places the verges were yellow with bobbing daffodils. The sky was blue with fleecy white clouds and in some of the fields sheep grazed with lambs at their sides. It was a lovely day and the dread he felt seemed to be lifting. The word 'fling' came into his head. A fling in spring. It sounded careless and rapturous. What harm could it possibly do?

By the time he reached Okehampton he saw a lay-by with a snack van and pulled off the road. Roger sat up and looked interested and David clipped on his lead and let him out to snuffle along the hedge and cock his leg vigorously at intervals. He bought a cup of coffee and a bacon bap and went back to sit in the car and consider his options. He would shortly reach the point where he either went in the direction of Edwin's cottage, which would obviously be the wise and sensible choice, or took the road towards Tavistock, Cornwall and Julia. He gave the last of the bap to Roger and started the engine.

Annie had had a response from her editor, who suggested a day for lunch later in the week. This had thrown her into a state of emergency that got her thoroughly rattled. What had motherhood done to her, that the mere prospect of a London lunch with her ex-boss had her in a state of jittery nerves and apprehension? A few telephone calls later and she had the boys fixed up. Fiona was going to collect Archie after nursery and take him home for the afternoon, and Rory, who had swimming after school on that particular day, was fixed up with Oscar, another boy in his class. Oscar's mother had said it would be no problem. In fact, she said, she was feeling guilty that it was always Annie who had the boys after school – little knowing that Annie did so because it was better than being with her children on their own.

Upstairs she went through her entire wardrobe. While she could no longer be cutting-edge fashionable, she still had a few good pieces that would work: a pair of black McQueen trousers with a cashmere sweater and a swash-buckling Vivienne Westwood coat. She added a pair of boots and a Chloe bag. The pleasure of wearing her good clothes again was enormous. It gave her an actual physical thrill to handle the expensive materials and see the effect of cut and tailoring. At least she had kept her figure – in fact she was a bit thinner than before she had children. Her boobs had almost disappeared, sucked away to nothing by babies, she thought. They were like two flat cherry-topped biscuits stuck quite low down on her chest.

The problem now was her hair. It was, frankly, disastrously nondescript in colour and shape. On an impulse she tele-phoned her old hairdresser and booked a cut and colour with the top stylist for the morning before the lunch. It would cost hundreds of pounds but she didn't care, and after a moment's thought she rang back and booked a mani-cure as well. Think like a bloody man.

'Now you need a strategy,' said Fiona when she and Damon came to tea. It was strange having her as a visitor. Annie noticed that she never commented on anything in the house, not the astronomically expensive sitting-room curtains that had come from the London house, or the knocked-through kitchen that gave a pretty outlook on to the secluded garden. She looked at photographs with interest and ran her eyes along the rows of books, picking one out at random to flick through the pages and read a paragraph or two.

Damon and Archie were upstairs, probably wrecking Archie's bedroom, and for the moment there were no blood-curdling shrieks. The large hairy dog lay peacefully under the kitchen table.

'So about this lunch,' said Fiona. 'What are you hoping to achieve?'

'I want to put it about that I would like to come back to work. Sylvia is the best contact I have. I want her to put out some feelers for me.'

'Yes, I see that, but I think you need to be more aggressive, or proactive or whatever. As you put it, all the wanting is on your side. You need to make the publishing world feel that it wants you and what you have to offer.'

'That's hard to do when I have been out of it for four years and haven't published a noteworthy thing meanwhile. Having children, being at home, not working on anything worthwhile – it's sapped my confidence, Fiona.'

'It was fashion that you covered before, wasn't it? I take it that you don't want to go back into that particular world?'

'No I don't. It's too demanding to combine with a family. The unpredictable hours nearly killed me when I went back to work after Rory was born, and also it is the favoured field of bright young things straight out of university with first-class degrees.'

'So what now? Features? Beauty? Travel? What else is there in the world of women's mags?'

'I think I could do family-related pieces – education,

health, holidays, relationships. I could write for more than one publication.'

'Have you got any new material that you can show to this Sylvia person?'

'Yes, I have,' said Annie. 'I've written the outline for an article about exactly what I am trying to do – go back to work after having children. I need some strong interviews to hang it on – the managing director of John Lewis, for instance, or Boots the chemist, who employ a largely female staff – and I need the statistics for the cost of childcare and some health data. Are working women less likely to see a doctor? Do they have less need of antidepressants? That sort of thing.'

'But hasn't all this been done before? I'm sure I've read it already. They're not very fresh, these women's issues, are they?'

Annie felt affronted and fell silent.

'Have I annoyed you? I'm afraid I'm no good at dissembling.'

'No, no. I appreciate your point of view.'

There was a silence for a moment before Annie said, 'Okay. So what line would you take?'

'I don't know anything at all about the world of women's journalism. You only have to look at me to see that beauty and fashion advice have passed me by. I am interested in issues of equality and employment, though, because they have touched me personally. I suppose it occurred to me that by coming back into work you have the advantage of seeing things with fresh eyes, and that perhaps you could do something completely different – like that female journalist who hated sport who was asked to become a football correspondent.'

'I couldn't do that! I need to write about what I know.'

'But do you? That's exactly my point. Perhaps you could write about something you don't know – like women in banking, or prostitution, or racing stables, or in prison or girl gangs, or those that care for elderly relatives . . . writing that gives an insight into their lives.'

'I've never done investigative pieces. I've never done full-blown interviews.'

'Does that mean you can't do them now?'

'It would be way out of my comfort zone.'

'Maybe a good thing.'

When Charlie came home, relatively early, he found Annie sitting at the kitchen table with her open laptop, in the company of a large, unkempt woman he didn't know and a hairy dog asleep on the sofa in the sitting room. Upstairs, his sons and a visiting boy were jumping on the beds and shrieking with laughter.

'Hey! Hey!' he said. 'What's all this? Hello, I'm Charlie.' His good manners never failed him.

'Fiona.' Fiona stuck out a large hand.

Annie began an explanation. 'Fiona's been giving me ideas for some articles – stuff I wouldn't have thought of.'

'Are you a writer?'

'God, no! I'm a lecturer of sorts.'

'In what? Where?' That was typical of Charlie. He always wanted to get people sorted into categories, thought Annie. He seemed impressed when Fiona mentioned Oxford.

'Beer, anyone? G and T?' he asked, opening the fridge.

'Thanks, but I must go,' said Fiona, getting up. Annie saw Charlie take in her size and the eccentric clothing.

'Damon has had a wonderful afternoon. Thank you from us both.'

'Thank *you!*' said Annie warmly. 'Stay to supper if you like. It's only mince and potatoes. It hasn't quite made it into shepherd's pie.'

'No, I must take him home.' The screaming from upstairs had become high-pitched and hysterical. 'He needs calming down or it will take me hours to get him to sleep tonight.'

When Fiona had gone, after a prolonged display of resistance from Damon, Charlie said, getting another beer out of the fridge, 'Jesus! What a nightmare! How does she cope with that every day?'

'Very well, actually.'

'Should that sort of child be in mainstream school? Is he really going to be in Archie's class next year?'

'Yes he is, and yes he should. They're friends, actually.'

'I wouldn't encourage that, if I was you.'

'Why?'

'Come on, Annie. He's out of control and disruptive.'

'Charlie! Yes, he's got problems – obviously – but he's doing really well. He's very bright.'

Charlie made an exasperated face. 'Is she on her own? Fiona?'

'Yes.' This was not the time to go into Fiona's private life. Annie felt Charlie's hostility and it annoyed her. Fiona didn't tick the necessary boxes. She wasn't the sort of person who would send her child to his bloody school.

'She seems an unlikely friend.'

'Why?'

'Not your sort, I would have said.'

'Why?' Annie felt her anger rising again. Everything that

was unresolved between her and Charlie rushed to the surface.

'Well, she's obviously pretty academic, not interested in your world of fashion, and seriously uncool. She looks like a dyke, actually. Of the Russian shotputter variety. So what are these ideas she's helping you with?'

If Annie was predisposed to telling Charlie anything about her lunch date, his remarks had changed her mind. She was certainly not going to tell him now.

'I don't think you would be interested,' she said coldly.

Charlie felt affronted. Next he would be accused of *not* being interested. He just couldn't win.

'Why do you say that?'

'Because you are so bloody scornful of everything I do, that's why. You even criticise my friend when you don't know a thing about her.'

'Oh for God's sake!' Charlie sighed wearily. 'Loosen up, can't you? It was hardly criticism. A passing remark or two. I'm not allowed to say anything that might offend your tender sensibilities! Jesus!' He took his beer and went through into the sitting room with the newspaper.

'You might set the table!' yelled Annie after him. 'And get the boys to wash their hands – supper's almost ready.'

Set it yourself, you've got sod-all else to do, Charlie thought, but didn't say. 'Guys!' he called up the stairs. 'Wash your hands and come down for supper,' and he sat back down with the newspaper.

Sadie collected Tamzin and Georgie from school and piled them into the cab of the pickup. Georgie had something going on about a lost reading book and was near to tears, but Sadie said, as she drove, 'Don't worry, hon! I found it under your bed this morning. It isn't lost at all.'

'Where are we going, Mum?' asked Tamzin anxiously. 'Why have you come to pick us up?'

'We're going to have a treat, all of us,' said Sadie. 'I've booked you both a ride at the stables this afternoon. Your gear is in the back. Then we're going out for supper – a Big Mac if you like.'

This was so out of the norm that Tamzin was instantly suspicious. Georgie was clapping her hands and shouting, 'Yo!' but Tamzin knew that this sort of thing didn't happen without a reason. She looked at her mother's face and saw the dark rings under her eyes. Something was wrong, she knew it. She had heard arguments between her and Kyle and she knew he was angry about something. He had shouted at her when she dropped a pail of milk for the calves, when she was only trying to help because she wanted him to like her and she didn't think he did. She could tell he preferred Georgie, who made him laugh, and she had once heard him telling her mum that she got on his nerves. He said she was always trying to attract attention. Her mum had said he should perhaps consider why she was like that, and she was angry with him. Tamzin was glad to hear her mother defending her but Kyle's words struck deep into her heart, because it was horrible to feel that she could be disliked for something she didn't even know she was. She wanted him to like her, but it never seemed to work when she tried to muck about with him like Georgie did.

'I've got something to tell you,' said Sadie, and Tamzin tensed, knowing that she had been right, that something had happened. 'I'll start with the good thing, the thing that will make you both happy and excited . . . I am expecting a baby! You're going to have a little brother or sister in October!'

'Cool!' shouted Georgie. 'Tia Marie's mum's just had twins! I hope it will be a girl!'

'Tamzin?'

'Yeah. Cool,' but Tamzin was already thinking, how will we manage? Her mum was always saying they couldn't afford stuff and the cottage was so small. She imagined having to share a room with a baby, but then she thought about pushing it around in a pram and showing it things, like the new lambs in the lambing shed, and making it daisy chains and tickling it under the chin with buttercups like she had done with Georgie when she was a baby. 'I'll clean the old pram,' she offered. She and Georgie used it for their dolls and it was caked in mud from the farmyard.

'That would be great, darling! Now the second thing I've got to tell you is part bad and part good. I'm afraid that Kyle and I are going to split up. He doesn't want the baby, you see. He says that if I want to keep it, to have it, then he doesn't want to live with us any more.' She paused to allow this bit of news to sink in and glanced sideways to see how it was received.

She was surprised to see that there was hardly any re-action. 'Yes, but *we* want it, don't we?' said Georgie. 'Tia Marie gets to bath hers. They wee in the air like a fountain, she says. Mum, do you think you might get twins? Tamzin and I could have one each, then.'

'God, I hope not!'

Tamzin said nothing. Really, she didn't mind if Kyle was there or not. She liked things about him, like the farm, and

208

riding in the pickup, but she didn't mind much about him. She and her mum and Georgie and the baby would be fine on their own. Better, really. They could all get into bed together again on Saturday mornings and watch television like they used to.

'The other bad thing is that we'll have to leave the farm – move out of the cottage.'

Tamzin shot her a look, then, thoroughly alarmed. 'Why? Why can't we stay? It's our home now.'

'Yeah, I know, but the cottage goes with Kyle's job. He's going to give up the job – move away somewhere – so we have to move out.'

'But you work on the farm. Why can't it be your cottage?'

'I only do part-time, lovey, and I'd do less and less as the baby grows. They'll want to find another dairyman to take over the herd and he'll want the cottage.'

'Where will we go then? What will happen to us?'

'I don't want to go back to Yeovil!' Georgie started to cry. 'I hated it in Yeovil in that smelly flat.'

'No, we won't. I promise you we won't. We'll find somewhere nice to live. Until we do, we're going to stay with Granny and Grandpa. They said they'd love to have us.'

Tamzin felt a wave of such intense relief that she thought she might be sick. She had to swallow hard and stare out of the window. She thought of Granny, her round, comfortable shape, her specs round her neck on a chain, the funny way she talked back to the radio while she was cooking; and Grandpa, reading them something out of the newspaper or getting out an atlas to show them where penguins came from.

She liked the bedroom she and Georgie shared when they

stayed with them. She liked all the old toys and the drawer full of dolls' clothes and the shelves of books her mum said she read when she was a child. She liked the way Roger climbed up the stairs and lay on the floor, snoring, between their beds, while Grandpa read them a good-night story. She liked meals at the kitchen table, where there was no pressure to eat disgusting, healthy stuff and they had their own napkins and napkin rings – hers was shaped like a brown horse with a hole in his tummy, and Georgie had a yellow chicken – and there was always a proper glass jug of water on the table.

'Tam? What do you say, darling?'

'Okay.' That was all she could manage for now.

Sabine supposed that her stepfather had broken the news of Sadie's pregnancy as tactfully as possible, but when she and Agnes got home from school one afternoon, their mother was upstairs in her bedroom, her face swollen with crying. Sabine stood in the doorway, her heart filled with dread, her mind catapulting her back to France and hot afternoons in a darkened room, her mother crumpled on her bed, weeping.

'What is it, Mum?' wailed Agnes, rushing to her side. 'What's happened?'

'Nothing! It's nothing,' gulped Lisa, rubbing under her eyes with both hands. 'I'm fine. Honestly I am.'

'Then why are you crying?' Agnes began to cry in sympathy, plucking at her mother's sweater. Lisa, sitting on the edge of her bed, took her into her arms and smoothed her hair, making an effort to be calm. Her eyes sought Sabine's face and reading her anguish, she held out an arm to encourage her to come to her as well.

'Really, it's okay,' she said. 'I am just being silly. Ollie has told me that his sister, Sadie, is having another baby. That man she lives with, Carl or something, doesn't want it, so they're splitting up and she and the girls are moving out.'

She's not crying for them, thought Sabine. It's about the baby. If the man doesn't want it, why can't they give it to us? People did that. Some women had babies for people who couldn't have them. Maybe that was what Sadie could do. She'd always seemed a kind sort of person. If she knew how much her mum wanted another baby, maybe she'd hand it over when it was born. But it was more compli-cated than that. Her mum wanted her own baby – hers and Ollie's – and suddenly Sabine saw it all and understood. She couldn't put it into words, not even in her head, but she felt something of what her mother must be feeling, the deep jealousy and pain at hearing of someone having what you most wanted – apparently above everything else, certainly more than she wanted her or Agnes. Somehow when you got older you were less important than a baby.

Thinking this made Sabine feel angry and hurt. Babies were spoiling everything in her life. What was it that made them so much more valuable than the children you already had? Her father and Jacqui didn't want her around because of the horrid little thing in Jacqui's belly – the boy that her father seemed to want more than he did his daughters. She remembered what Jacqui had said to her yesterday on the telephone, 'Sorry, Sabine, but these holidays won't be a good time for you to visit. We're away, as your dad told you, and when we get back I will need to rest and take things easy.'

Ignoring her mother's appeal, she turned on her heel and

211

went to her room and closed the door. The new computer gleamed like a large pink sweet from her desk. She opened it and switched it on. She knew what she was going to do. A moment later, before she had a chance to Google what she wanted, the door burst open and Agnes barged in, crying, 'Why are you so horrible to Mum? Can't you see she's really, really upset?'

'Get out!' commanded Sabine. 'You're such a baby. You don't understand anything.' She jumped up and was strong enough to push her sister out of the door and slam it shut. She shoved her desk chair under the handle.

Agnes kicked at the bottom of the door all the time she was finding the airline site and booking her ticket to Bordeaux. Eventually she heard her mother knocking on the door and asking in an anxious voice, 'Sabine? Darling? I'm sorry, darling. I didn't want to upset you.'

'*I'm* all right,' answered Sabine coldly, although her hands were shaking. 'Just take Agnes away, will you? I'm trying to do my homework.'

'So,' said David, stopping to get in through the peasant-sized front door of the cottage, 'this is it?' He didn't know what he meant by the remark or why the question had issued from his mouth. Did he mean *this is it* in a philosophical sense, or *this is it* referring to the cottage at which he had just arrived? Or maybe *this is it* as in 'this is what I have been waiting for all my life'.

He did not have to explain himself because Julia didn't take any notice anyway. She was too eager to get him inside and kiss him.

'I'm so, so glad that you followed your higher conscious

forces and came to me!' she said when she broke off for air. 'I have been practising remote transference all morning. Look!' She pointed to a windowsill – the cottage was clearly very old and the walls were over a foot thick. 'There's my sacred space.'

What was she on about? thought David. It sounded as if she was going to sacrifice him. On the sill was a bunch of rather dried-out silvery-green leaves and a feather and a small glinting object. 'My crystal!' said Julia. The whole thing looked like a rather second-rate nature table at a primary school.

But Julia was lovely. Her hair was loose on her shoulders and she was wearing a pair of tight jeans and a small shrunken sweater that worked its way up when she moved her arms about and revealed a strip of smooth white stomach.

Although he had stopped for a pee before arriving at the cottage, David found that he needed to go again, quite urgently. Julia showed him to a downstairs bathroom that was very cold and smelled of damp. It would take weeks for a cottage like this, built into a stony hillside, to warm up after the winter. As he stood at the lavatory, David's eyes fell on Julia's wash bag on a table beside him. He noticed a strip of bubble-protected small pills. Birth control, he guessed, and thought of Sadie, whom he didn't at all wish to think of at this particular moment.

This is it, he thought again as he washed his hands at the basin. I suppose I am about to be unfaithful to Alice. It should have been a sobering moment, but it wasn't. Instead he felt an overwhelming eagerness.

He went out to find Julia making some of her vile tea

in an earthenware pot, which he took gently from her hands and set on the kitchen counter.

'Julia,' he said. 'Sweetheart.' He had never called Alice that in his entire married life, and he wondered where the word had come from.

'There's a dog barking outside,' said Julia, cocking her head to listen.

'Oh, hell! That will be Roger. I'd better go and get him out of the car.'

'Dogs aren't allowed in this cottage!' cried Julia. 'What on earth did you bring a dog for?'

Chapter Ten

SADIE HELD OUT hope to the end that Kyle might change his mind, but the day before the girls broke up from school for Easter, she woke to hear the cows creating a rumpus in the yard, and turning over and consulting the alarm clock, she found that it was six thirty and that Kyle should have been up milking them an hour ago.

His side of the bed was empty, and when she went to the window and looked out, she saw that his pickup had gone from the yard. With a feeling of rising panic she pulled on her clothes and went down the narrow staircase to the front door, which stood open. The object on the floor at the bottom of the stairs turned out to be a sock, and glancing round the sitting room she saw that the laptop had gone from the table and that his work overalls were hanging on their peg by the door.

'Fuck! He's gone! The fucking coward's done a runner,' she said out loud. There was no note, nothing. She ran back upstairs to fetch her mobile telephone and saw that she had a text message.

'*Its better like this. Take care hon*', with a smiley face.

Sadie felt so angry that she would have thrown the phone

across the room had she not known that she would be lost without it.

Pulling on her rubber boots she went out into the yard. The cows mooed when they saw her and she opened the gate to let them into the milking parlour. They progressed slowly, stiff-legged, bony-hipped, with bloated, swaying udders, each one taking a moment to stop and stare at her standing by the gate with curious, mild eyes. Each one seemed to be asking the question, 'What are you doing here? Where's Kyle?' I wish I knew, girls, she thought in reply. I wish I knew.

She couldn't begin the milking, she didn't know how, but after she'd got the first lot into the parlour she would ring the relief milker and get him round as quickly as possible. She hoped to God that he would be at home and not out milking somewhere else.

She was too busy after that to think much about Kyle or how he could be so base as to walk out on them. After she had organised the milking she had to get the girls up and pretend to them that it was a perfectly ordinary morning. She walked with them down the drive to catch the school bus, Georgie hanging off her arm while Tamzin lagged behind reading a book as she walked. Neither of them asked about Kyle. It was normal not to see him because he came in later for breakfast, after they had gone to school.

Sadie knew that when she got back to the cottage she would have to telephone the farm manager and tell him that Kyle had gone. It made her mad that he had left her to do his dirty work. She would have to feed the calves as well as her usual work in the polytunnels. Today was veg box day – her busiest of the week – and she was feeling as sick as a dog. Of course she had no transport with the pickup gone. She had planned to use it to cart their stuff over to her parents'. She mulled over all this as she tugged Georgie along the drive, trying to keep her out of the pools of liquid mud that lay half the year in the vehicle tracks.

It was a beautiful morning, but she didn't notice. Birds sang in the blackthorn bushes that followed the drive and the grass on either side was studded with yellow celandines and the delicate white of garlic mustard. Little dog violets peeked blue from the banks, amongst the first tangles of purple vetch. On either side the meadows where the cows would soon be turned out to graze were springing green, and beyond, the blue Dorset hills rose to meet a high blue sky.

The three of them trudged along in silence. Tamzin's lunch box banged against her legs and the straps of her backpack slipped off her round shoulders to rest in the crooks of her elbows. Georgie seemed to lack the energy to lift her feet – she was terrible in the mornings, her face puffy with sleep, her hair a mess. 'Come here,' said Sadie, searching in the pocket of her denim jacket and pulling out an array of hair clips. She jammed one in the front of Georgie's fine, tangled hair, lifting it away from her forehead. She looked more kempt like that, as if she had an organised mother and maybe even a father, too.

They rounded the last bend of the drive, not very far from where it joined the lane at a clump of tall trees, still dark and leafless after the winter. Sadie could see the school bus down at the bottom of the hill, where it stopped to collect children from the council houses by the old mill. 'Come on!' she said. 'Get a move on! The bus will be here soon. You'll have a nice day today. There'll be no work on the day before you break up. It will be the holidays after tomorrow!' She tried to make her voice sound jolly, but it was an effort when she was weighed down with misery because of Kyle. She felt an aching sadness that what she had had with him, which some of the time had seemed to be complete happiness, had proved to be worth so little. Where was he, the bastard? Where had he run to?

She saw the girls on to the bus and stumped back to the farm. She was angry that he had taken the laptop. He had bought it for her and it had all her stuff on it: all her personal stuff, all her contacts. She would have liked to have got straight on to Mumsnet and publicised the latest development in the drama of her life. She could guess at the female outrage that the news of Kyle's defection would arouse. Instead, she thought she would telephone her parents. She took her mobile out of her pocket and tried their number, but there was no answer. Her mother's mobile was switched off. Sadie guessed that she would be driving to work. She tried her father's mobile, which went unanswered. Where was he? In bed, asleep, she guessed. She would have liked to have spoken to him. She wanted to hear the anger in his voice on her behalf when she told him the news.

Roger's presence had caused Julia to have what David would term 'a fit', and completely spoiled the opening movement of their reunion. He had been forced to leave her wringing her hands in the cottage and go to let the dog out of the car and take him for a little walk up the lane. Roger investigated the new smells with enthusiasm. As they went past the cottage next door, a woman came out and stood at her gate with her arms folded. 'Dogs aren't allowed,' she said, ignoring David's 'Good afternoon'. 'They don't allow dogs in the cottage. It says so in the brochure. And on the website.' Although she was quite young, she had the determined air of the resolutely bossy, glad to have the opportunity to point out the deficiencies of others. She was one of nature's prefects.

'I'm only visiting,' he said coldly, thinking, interfering cow. 'And should I stay, he can sleep in the car.'

'Yes, but you can't leave him barking like that all night. I wonder why you brought him when it's quite clear on the website. No dogs allowed. I just look after the place. It's not up to me.'

'No. Okay.'

'They're very particular. No children. No pets.' She was fat and wore a smock top over tight three-quarter-length black leggings. Her sturdy mauve calves continued down into her trainers with no visible ankle indentation.

'I get the picture. Thank you. I trust I am allowed to walk up the lane? I don't need permission?'

The woman fell silent, not knowing what point he was making.

'You can do what you like up the lane,' she eventually conceded regretfully.

'Good. Thank you so much.' Politeness was generally more discomforting to the aggressor than hard words, but the young woman seemed impervious. She remained at her gate, glaring. David felt her eyes boring into his back as he continued up the lane, which was sunk between deep banks that excluded the view on either side. It was like walking up a tunnel.

Bloody dog! Roger had wrecked the ambience of the reunion between him and Julia; completely taken the thrill out of that first rapturous contact. David felt angry and frustrated. It was all Alice's fault, insisting that he should bring him. He wondered why he hadn't resisted. He could have made up a story about Edwin being allergic to dogs or something.

Roger ran on ahead, stopping to examine the sides of the banks with great concentration. His tail wagged and his pink tongue lolled from side to side. He was having a lovely time, damn him.

At the top of the hill, David turned round and looked over a gate at the surrounding countryside of small wintry-looking fields separated by stone walls and banks and a few wind-blasted trees. There was no softness in the landscape as far as he could see. It looked cold and uninviting. Calling to Roger, he set off back down the hill. When he passed the woman's cottage she was nowhere to be seen. Her front garden had a beaten-up look with scuffed grass and broken plastic toys. The whitewashed cottage had a map of green mould growing on the walls, under a grey slate roof. It was a miserable, cheerless place, even in the bright sunshine.

He went back to his car and collected Roger's blanket and bowls out of the back and took them into the cottage. Julia was sitting hunched on the sofa nursing a mug.

'You can't bring him in,' she said, looking up. 'I told you.'

'He can stay out here, in this porch thing,' said David. There was an enclosed glass lean-to over the front door. 'Then, technically, he isn't in the house.'

'Brilliant!' said Julia, and laughed.

David made up Roger's bed and got him a bowl of water.

'There you are,' he said. 'Lie there.' He pushed Roger's hindquarters down on his blanket, and closing the glass door on him, went into the cottage. He looked back to see how he had taken his banishment and saw that he had got up and was standing at the glass looking hurt.

Going over to Julia, he sat down next to her on the sofa and took the mug out of her hands, and a moment later they were locked in an embrace. Roger watched, whining, for a minute or two, and then went to lie on his bed and put his head on his paws, sighing deeply.

As it turned out, Annie's clothes for London were an unsuitable choice. It was quite cold when she set off early in the morning, having dropped the boys off with Fiona, and as she stood on the platform with the London-going commuters waiting for her train, she was glad she had worn the black coat. However, the sun came from behind the clouds, the sky cleared, and by the time she had ploughed through Waterloo and down on to the Tube, she was far too hot.

She sat for three hours in her old hairdresser's and had to endure the dismay of the stylist as he lifted the heavy clumps of her dark brown hair in his hands and exclaimed at its poor cut and condition.

'I know, I know,' she said humbly. 'That's why I'm here, actually.' Although she had gone to the salon as a regular when they lived in London, Mark had hardly acknowledged that he knew her. His attention was distracted each time the door opened and another attractive and important woman came in to have her hair done before work.

'I think we should go for a shortish, blunt bob with a

full fringe,' he said, turning back from greeting a woman Annie recognised as head of one of the top City fund managers. Her miraculous combining of high-level career and four young children was always being written about in the press. 'Your hair has the weight to hang straight, and I would like it to curve along your jaw line, with a bit of movement when you turn your head. It would suit your gamine face. I'll get the colourist to come and talk to you. I am going to suggest we go for conker, mahogany, through to burgundy and orange pekoe. What have you been doing to get the ends in this condition?'

Gamine? A no-longer-young woman with a small, tired face was more like it. Staring at her reflection in the mirror, she looked like a stranger in the make-up she hadn't much bothered with for several years. She didn't care what they did to her. Just get on with it, she thought. Do something to turn me back into what I was. I'm in your hands.

Fortunately the manicurist was a small Spanish girl who could not manage much conversation and Annie sat with eyes closed and had her neglected cuticles pushed back at the same time as her hair was painted in strands by a snake-hipped boy.

She paid a vast amount at the end of it all and could only stare in surprise at her new image. Her hair swung round her face like a shiny tortoiseshell bell. She looked very much smarter and sharper. She didn't know that Charlie would like it. He preferred her with long hair – like most men. Long hair was non-threatening, whereas her new haircut meant business.

She had half an hour to get to the restaurant in Great Portland Street where she had booked a table. It was a place she had used a lot in the old days and was frequented by people in publishing and entertainment, and there was always a sprinkling of celebs to cheer things up and provide a talking point if conversation was sticky. Walking along in the warm spring sunshine, she took off her coat and carried it over her arm. Her cashmere sweater was high-necked and her face felt hot. Women coming the other way were dressed in wrap dresses and little cardigans. Some were even bare-legged. She had forgotten her sunglasses and her high-heeled boots began to rub.

Wildly, she considered dashing into a shop and buying something completely different to wear, but she didn't have time. She walked briskly and was sitting at the table in just over twelve minutes, nursing a glass of house white and hoping Sylvia would not keep her waiting. She felt a knot of excitement in her stomach. Part of it was being out on her own – childless for once – and sitting in a sophisticated London restaurant with smartly dressed people. She also enjoyed the fact that Charlie had no idea where she was. She had decided that there was no need to tell him anything about today. It was a way of paying him back. A nice revenge.

He had gone off to work before she packed the boys into the car and drove them round to Fiona's. They were curiously unbothered by the change of routine, although she had had to shout and threaten to get the shoes and backpacks and lunch boxes and reading books and swimming stuff collected and the whole lot into the car. There was no hanging on to her or asking questions when she pushed them through Fiona's front door. There had been no need even to tell them where she was going.

She was starting to enjoy the way her hair swung forward and the feeling of the air touching her newly exposed neck. At the end of the month, when the credit card bill came in, Charlie would see what it had cost. By then, maybe, she would have something lined up and the expense wouldn't matter.

'Hi!' said a man's voice, and Annie looked up to see a tall man in a well-cut grey suit smiling down at her. 'It's Annie Thorne, isn't it?'

'Oh! Hi!' It took her a moment or two to recognise Peter Maguire, chief accountant on the magazine for which she had worked. It was strange to be addressed by her maiden name again.

'How are you? It's been years!' Peter looked over his shoulder to where the waiter was holding out a chair for him at a nearby table, where three other men were already seated. He gestured that it was okay, he would look after himself.

'It has. I moved to the country, if you remember. Had kids. Went off the radar.'

'Are you back?'

'Not yet, but I hope to be. I'm meeting Sylvia, actually. I'd like to start again. I feel ready for a challenge, so I'm looking for something a bit different. Not back in fashion, though.'

Peter made a face. 'It's tough out there right now. You know *Glitz* is folding? There have been a number of failed start-ups in the graveyard of women's mags recently. Not a good time, I'm afraid.'

Annie thought of Fiona and swung her shiny bob. 'Yes, but come on, Peter, I was good, remember. I have a hard-earned reputation and a wealth of experience. I can do the job. No magazine ever folded that I had a hand in.'

Peter smiled down at her. 'You're right, of course. You were a good editor. Have you got a card? No? Well look, here's mine. Give me a ring in a week or two. I'll have a nose-round for you. You're looking well, by the way. Great, in fact. I like the hair. You haven't got fat and boring in the country!'

Annie remembered kissing Peter at a long-ago drunken Christmas party. After she was married. He wasn't exactly good-looking, but there was a lupine attractiveness about him. He had the reputation of being dangerous. She smiled up at him. 'Thanks. How's Sarah? You've got children, haven't you?'

Peter made a face. 'Marriage over, I'm afraid. Sarah's taken the kids and gone to live in Surrey. She *has* got fat. Look, I must join the others. Don't forget to call me.'

At that moment Sylvia appeared at the table, looking dramatic in a peony-coloured silk coat and drainpipe trousers. She and Peter exchanged warm greetings before he went back to his table and she could turn her full attention on Annie.

'Dreadful man!' she whispered in Annie's ear as she got up to embrace her. 'It was thanks to his manoeuvring behind the scenes that I was axed. But darling, how lovely to see *you*! Fab hair! You didn't get a cut like that in the country!'

'Champagne? Shall we have champagne?' asked Annie. 'It's so great to see you, Sylvia.'

Sabine kept her eye on the departures board at Southampton airport. Her flight to Bordeaux was on time and in a minute she would say goodbye to her mother and go through the departure gate and begin her journey. She was travelling with only hand luggage and was dressed in jeans and a sweatshirt, her hair in a ponytail. Round her neck she wore a small pink leather satchel – a gift from Jacqui – containing her passport and e-ticket and a purse of euros. She had done this trip so many times that she wasn't nervous, and although her mother had checked her in as an unaccompanied minor, Sabine intended to avoid an escort. She was perfectly capable of managing on her own.

'Now, you must ring when you get there. Okay? If I'm out, leave a message or send a text. Have a lovely time, darling. It's going to be so strange without you and Agnes. Quiet and tidy! Don't forget to tell Papa about needing a tennis racket, and that Ollie had to buy you a new laptop, and tell him about the choir trip to Italy next term. Now have you got everything? Just check again. Okay, sweetheart. Big hug!'

Sabine was glad when all of that was over and she was through passport control and walking towards the queue for security screening. Nobody took any notice of her and she was through in no time. Once in the departure lounge she bought a bottle of water for herself and a small white rabbit with a blue bow round his neck for Jacqui's baby. She wanted to show Papa and Jacqui how pleased she was to have a stepbrother. She mustn't appear jealous or resentful, because the important thing was that they should see that they were really a proper family – her and Agnes and the baby – and that they would all spend time together and go on holidays and stuff, and that Pompignac would still be home even if they lived in England with Mum most of the time. It was the only way she could think of managing her life as it was — loving both parents as much as she could and trying to be fair to them both and hoping that by doing this she could save either one from ever feeling that she and Agnes didn't *mind* about not being with them.

She liked Ollie and she liked Jacqui, so that made it easier, but she knew in her heart that they could never love her and Agnes as if they were their own children, just as she could never love them in the same way that she loved her real parents, and this baby boy, who would belong to Papa and to Jacqui, would be more beloved of them, because he would be truly theirs and not a leftover of an unhappy marriage.

Now that she understood about her mum wanting Ollie's baby so much, she saw it was exactly the same. The baby would be like something to show off their love for all to see, whereas she and Agnes had to be explained to people as part of Lisa's past, which she now bitterly regretted, and which had made her unhappy and was still a burden, what with money and everything.

She thought about stuff like this so much that her head ached, and sometimes she wondered whether they really belonged anywhere, her and Agnes. It seemed like they were a bit wanted and a bit not, everywhere they went. She once had a non-speaking part in a play at primary school and she was called an 'extra', and this was what she feared she had become in her own life. She knew Mum and Papa loved her, nobody was cruel or anything, but there was always a reservation, a *but*. The only people who made her feel that she and Agnes were just fine as they were were Ollie's parents, who were quite okay about France and all the complications, and seemed to be pleased that they had joined their family when Ollie married their mum. They seemed sort of glad about them just as they were.

Papa's family were not like that. Their French grand-mother called them 'the Englishwoman's children'. Sabine knew that she disapproved of the way they had been brought up. Sabine had heard her and Papa arguing about it. She had been glad when they had moved to England, although she had cried when Papa took her and Agnes to say goodbye.

Maybe she should get a present for Papa and Jacqui so that she had something to give them when she arrived so unexpectedly. She counted out her pounds and trawled through the shops. She could afford a packet of shortbread and tea bags in a tin shaped like a London bus, and maybe some sweets. Papa liked sweets, especially the sort that you couldn't buy in France. English sweets.

She paid for her purchases and then went to sit down with her case between her knees where she could see the board for her flight to be called. She looked at her watch. Counting the time difference, she would be at home in Pompignac by late afternoon.

She sipped water from her bottle and thought of her mum driving home on her own. She was anxious, of course, about using her credit card without her permission and fibbing about Papa buying her flight, but that would all be put right when she explained to him. He would under-stand why she needed to see him and he would pay for her ticket as he always did. It was funny to be at the airport without Agnes and she was quite glad when an airline lady came up to her with a clipboard and asked her name.

'We've been looking for you, Sabine,' she said. 'If you'd like to follow me, I'll see you to the gate and hand you over to the flight crew.' She smiled, not very kindly, and walked off fast, her high heels clacketing. Sabine followed, trundling her little suitcase. She hadn't got very far when she realised that she had left the carrier bag containing the presents where she had been sitting and she had to run back while the clipboard lady sighed and stood with one hand on her hip, the big red tartan bow tied under her chin making her look like a large disgruntled pet.

'Are you French, then?' she asked when they got going again, reading the name on her list. 'You don't sound it.'

'Half,' said Sabine. 'My father's French.'

'He'll be meeting you, will he, at the other end?'

'Yes,' Sabine lied. 'Oh yes, he'll be there.'

Of course he wasn't. How could he be there when he didn't know she was coming? But she couldn't help looking hopefully at the crowd of people waiting to meet passengers off her flight. With only hand luggage she was one of the first through customs and she paused for a moment getting her bearings. She knew how to get to Pompignac on public transport, by tram and bus, but it would take a long time and she thought that perhaps she would telephone Papa at his office and see if he was in the city today, and then they could drive home together.

This was when her tummy started to flutter and she began to lose courage. Exactly what she had done was now inescapable. She had got to face Papa and she knew that he might be very angry. She rolled her suitcase to a quieter corner and took out her mobile and found his number.

He answered almost at once and his voice sounded abrupt, as if he was annoyed at being disturbed.

'Hi, Sabine. I am sorry, darling, but this isn't a good moment. I am waiting for some big American buyers. The 2009 first growths are going to top even 2005 prices. It's a big moment. I can't speak now, my sweet.'

'Papa! I'm here! I'm at the airport!'

'What airport? What are you saying? You are in Bordeaux? Now?'

'Yes, Papa! I came this morning. I wanted to see you. I know you said not to, but I really need to see you.' Sabine heard her voice start to crack.

'Your mother let you? She allowed you to come? Sabine, this is ridiculous! I don't have time for you now. I told you that it is impossible. This is the busiest possible time for me. How could you be so disobedient? Is this your mother's doing?' His voice rose, really angry.

'No, no, Papa. She didn't know that you said I couldn't come. It's not Mum's fault. I bought my ticket on her credit card without her knowing.'

'What is this about? How could you be so naughty? Really, I can't deal with this now. Jacqui is at her mother's for a few days. There is nobody at home to look after you.'

'I don't need looking after. If you are on your own, I can look after *you*!'

'Don't be ridiculous! I am very late in the office. I am taking clients out to dinner. I cannot also be responsible for you.'

'Papa! Don't say I am a nuisance. I am your child, and I haven't even seen you for three months. I need to see you! Papa, I can't live without seeing you!' Her voice had gone high and trembly. People walking past had started to look in her direction, and she turned away to stare blindly out of the plate-glass window, her telephone clamped to her ear.

'All right. All right. I am thinking here.' His voice had softened. There was a pause. 'Sabine, can you get the airport shuttle into town? You can come to my office but you will have to wait on your own. Have you got money? Buy yourself a sandwich or a burger. I won't be free until the evening, and even then only for an hour or so. I will try and work something out. Now I have to go. Really, Sabine, you couldn't have chosen a worse time to spring this on me.'

'Sorry, Papa,' she whispered. 'I didn't realise. I thought you'd be pleased to see me.'

'No! I am angry to see you! This is no way to behave. You can't just arrive like this, expecting me to say okay, it's fine. It's not fine. Not fine at all.'

'Papa?'

'What?'

'Papa, please don't tell Mum. Not just now, anyway.'

'Of course she must know, but I don't have time now. We'll talk about this later. You must understand, Sabine, that I am very angry with you. Very.'

All the way into the city Sabine sat on the shuttle bus and sniffed back her tears. Things had gone far worse than she expected and she had no idea now how it would all work out. If I was a different sort of person, she thought, I would somehow make them sorry, Papa and Jacqui. She could just get off the bus and disappear and give them a terrible scare. They would have to go on TV and beg for news of her, plead with her to get in touch with them. She would show them how much they had upset her and then they would weep with joy when she allowed herself to be found and returned to them.

She could dream of being like that, but she could never do it. She didn't have the courage to find somewhere to sleep at night, to wander the streets all day with no one to talk to, and really, she didn't want to cause her family so much anguish and bother. Instead she would just have to face their anger. She had never done anything bad before. She had always been good and never made a fuss about anything, unlike Agnes. I've always tried to be good so that they would love me, she thought, but it doesn't work like that. They didn't love her any more than Agnes, who shouted and screamed and kicked the furniture and often refused to do what she was told. There was no reward for being good. In fact telling Papa on the telephone that she loved and needed him seemed to make him more exasperated. He would have preferred her to be like Agnes, who went off for the holidays without giving him a thought. That way it was easier for him, less of a bother. Loving people could be a burden to them, an inconvenience.

She got off the airport bus at rue de L'Esprit des Lois and began to walk slowly towards Papa's office. It was a bright windy day but no warmer than in England. She didn't feel hungry but he had told her to get something to eat, so she stopped and bought a baguette and some chocolate. When she reached his office in the Rue Notre Dame, she rang the bell and Monsieur Robert from the antique shop on the ground floor came out and told her that Papa had gone to his meeting and that she was to go up and wait for him. Monsieur Robert's breath smelled of alcohol and his silly white moustache was stained yellow. He reminded her of the disappointment of seeing polar bears in the zoo, and finding that instead of snowy white they were a dirty brown.

Papa must have told him about what she had done, because he sighed and tutted as she hauled her case up the stairs. Papa's office was untidy and stank of cigarettes. At any other time Sabine might have set about putting things straight, but today she didn't feel up to it. She went to the window and looked out at the grey roofs and the chimneys. She could remember coming here with her mum when she was very small – before Agnes was born – and her papa holding her up to see the pigeons.

Everything must have been easy and happy then. Sabine couldn't remember any rows or anything. It was before Papa's business grew much bigger and moved out to Pompignac and before he employed other people, including Jacqui, to help him run the company.

She turned from the window and went to sit on the sofa, the very sofa on which Papa used to sleep when later on he and Mum were quarrelling and he used to slam angrily out of the house and drive his car furiously out of Pompignac towards the city.

Sabine smoothed the blue checked sofa cover with her hand. She felt very sad and lonely. She didn't want to be here on her own, but then she didn't know where else she wanted to be. She had tried to make things better but she had only made them worse.

Sadie arranged an emergency meeting with the farm manager, Bob Davis, a smooth middle-aged man who wore

a waxed jacket and a flat cap and drove a Land Rover
Discovery. His face flushed red with anger over Kyle's defection before he had the decency to work out his notice. The
relief milker could be brought in for a week or two, he said.
After that there were plans afoot to amalgamate the herd
with another on an estate farm that was better situated for
milk collection. It made economic sense, he said, to double
the size of the herd and reduce costs by cutting down
on the workforce.

'So are you telling me Kyle would have been made re-
dundant anyway?'

'There was a chance. Or we might have kept him on
over at Bishops Barton.'

'Did he know this?'

'We had talked about it. In general terms.'

So they might have been chucked out anyway. Sadie lost
any sense of guilt that they were letting anyone down.

'What about this place?'

'We've looked at plans to go in for asparagus and straw-
berries – in tunnels, of course, using Eastern European labour
during the peak cropping times.'

'And the box scheme?'

'That would have to go. It struggles to make money,
especially when we have to buy in stuff that we don't
grow here.'

'Well sod you!' said Sadie. 'Here was I, feeling we had let
you down. You couldn't give a twopenny fuck for us, could
you? Kyle was quite right.'

Bob looked pained. 'I don't think—' he began.

Sadie interrupted him. 'Well we're going, obviously, the
girls and me. We'll move out in the next few days.'

'That would suit me. If and when the herd moves, we were planning to renovate the cottage.'

'Renovate it for whom?' asked Sadie coldly.

'Holiday lets. We'll have no need for dairyman's accommodation, you see, although to be frank we could do with you here from the veg point of view – we're coming up to our busiest time, as you know.'

'Yes, I bet you could, on your miserable hourly rates. Thanks, but I'm not interested.'

'And your furniture that you want to store here? How long is that going to be for?'

'I'll come and get it when I've found somewhere else to live. It sounds as if you would have been paying Kyle redundancy, so you can at least do that for me.'

'It's a question of insurance—' began Bob, at which point Sadie burst into noisy tears.

'My partner's left me,' she wailed. 'I've got two kids to look after on my own and you're going to throw me out of the cottage. I've no money, no car and I'm pregnant. Make a bonfire of my stuff if you like, because frankly, it's the least of my worries.'

Bob backed off, alarmed. His Estate Management course at Cirencester when he had come out of the army hadn't prepared him for this sort of thing. He wished that he was safely back in his Discovery or dealing with paperwork in his office. He was basically a kind man and he had always liked Sadie, who was cheerful and a good worker. He had never been able to understand what an educated girl like her was doing with a young man like Kyle, who, frankly, seemed a bit brutish. He had mentioned her to his wife, Antonia, who had said, 'Oh, she sounds like one of those modern-day hippies, like that lot that go round in gypsy caravans pretending to be travellers when really they live off trust funds. I expect she's just playing at being a milk-maid. To the detriment of her children.' She was always disparaging of any mother who didn't appear to understand the importance of sacrificing all to send one's offspring to a good prep school.

'Look, I'm sorry,' he said, holding up his hands. 'I didn't mean to put pressure on you. Don't worry about the storage. Let me know if there's anything I can do.' Within reason, of course, he thought. Another baby on the way and appar-ently no father for the two she'd already got. The girl didn't make life easy for herself.

When he had gone, Sadie went into the cottage and shut the door. She sat at the kitchen table amongst the toast crumbs from the girls' breakfast. There was no point in continuing to cry but somehow she had to deal with the anguish she felt at being abandoned yet again by a man she still loved. This isn't just fate, she thought sadly. It's not just bad luck. It's my lack of judgement that's landed us in this mess. I see that, but I can't see how I'll ever change. I still love the bastard and I'd have him back tomorrow. Why can't I fall in love with a man like Dad? Someone sensible and reliable.

David and Julia remained on the sofa, and she seemed to enjoy his efforts, judging from the amount of noise she made. From what he gleaned from film and television, this was the norm these days. He and Alice belonged to a gener-ation that had grown up making silent love, just as they played tennis without feeling the need to grunt. Discovering a new body, where everything was arranged slightly differently, was a strange experience and, unfortunately, made him think of Alice. It was only a small step to wondering what on earth he thought he was doing.

'Come upstairs,' groaned Julia.

'Look, I don't think I can do this!' he said in a desperate tone. 'I'm afraid I feel bad about it. I should be here to help you sort out your life a bit, not make it more complicated.'

'Come upstairs!'

'I can't *offer* you anything, Julia. I'm a very married man. I can't even have an affair with you – not a proper one. It just wouldn't be possible.'

'That doesn't matter. We're here together now. You responded to a karmic pull and came to me.'

'But I shouldn't have done.' David sat up and put his head in his hands. 'It feels like using you. I can't do it. Given the age difference between us, and your present situation, it makes me feel as if I am taking advantage of you.' He thought it best not to mention that he was also feeling bad about Alice. This was the worst possible moment to realise how much he loved his wife. Damn, he thought. Damn, damn. Why had his conscience chosen this moment to wake up and interfere?

'Oh for goodness' sake!' Julia reached for her sweater. With her arms over her head, her hair bunched up and her little pointed breasts, she had never looked more lovely, but she stood up and glared at him. 'Why the fuck did you come, then?' she said in her little-girl voice. 'Why did you come if you were going to cop out? Sorry, David, but I think you're being pathetic with these bourgeois scruples of yours.'

'I'm evidently not cut out to be a Lothario. It's too late in the day. I came because I wanted to see you again and I hoped that it might work out. You're a very attractive girl and I felt flattered. I have to agree, it's pathetic.'

Julia looked at him coldly for a moment, and then her face softened and she sat down next to him and took his hand and said quite tenderly, 'I'm sorry. I shouldn't have hurried things. I've shown no respect for your feelings and I know that you are a principled man.'

'No, no, it's entirely my fault. I shouldn't have come.'

'Yes you should. I'm glad you did.'

'Do you mind if I stay for tonight? It would save me having to explain to Alice.'

'Of course you can. You don't have to make love to me, but it would be nice if you found you could change your mind.'

Because he felt he had let her down and had generally behaved in a dismal fashion, David took Julia to a ludicrously expensive fish restaurant and gave her a very good dinner. It was the sort of place Alice would have liked, he thought guiltily, with crisp white napkins and a wide view of the bay, where the tide was out and small, picturesque fishing boats lay on their sides.

He sat and listened to Julia in a sort of stupor. His failure to come up to her expectations appeared to have activated the Declan theme in her mind, and she gave him a detailed catalogue of Declan's various shortcomings as a husband and an ex-husband-to-be, and how, despite the suffering he had inflicted on her, her recent spiritual evolution had aided her healing.

Although David believed her to be a vegan, she could, apparently, eat fish, expensively, and she could certainly drink. Two bottles of exorbitant Sancerre were dispatched, and he shouldn't have driven back to the cottage up the road from the bay, with its hairpin bends, but somehow he managed it without passing a single vehicle coming in the other direction.

Roger required to be taken for another turn up the lane and David noticed that the dog's previous holiday spirits seemed to have dissipated. He plodded along quite dejectedly, as if he felt the whole trip was a let-down. When they got back to the cottage he went to lie on his bed in the porch with a gloomy sigh. If a dog could be disapproving, that was Roger.

Earlier David had sent Alice a misleading text, and now he switched off his telephone. Julia had already gone upstairs, and he cleaned his teeth in the freezing bathroom and went eagerly to join her. Despite his age he still felt vigorous and full of desire, and his wine consumption seemed to have stilled the nagging of his conscience.

He undressed, tossed his clothes on the floor and got into bed beside the naked Julia. It was when he turned to take her into his arms that he started to wheeze. At first he thought it was just a little cough, but as his chest tightened he had to sit up in bed and struggled to breathe.

'Oh Lord! I'm having an asthma attack.'

'Oh for God's sake!' Julia sounded irritated. 'Can't you take something?'

'I haven't got anything with me. I haven't had an attack for years. I'm going to have to sit up for a minute.'

'Okay. Whatever.' Julia turned over and appeared to go straight to sleep.

David sat upright in bed. The unfamiliar headboard cut into his neck, and he got out and went to sit in a chair instead, which made his breathing a bit easier. Now that he thought about it, he wondered if the duvet was made of feathers or down, to which he was allergic, or maybe he had eaten some strange bit of seafood in the restaurant and was now having an adverse reaction. He felt his heart thumping and wondered whether he should call 999. Asthma was not to be treated lightly. People died of asthma attacks. It was a bit hurtful that Julia seemed so unconcerned.

Maybe a glass of water would help. He found his way downstairs in the dark and turned on the kitchen light. Something scuttled into the shadows. Mice. That was what the place smelled of. He sipped the water and tried not to panic. He wished that it was Alice upstairs. She would know what to do. She would have packed his inhaler, for one thing. He wondered if it was too late to ring her. He could say that he was staying in a pub with Edwin, that he felt unwell and didn't know what to do. Trembling and gasping, he reached for his mobile telephone, which he had left on a table in the sitting room.

When Alice got back from work, she made herself a cup of tea and went to lie on the sofa in the sitting room although it was only mid-afternoon. The thought of not having to cook supper for David and having the house to herself seemed like a luxury. It was very quiet with even Roger away, and after a few minutes she felt her eyelids droop and she dozed.

She woke with a start as dusk crept into the corners of the room and looked at her watch guiltily before she remembered that she had nowhere to go and no one to worry about. This is what it will be like, she thought, when I am old and on my own. It was strange that she could imagine life without David, but not the other way round. Now that she thought about it, how on earth would he manage if she died first? Would he even bother to get up in the morning? She doubted it. Would he cook for himself? Perhaps she should start him on a training programme so that he would be better prepared. She knew he would ruin her non-stick pan and fail to wipe the stove properly when he spilled things.

On the other hand, perhaps he would marry again, or replace her with a more dominant sort of woman, like widowed John next door. Yesterday she had seen his lady friend, Carol, marching towards his front door with a small travel bag over her shoulder while John lurched after her with a large suitcase that he had hauled from the boot of her car. Alice had stopped and offered to help but Carol had called across, 'No need – it's got wheels! He can manage! We're off on Monday. A luxury Mediterranean voyage – we've got a de luxe balcony stateroom upgrade. John is going to pop our itinerary through your door.'

'Oh, how lovely for you.' Alice noticed that John had undergone a clothes overhaul and was looking quite jaunty in an improved style of trouser and a pink checked shirt. She remembered when Betty was alive, and the modest caravan holidays to the Lake District, when Betty could polish and clean and cook in exactly the same way she did at home. It hadn't taken Carol long to change all that.

Maybe the same thing would happen to David and he

would turn into someone quite different under the influence of another sort of woman in his life. Perhaps he could be trained to become sociable and go to drinks parties and have friends round without grumbling.

She tried to imagine how her life might be with a new man. Would she like it if he interfered in the kitchen or criticised her cooking or how she dressed, or wanted her to accompany him to vintage car rallies or go potholing? She didn't think she would.

She wondered how David was getting on. He had sent her a text to say that he had arrived safely. She hoped he would look after Roger properly and remember to towel him dry if he got wet. She might just see if she could get him on his mobile telephone. It would be nice to know how his day had been. Then she would have a boiled egg for supper and make a start on clearing the bedroom for Tamzin and Georgie. They would be here next week. The house wasn't going to be quiet for long.

There was no reply from David's telephone. Alice pictured him and Edwin leaning their elbows on the bar of a Cornish pub with two pints in front of them. It had been such a nice sunny day that they would be looking quite tanned from the spring sunshine and the wind off the sea. A pasty would make a good supper – with a green salad – and Roger would be lying at their feet, the kindly landlord having offered him a bowl of water. He would be quite worn out from all the unaccustomed exercise.

She was just thinking about getting up off the sofa when there was a knock on the door. She went to answer it and found Mandy, the grown-up daughter of Mr and Mrs Baker from next door, standing on the step with two large flat boxes in her arms. 'These came for you today,' she said. 'Mum took them in.'

'Oh, thank you. How kind of her.'

'She didn't like seeing them on your step. You never know, round here, not these days.'

Mandy had a theatrical view of life, Alice always thought. Although she must be over forty, her father still picked her up in his car if she'd been to the cinema after work with her friend Karen. She apparently thought she'd be kidnapped and murdered if she waited at the bus stop.

'No. Well, please thank her. By the way, there's an invitation coming your way. We're having a party. A proper one. That's what all this is about.' Alice indicated the boxes. 'I've ordered some things to try on.'

'A party!' said Mandy, full of wonder. Her marriage had lasted only a few weeks and she was still looking for a replacement husband ten years on, consulting horoscopes and clinging to the belief that the right man would turn up one day. A party sounded hopeful. Alice was sorry that there wasn't a chance, in this case.

'Yes. You'll be getting an invitation soon. A marquee and everything!'

'Well! I'll tell Mum.'

'It's Sunday May the sixth. You must keep it free.'

As Mandy turned to go down the path, Alice saw that she was wearing cut-off cargo pants. She did not consider them a wise choice. If one was talking cargo, it was a hefty one.

She took the boxes upstairs and laid them on her bed. It was much more exciting to unfold dresses from tissue paper in her bedroom than search through racks of clothes in a department store. The first one was silk in the colours of the sea and sky on a mild day; slightly grey, slightly blue, slightly green. She slipped it over her head and it fitted her perfectly, skimming her hips and ending just on her knees. Her legs were still shapely. They hadn't got fat with the rest of her. She wished the sleeves were longer because she hated her arms, but the neckline was pretty and not too low. Older bosoms were not a particularly attractive sight in her opinion.

She twirled about and smiled into the glass behind the door. It was pretty. It was dressy. It was suitable for a party in the garden. It would do very nicely.

She would have to find a jacket or a pashmina to wear over her shoulders. It could still be cold in May and she liked to have something to hug round her, to hide the heaviness that had crept around her waist. It was sad that her clothes these days had such a camouflaging role, rather than being a celebration of her figure. Still, it couldn't be helped, and the dress was really very pretty.

She opened the second box and shook out a dark crimson dress with a slim skirt and heart-shaped neckline. She might as well try it on, although it was very expensive. She struggled with the zip because the top was tight and fitting with narrow elbow-length sleeves. When she looked in the glass she saw herself transformed. The dress hugged her curves and accentuated her womanly shape, and the neckline framed her face. It was a miracle dress. If she looked for weeks she wouldn't find anything that suited her better. She beamed at her reflection and shook back her hair. A glamorous stranger smiled back. Excitement and happiness flooded her heart. There was no question that this was the dress she would buy. This was the dress she would wear to her party.

She replayed her vision of the great day in her head, but this time the original navy linen suit with white piping was replaced by the dark red dress, and she was very pleased with how it looked. Margaret would be proud of her.

Chapter Eleven

SABINE PASSED THE afternoon alone, nibbling at the
baguette and eating the chocolate in small squares, and
watching the pigeons quarrelling on the roof of the next-
door building. She texted her mother to say that she had
arrived safely, and several times the telephone rang and
switched immediately to answerphone mode. She heard
her father's recorded voice ask the caller to leave a message,
or alternatively to telephone his secretary, Michele, in
Pompignac.

She made no more plans and had no expectation of how
things would turn out. She had exhausted her efforts to try
and order her life. She would have to let the grown-ups
take over.

She must have dozed, because at five o'clock she heard
her father's voice from the street below and the front door
of the office opening. He was talking to Monsieur Robert
and he sounded cheerful and in a good mood. He had just
come from lunch with the Americans, he said. Tomorrow
he would be taking them to Chateau Pontet-Canet, where
they were likely to buy the whole 2009 vintage. There
would be a lot to celebrate.

'She's waiting for you,' she heard Monsieur Robert say. 'I

have been keeping my eye open but there hasn't been a squeak since she arrived. She's like a frightened rabbit, your daughter.'

'So she should be.' Then she heard his step on the stair and she stood up to meet him, pulling her hair back into its ponytail with both hands.

The door opened and there he was, her papa, wearing a smart grey suit and carrying a briefcase, which he put on his office chair before opening his arms to embrace her.

'Oh, Sabine! Sabine!' he said. 'My little one!' and she went to him and put her arms round his tight, hard chest and laid her head against his cream shirt front.

'I'm sorry, Papa. I'm sorry I've made you so cross.'

'Yes, I am mad with you. Really mad. You don't know the problems you have caused me. I have had to alter my arrangements for this evening and it has been very difficult. This is a huge deal I am negotiating and I don't have the time for you now.'

'I'll go to Pompignac. I can go on my own. I've often done it.'

'There is no one there. You cannot be on your own. I haven't had time to telephone the families of your friends to see if they can have you.'

'I don't mind being on my own.'

'Then why did you come? Why did you deceive your mother and come here, if you don't mind being on your own? You can be on your own in England, can't you?'

'Papa, I came because I wanted to see *you*! I wanted to be at Pompignac with you and Jacqui – just for a few days. I grew up here! It's still my home!' Tears began to stream down her cheeks.

'Okay, okay.' Her father patted her hair and pulled a

handkerchief from his suit pocket. 'Here. Use this. This is my best shirt – especially for the Americans!'

Sabine mopped her eyes while her father took off his jacket and put it on the back of his chair. He sat on the corner of his desk and observed her.

'Look,' he said. 'I have been terribly busy – no, really! I don't always have the time to answer your e-mails and speak to you. I know that, and I am sorry for it. It makes me feel bad. It has nothing to do with Jacqui, you understand? She is very fond of you and Agnes. She doesn't intend to come between us. It would be just the same if you were here, living at Pompignac – I would still be too busy to spend time with you. Jacqui too feels neglected, but she under-stands that it's the nature of my business, and the fuss about this exceptional vintage – it will calm down soon and then things will be different.'

Sabine, sitting on the edge of the checked sofa, sniffed and nodded. Her father's words calmed her thumping heart. The muddle in her head began to clear.

'It really is impossible for me to spend time with you now, and you know that Jacqui and I are going on holiday because she needs to rest before the baby is born.'

Sabine nodded again. She longed and longed for him to say that she could go too, but she knew that wasn't going to happen.

'But I have been thinking. Jacqui has elected to have a Caesarean birth, so we know the date. How about I book you and Agnes flights to come and see the baby a few days later? When she is out of hospital and back home? I am taking time off myself, so we can all be together. It will be a special time for us.'

'What about school?'

'Fuck school! You don't have a baby brother every day.'

Sabine, sniffing and grinning, jumped up to hug her father. It was better than anything she could have dreamed up herself. Then an awful thought struck her. What about Mum? How would Mum feel about it? The confusion closed in again like dark water over her head.

'I don't know if we can . . . I don't know . . .' She hesitated.

'Why? What's the problem? I will take care of it.'

'It's just that Mum . . . I'm not sure . . .' She knew instinctively that she couldn't tell her father that her mother was desperate for a baby with Ollie. It would be wrong, although she couldn't explain exactly why. She just knew that Mum wouldn't want Papa to know. It seemed like having babies was a sort of competition in which Mum was a non-starter.

'It will be fine, I promise you. Your mother will understand that it's important to you, and she will put you and Agnes first — before her own feelings. I understand that it's complicated — but hell, your mother and I are the adults here.'

'Yeah, okay,' she said with little conviction. If only real life was as easy as that. She remembered her mother's terrible tears when she heard about Sadie's baby. She didn't think she could bear to witness her pain. For instance, it was too awful to think of Mum having to take her and Agnes to the airport, armed with presents for Jacqui's baby.

Suddenly Sabine understood that it was never going to be all right, however much she wanted it to be. When people had once loved each other like Papa and Mum, and had children and then fell out of love and got divorced, it left a sort of scar that would always be there, and although it was quite possible for them to be happy again with someone else, their shared past could never be forgotten, and the shadow would always be present in the lives of their children, too. Maybe it would get better and easier, especially if Mum had her own baby, but sitting there in her papa's office Sabine understood that her own life would never be like that of her friends whose parents were still together, however much she wished it. This knowledge made her feel very weary and very sad. She realised that she couldn't make herself responsible for her parents' feelings any more. I'm just an extra, she thought. I don't make any difference, and she began to cry again.

'Sabine! Sabine! Don't do this to me, baby! Haven't I promised you to come out in May? What more can I do?'

Sabine couldn't help it. Her tears seemed uncontrollable, even though she tried to stem the flow.

'We can't always have what we want, you know, baby. Life's not like that.' Her father spoke tenderly. He lit a cigarette and watched her through the smoke with narrowed eyes.

But Sabine was crying less for herself and more because for the first time she understood that whatever grown-ups said and did, there would always be pain and suffering. There would always be someone's mother dying of cancer, and children born with harelips and pleading eyes, condemned to misery in Africa, and dogs tied to posts and tortured. That was life. Her own sadness was just a drop in the ocean. She had got to learn to live with it.

'Now stop crying and listen to me. We'll go home now and I'll cook you supper. We'll have the evening together. Tomorrow I shall have to leave you when Michele arrives in the office. She'll put you in a taxi in time to get to the airport for the late-morning flight. I've booked you a seat, and I have transferred the cost of your return ticket to your mother's account. You must telephone her this evening and let her know.'

'Thank you, Papa, thank you.'

'Yes, well, come on! Let's go! Maybe we'll pick you up a pizza on the way. Eating is not on my mind at the moment. Five courses for lunch have seen to my appetite for a while.'

Sabine trailed after him, waiting while he locked the door on to the street. He called to say good night to Monsieur Robert, a gloomy figure slouched on one of his Louis XIV chairs, a bottle and glass on the floor beside him. Then he carried her case, his jacket hooked over his shoulders, to the underground car park on the corner.

In the car, they travelled in silence through the grand city that Sabine had been pushed round in her stroller when she and Papa and Mum had lived in the apartment below the office. Papa stopped in St Pierre and sent her into a pizzeria to buy whatever she wanted, and then they drove through the straggling suburbs to the beginning of the country-side, and Pompignac. It was nearly dark when they turned in to the courtyard of the old farm, and Sabine felt so tired that she could hardly speak. ·

The house looked different – tidier, more stylish. Jacqui had clearly been making some changes. She had got rid of all Mum's old sofas and chairs and now there were uncom-fortable-looking modern pieces instead. It seemed that she and Papa didn't relax in the salon any longer. Her father saw Sabine looking through the door and nodded at the interior. 'Those pieces are Charlotte Perriand. Very, very special. School of Le Corbusier. She worked with him. Jacqui is amazing that she finds these things.'

The kitchen looked the same, and Sabine sat at the table and ate her pizza out of the box. Her father poured himself some cognac and sat opposite her, pulling at the pizza with his fingers and putting pieces of it in his mouth as if he were hungry.

'You're tired, aren't you? Have you tried to ring Maman? We must do it when you have finished. Best not leave it late. How is she, your mother? How is Oliver? Does he make her happy, eh? He is a so typical Englishman. Pussywhipped. I shouldn't say it to you, but it's true.' He was slightly drunk.

Sabine didn't want to talk to him about Ollie. She shrugged. 'He's fine. He's cool.'

'Good! Good! I am glad to hear it. Second time lucky, eh?' Sabine said nothing. This was not a conversation she wanted to continue, because she could hear in Papa's voice that he was mocking Ollie and that he wanted her to join in and run him down in some way. She remained resolutely silent, looking round the kitchen and noticing all the small changes that she hadn't at first seen. All the country stuff that her mum liked had gone, and there was no clutter on the work surfaces.

Her father lapsed into silence and stared into his glass. His face had fallen into an expression of deep sadness. He held out his hand to Sabine across the table, and when she placed her own in his, he stroked it with his thumb.

'I loved her, you know,' he said, mournfully. 'I loved your mother. She was so beautiful when I first met her. Tall and golden, with that fabulous hair. She was unlike any girl I had ever met. What we had, your mother and I, was real love and passion. I have never got over her, you know? I will never get over losing her.'

Sabine removed her hand and got up. She pushed the pizza box across the table to him.

'Here,' she said. 'You can finish this. I've had enough.'

She lugged her case upstairs and opened the door of her old bedroom. Her hand felt for the light switch, and when the room jumped into view she saw that it was exactly the same as when she had left it at Christmas. Her clothes were still draped over the chair and the Advent candle was still beside her bed. Her heart filled with affection and gratitude for Jacqui. Sitting on the bed she took out her telephone and rang her mother.

'Hi, Mum. It's me.'

'Sabine! All right, darling? Everything all right?'

'No, not really. I have to come home, Mum. I'll be coming back tomorrow.'

'Why? What's happened? Sabine? What's happened?'

'Nothing. Everything's all right. It's all fine, but I got it wrong, Mum, and, like, I shouldn't have come. Jacqui's not here and Papa's busy and stuff. I'll be back tomorrow. I'll explain then.'

'Why? What's happened? Sabine! Tell me!'

'I'll tell you tomorrow, Mum. I'll text you with the flight details.'

'I think I should speak to your father. Where is he? Can you put him on?'

'No, I can't now, Mum. I'll see you tomorrow. And Mum?'

'Yes?'

'I thought I might go to stay with Ollie's parents, if it's okay. Like, while Agnes is away.'

Annie had forgotten how much Sylvia liked to talk about herself and how her professional life had always been a series of stand-offs with the people with whom she worked. At the magazine, she had been permanently at war with one department or another, often changing sides with dazzling footwork. This pattern had evidently continued at the newspaper but with added intensity, as war was waged between the serious part of the daily broadsheet and the more frivolous monthly magazine section. This centred mainly on allocation of budget – particularly, in Sylvia's case, because writing articles about luxury demanded, in her view, a fat expense account.

Meanwhile, her husband, the Labour peer, was engaged in various diverting feuds of his own, and because their entire life was centred on London and fashionable parties, the sprinkling of A-list names in Sylvia's conversation was jaw-dropping. Annie listened, open-mouthed, and entirely unable to contribute any gossip of her own.

'So, darling, how are things with you?' asked Sylvia, pausing for the first time over panna cotta and raspberries.

'Well, they are all right,' said Annie, 'but I am ready to come back to work and I hoped that you might be able to help.'

Immediately Sylvia's tone changed and her voice became confidential and serious. 'Terribly difficult times, you know, darling. There just isn't anything happening at the moment. We all live in fear of the axe falling.' She glared at the table of accountants, who had just called for a second bottle of dessert wine.

'Look, I'm serious,' said Annie. 'I want work, Sylvia, and you know I am good at my job. I was ten years with you. I was your protégée. There must be something you can do.'

Never in her life had she been so pushy on her own behalf.

Sylvia considered, greedily spooning down the silky white pudding. 'Well, I am thinking of commissioning an article on top London hotels – from the angle of beds, pillows, sheets, thread count, that sort of thing. The discerning top-end hotel guest wants to know the provenance of *everything* these days. It's not your sort of thing, though, is it? I had someone else in mind – one of my regular contributors – but I've gone off her slightly. She was late with her last piece on vintage couture, and when it came in I couldn't use it. She's gone off the boil since she moved in with a minor European princeling. She's lost her edge.'

'Now *that's* something I could write about.' Annie dreaded the idea of investigating the thread count of organic linen sheets in housekeepers' cupboards all over London. It seemed only marginally better than stepladder safety. However, vintage couture was right up her street.

Sylvia paused and looked at Annie shrewdly. 'You do remember, don't you, that I absolutely don't do children? I don't want, ever, to hear about chickenpox or ear infections or sports day or nativity plays. Okay? If I use you for the mag I want none of that. No kiddie excuses!'

Of course I remember, thought Annie. That's what made my job so bloody stressful.

'Sylvia, look – I gave up work when I knew I couldn't give one hundred per cent, and now that the boys are both at school – well, almost – I'm ready to start again. I have the total support of my husband, of course, who can be as flexible as necessary.' Liar, liar, she thought. She wished she could believe her own propaganda.

'How is your husband?' Annie remembered that Sylvia had a soft spot for Charlie – when he was a sharp-suited hedge fund manager who played club rugby at weekends and was fit and lean.

'He's fine.' She moved on swiftly. 'Very involved in his school.'

'Well you'd better come and see me at my office. I'll get my secretary to call you. You've looked at the website, I take it? It's taken a lot of time and effort to develop that particular sophisticated online format – we had to carry over our trademark of luxury and indulgence, you see. You'll need to be able to prepare website content as well as articles for the print edition. Are you up to that? It's a different skill, you know, but I use the same team for both. That's important to the continuity of the core values of the magazine.'

'I've been editing an online trade magazine,' said Annie, keeping it vague. 'I'm well up to it.'

'Being a high-end product has helped us weather the recession. We have a mostly A-class, affluent and very discerning readership, and the magazine has proved to be resilient, with a twelve per cent increase in readership for the weekend paper in the last year.' Annie heard Sylvia switch from her gossipy self to the hard-nosed editor that she remembered. 'I can only give you this one piece for now,' she added. 'We'll see how it goes from there.'

'Thank you, thank you,' said Annie, feeling pathetically grateful.

Lunch came to an end. Annie discreetly settled the bill

for a shockingly huge amount. The tip alone would have fed a family of four for a week. Sylvia chose that moment to turn away and talk to the accountants in an animated fashion, and then they threaded their way through the tables and stood for a moment in the warm sunshine on the pavement.

'My secretary will be in touch. I'd like to see you next week and we'll talk through some ideas. Now, I need a taxi.' She paused to peck at Annie's cheek before hailing a cab and hopping nimbly in. 'Lovely lunch, darling! Thank you!'

Annie waved after her, at last able to allow herself a grin. She had done well. She had made a start. It was only one article, but it was a beginning.

'Back together, are you?' Peter Maguire appeared at her elbow, smiling his wolfish smile. 'You and darling Sylvia?'

'Maybe. Who knows?' Annie was far too wise to give Peter any information.

'Don't forget to give me a ring. I may be able to point you in the direction of something interesting. We'll do lunch one day soon. But how are you fixed now? Would you like a coffee somewhere?'

'Don't you have an office to go to?' said Annie lightly. She glanced at her watch. 'Thanks, Peter, but I've really got to dash. Back to the country!' and she gave him one of her most winning smiles.

The train that she just caught out of Waterloo was crowded and she was unable to find a seat until Basingstoke, but as she stood in the corridor she thought about what she had accomplished. She was already planning her piece on vintage couture. She had plenty of material to draw on and she knew the best person in London to go to – a specialist dealer who could always source a fabulous ballgown for a film star to wear on the red carpet.

The money wouldn't be great, she knew that. Sylvia would pare it down to the minimum, knowing that Annie would probably pay to see her work in print again, but it would be a start. She totted up in her head what the day had cost her. It was disastrous. Charlie would have a fit.

Charlie. How was she going to tackle Charlie? It was all very well to have seen Sylvia surreptitiously, but tonight she would have to tell him what she had done, especially if next week she was going to have to be in London again. The subject of childcare had got to be sorted out. The holidays were about to start and she couldn't work if she had the boys to look after. The problems suddenly seemed overwhelming and the forthcoming battle with Charlie was what she dreaded most. She imagined telling him the subject of her article and already felt defensive. I've got to stop being like this, she thought. I must stop thinking of going back to work as a battle between us, because it makes me aggressive towards him and oversensitive to anything he says.

It wasn't hard to step into his shoes and see what a pain she was. He knew she resented the satisfaction he took from teaching and she was bad-tempered when he got home at night. What she had got to make him understand was that the only way to get the old Annie back was to support her in her decision to start work again. The trouble was, she didn't know how she was going to do it. She wasn't confident that there was enough goodwill between them at the moment, and that was a sobering thought. What had happened to them if it appeared that they didn't really like one another any more? Was it possible to rekindle affection? Of course it was, she told herself. All marriages had these bad patches that had to be worked at. They had been married for nine years – a dangerous time – and she knew that what they were going through now was a temporary difficulty – or at least she hoped it was.

The champagne had given her a headache, and by the time she stepped off the train and went to where her car was parked, the euphoria had completely dissipated.

She collected Rory first. He had been fine, Oscar's mother, Melanie, told her. He and Oscar were sitting side by side on the sofa glued to a Ben 10 DVD.

'They haven't been watching long, I promise,' said Melanie apologetically, 'but swimming always seems to tire them out. It seemed okay to let them sit quietly for a bit.'

'Don't worry. How would we survive without DVDs?'

'Your hair looks fantastic. Is that why you were in London? To get a cut like that?'

'Well I had a business lunch to go to. Perfect excuse for a makeover.'

'Yeah! Nice hair, Mum!' said Rory, looking over and then back to the screen again.

'Come on, kiddo. Time to go. Thanks so much, Melanie.'

'Any time. It was a pleasure. They get on really well. It was great for Oscar. His brothers are older, as you know. He gets left out of things.'

She was a nice woman, thought Annie. She had been a primary school teacher and was married to a man who worked in IT and caught the train to London every morning.

259

She had once confided in Annie how much she loved being at home with her three boys; how lucky she felt, and guilty that she wasn't contributing to the family income. Annie looked at her now and almost envied her. If only she could feel the same. It would need a head transplant, unfortunately.

When at last she got Rory in the car, with his collection of stuff, she felt like part of a baggage train. Now to get Archie. She had left him last because she wanted time to talk to Fiona about her day. The boys would be late home but they could skip baths and go straight to bed. Although it wasn't the best evening for a scratch supper, she and Charlie could make do with whatever she could lay her hands on.

When she parked outside the house she could see through the front window that Fiona, Archie and Damon were sitting at the table poring over a puzzle. When did I last do something like that with the boys? she thought. God, I am a rotten mother. It seems that I would rather suck up to a woman like Sylvia and write articles to encourage the affluent to spend their money in enjoyable ways.

They looked up when they heard the click of the gate latch and Pat began to bark. When Archie saw his mother and brother standing outside, his face underwent first surprise and then pure pleasure.

Fiona came to open the door to them and Archie pushed round her to shout, 'Mum! You look like a different lady! Your hair has all gone! I've had a lovely time. Me and Damon played football.'

'Good! You must tell me all about it. Hi, Fiona. Thanks so, so much.'

'You certainly do look different. Come in. Have you got time to tell me how you got on?' She inspected Annie's hair. 'Goodness, it looks rather high maintenance. Very smart, though. Would you like a drink?'

'What I'd most like is a cup of tea.'

'That's easily done. I'll put the kettle on. No, Damon. Don't do that. Show Rory how much of the puzzle we have done. See if you can finish the sky.'

'Well, then?' she said as she passed Annie a mug of tea and they leaned side by side against the kitchen units.

'It was good really. I've been commissioned to write an article by my ex-editor for her monthly magazine devoted to luxury lifestyle.'

'Just the one?'

'Yes. It's a start.'

'Of course it is. An excellent start. And the subject?'

'Vintage couture. I can do it. I can do it well. I've got to go back up for a meeting next week and I shall have to go again to do some research. That's the difficult part. The children break up in a few days, and I'm sure there'll be some reason why Charlie won't be able to step in to help, and then I will have to have someone to look after them while I work at home. I know it's only one article, but it's my starting point.'

'How do you know he won't help? Have you asked him?'

'No. He doesn't know anything about any of this.'

'Well why don't you start with him? If it's the holidays, it sounds as if you are halfway there. Maybe he could do a bit and you could find someone to take over what he can't do.'

'Does such a person exist?'

'Funny you should say that.' Fiona grinned. 'You know

I have a spare bedroom here? I've often thought about a lodger but never got round to it, partly because I would have to find a very understanding person because of Damon. As it happens I have a Czech girl, Nadia, in one of my tutor groups – a very bright, charming young woman in her late twenties, who is struggling to find the means to go on with her degree. I have talked to her about coming to live here, and instead of rent she would do a bit of babysitting for me when I have to work. At the moment she's a cleaner for a firm in Reading, but it's unpleasant work and disgracefully badly paid. I imagine she would jump at the chance of a bit of nannying for your two, as and when you need her: ferrying to and from school and so on. She's away at the moment, seeing her husband and her child – a boy of six, I think – in the Czech Republic, but I was going to suggest that she might move in on a trial basis after Easter. You could meet her and see what you think. It's an arrangement that could work, I think.'

Annie looked at her with a smile. 'I can't really take this in, Fiona. It sounds fantastic. It doesn't help me next week, though.'

'Can your family help out on this occasion?'

'I suppose I could ask my mother, but I can't see her agreeing. She doesn't have a close relationship with the boys. She only sees them about twice a year. She still works, for one thing.'

'What about your husband's family?'

'There's always Alice. She only works part-time, and David, her husband, has retired. She's very family-orientated and the boys like going there. But one of Charlie's sisters is just about to move back home with her daughters. Her partner's chucked her out because she's pregnant and he doesn't want the baby.'

'Good lord! And Charlie's parents are taking them in? Are they up for sainthood?'

'Oh, they're like that. Family first. It gets up my nose sometimes. I think it's only temporary with Sadie, while she sorts something out. I like her very much, but she's her own worst enemy. I mean, her girls have no contact with their father. He doesn't support them at all. She seems to have a predilection for hopeless men.'

'Look, Annie, I'd like to help you next week, but I'm not in a position to offer to have the boys here while you research this article. I have my own work, and Damon has to be considered. A bit of socialising is great, but I have to manage it carefully, and it just wouldn't be fair to your boys or him. He's completely knackered by the end of term and he needs to recharge, very quietly, for at least a week after he breaks up.'

'No, I understand. I wouldn't dream of asking you.'

'It sounds to me as if you need to get Charlie on your side. What's a husband for, for heaven's sake?' Fiona grinned. 'Surely it would be a good idea to get him in a supportive role from the start. Then he would feel that he had a controlling interest in the situation, which men like to believe, in my experience.'

'That's exactly what his mother said, but Charlie and I seem to have got on a collision course over this. We aren't exactly getting on well. We haven't been for some time.'

'Can't you put that right? How about humble pie? That's another offering that men usually can't refuse. Frankly, Annie, I don't see how this career restart will work unless you have

Charlie's support. If you really can't see that happening, maybe you should consider mediation, or even separation.'

'Separation! Fiona! No!' Annie was shocked. 'My marriage is, well, it's the most important thing to me after the children.'

'I have to say that it hasn't sounded like that. You have described it as non-functioning, to be frank, and a source of a lot of your difficulties.'

Annie fell silent. She couldn't believe what Fiona had just suggested, but she was struck with a sudden clarity by how she had allowed her unhappiness to corrode the foundation of her relationship.

'Thank you, Fiona,' she said quite briskly. 'We must go. Come on, boys!'

'I'm sorry if I have spoken too bluntly. I know nothing about you or your marriage, so I shouldn't comment.'

'No – it's not that. I'm just a bit shocked that I've given you the impression that my marriage is on the rocks.'

'Of course, I'm glad to hear that it's not.'

'Yes. We really must go. Thank you again. Come on, you two! I'll be in touch, Fiona. I'll let you know where I go from here.'

Alice was in bed reading a novel when David telephoned, and it took her a moment or two to collect her thoughts and take in what he was saying.

'Asthma? Have you got your inhaler?'

'No!' David's voice was rasping and full of effort.

'Well how bad is it? If it's severe, you should ring 999 and get an ambulance.'

'I don't want to do that unless I really have to. It seems a bit melodramatic.'

'What on earth has triggered it off? Maybe if you sit upright for a while and try not to panic it will wear off.'

'That's what I'm hoping.'

'What does Edwin think? You're sharing a room, aren't you?'

'Um – well, he's asleep. I don't want to disturb him.'

'You might have to. Really, David, you will just have to be sensible. If it gets worse, you must get help. Do you think it could be an allergic reaction to something? Have you been stung? No? Well what did you have for supper?'

'Shellfish of various sorts.'

'That's it, I expect. You could have developed an allergy, don't you think? Lots of people are allergic to shellfish. Have you got antihistamines with you? Then take one, now. It couldn't do any harm.'

'Okay. I'll do that. Thanks, Alice.'

'Just sit quiet for a bit and try to breathe and relax. Ring me, won't you, if it gets worse? And you must make sure that Edwin knows that it could be serious. Okay?'

'Okay. Thanks, Alice.' David felt better just from talking to her.

'Let me know how you are in the morning.'

'Yes, I will. Good night, then.'

'Good night. I hope you sleep now.'

'Thank you.'

Alice rang off and thought about her husband. He actually didn't sound too bad. He was more panicked than anything else. It was reassuring that he was with Edwin, who she remembered as being very sensible and capable. He could be relied on to deal with the situation if it became serious.

Really there was nothing to worry about. David would be okay. He had telephoned her because he needed reassurance. It was quite endearing that he still turned to her in an emergency. Switching out the light, Alice prepared to go to sleep. The last thing she saw before she closed her eyes was the miraculous dress in its plastic sheath hanging on her wardrobe door. It made her happy just to see it there. She ran through the vision of the party in her head, and for once she felt that the reality might be better than anything she could imagine.

David took his antihistamine tablet and sat downstairs trying to do what Alice had told him – to relax and take even breaths. She could be right about the seafood. Maybe he was allergic. He would probably come out in a hideous rash from head to toe. Or maybe the attack was triggered by the stress of adultery. It could be divine retribution. He was aware that this was a ridiculous thought, but he did wonder exactly why he should have an attack now of all times. It seemed like the hardest possible luck.

It was slightly galling that Julia hadn't appeared to see how he was. He could have collapsed by now and be lying on the floor gasping his last. She would then have to deal with the hoo-ha that surrounded a sudden and unexpected death, which would serve her right.

He heard a whining noise and saw that Roger was sitting with his nose to the glass of the porch door, looking anxious. Dear old Roger. He appeared to have picked up on David's distressed condition, like dogs that predict natural disasters or know when their owner is about to have an epileptic fit. David got up and opened the door and let him in. He could now be classed as a caring dog for the disabled. Roger rushed into the room and lay beside the armchair where David had been sitting. David sat back down again and then looked round and saw a tartan rug folded on the back of a chair. He wrapped himself up in it. He would just sit here until he felt better.

Chapter Twelve

'SO CAN WE talk now?' Annie asked Charlie as he came downstairs from reading the boys their bedtime story.

'Yes, I think we should. I want to know what's going on here.'

'Would you like a drink?'

'No, I don't think so, thanks. I want to know why you went off to London without telling me. For one thing, quite apart from keeping me in the dark about where you are and what you are doing, I should know where the boys are after school if you aren't going to collect them yourself.'

Annie swallowed hard. Don't say it, she told herself. Don't spit back that he's not usually bothered where any of us are.

'Yes, you're right. I should have told you. I'm sorry about that.'

'I mean, I always tell you if I am going to be late and where I am. I think as a general principle we should know what each other's movements are.'

'Yes, you're right!' Annie saw a muscle in Charlie's cheek relax. It was as if he had established his position of moral superiority and put her in the wrong, and that gave him satisfaction.

'Okay, Charlie. Cards on the table. Today I went to London,

as you now know. I had my hair cut properly for the first time in four years and then I met Sylvia for lunch.'

'So you arranged all this without telling me?' Charlie's voice was hurt and incredulous.

'Yes.'

'Why?'

'Because I know that you aren't sympathetic to the idea of me going back to work and I wanted to take this first step without you knowing. Maybe that was a mistake, and I'm sorry if it has upset you. And also, I think you'll admit that things between us have not been exactly harmonious lately. We haven't been communicating openly about anything very much.'

'Well I agree with you there. Any time I try to talk to you, you jump down my throat.'

'Charlie, I know I have been difficult, and losing that pathetic job was the last straw. I *know* I have been horrible to live with, and I am sorry because it has made me bloody miserable as well. I can tell you now that I have resented that you don't seem to even try to understand what it is that makes me such a pain, and I've diverted a lot of my angst towards you.' Whoa, Annie thought. She was determined not to be critical in this discussion. Throwing criticisms was not helpful. It was not a way forward.

'I like your hair, by the way.'

Annie stared at her husband. 'You do?'

'Yes. Why? Are you surprised?'

'Yes, I thought you'd hate it.'

It was Charlie's turn to look at her, and then shake his head. 'Why do you always do this? You always cast me in a role as heavy-handed and disapproving.'

269

'Let's just leave my hair out of it for the moment, Charlie.' Annie was amazed by her self-control. She could so easily have parried with a counter-accusation. Fiona's remark about her marriage had shaken her so profoundly that she was determined that this discussion should not spiral into acrimony. 'Let me be straight with you. Lunch was about getting myself back to work. Proper work. I had a useful chat with Sylvia – who sends her love, by the way – and she has commissioned me to write an article for the monthly magazine she edits.'

'Okay. Is that a big deal?' Charlie went to the fridge and took out a bottle of beer. A good sign, thought Annie. He's more relaxed now, less combative.

'It is a big deal because I hope it will be the first of many. I would like to ease myself back into journalism, possibly freelance. That way I can work from home and reduce the office hours, and have an element of control over what I choose to write.'

'Yeah, I see all that. Part-time would be good.' He thinks I can go on exactly as before, thought Annie, fitting round the children, suiting him.

'If I take on this work – and I have told her that I will write the article she wants – then I have to go and see her in London next week. The article itself will need a bit of research, some of which I can do from home, though not all of it.'

'So?'

'Well, isn't it obvious? It's about the boys. They break up the day after tomorrow. I can't work and look after them. I need some immediate childcare arrangement and long term I will – we will,' she corrected herself, 'have to work out something more permanent.'

'So this is it, is it? Not just the odd article here and there. You want to go back to work? To go back properly? Full-time?'

'Yes, I do.'

Charlie sat with the beer bottle balanced on his broad, round knee, his face downcast.

'Why? Can you tell me why you prefer to work with people like Sylvia, for a magazine peddling luxury goods to the obscenely rich, than look after your own sons?'

Annie took a deep breath. 'The magazine is not necessarily where I will end up, or even want to, come to that. It is just a start. I feel that going back to work is the time to try something completely different. Maybe I can find a way to write about what I like, and what I am interested in.'

'You want to do this more than looking after your own children, even though they are still so young and need you in a way that they won't when they are a bit older?'

Annie had to summon all her resolve to remain calm.

'The two things don't have to be mutually exclusive. You work and look after the boys, and so will I.'

Charlie sighed. There was a moment's silence, heavy with what lay between them, until he spoke in an altered tone. 'Do you know what? I've dreaded it coming to this, but in my heart I knew it would.'

'What do you mean?'

'When we had children I wanted them to have the sort of old-fashioned upbringing that I had at home. Wait a minute, don't look like that. I'm not saying it was perfect, but it provided a proper childhood in my view: stable, healthy, disciplined, where there was always someone there for us at home. Always. The security that gives is priceless and I put it down to having a non-working mother, and I suppose that's what I have tried to force on you.'

'Times have changed, Charlie, and you haven't married your mother.'

'Yes, and to be truthful, I could see that you weren't happy when you were stuck with the children, especially when they were younger. I suppose I put my head in the sand and hoped things would improve. I hoped that you could be different if you saw that the job you were doing with the kids is the most important job in the world.'

'I'm sorry, but I can't become something I'm not. I have tried, you know.'

'I know you have, but it makes me desperately sad that we aren't going to give Archie and Rory what I had. You'll never get me to agree that childcare is a good alternative to being with a parent, but I can't work any less, and you want to work more, and so there's nothing else for it. I hate them having second best. It makes me feel that we have failed them.'

'Listen, the most important thing is that they know they are loved and valued. I'll be a better mother, I know it, if I don't feel trapped by them in a life I hate.'

'You *hate*? You really *hate* it?'

'It doesn't suit me. It doesn't make me happy. It makes me feel hopeless and a failure.'

Charlie shook his head in despair. 'It's terrible to hear you say that. Imagine how it makes me feel.'

'Charlie, it's not about *you*! You didn't marry a housewife and a potential full-time mother. You married me! I was a successful journalist, a career girl who had worked hard to get where I was. Look, I love you, but I don't love myself like this. I haven't for a long time.'

'Oh, God!' Charlie put his head in his hands. Annie knew that his emotion was real and not put on for her discomfort. She was moved by his sadness. 'How could everything go so wrong? This life, here, was supposed to be the answer to everything.'

'It was for you, but not for me. I don't think an unhappy mother is good for the boys, whatever you say.'

'So where do we go from here? Next week is already a problem?'

'Yes.'

'My school breaks up the same day as the boys, but I shall have to go in for a couple of days after that. I won't be able to be here to look after them.'

'No, I guessed that.'

'Then there's my First World War battlefields trip. I'll be away for five days at the end of the holidays and I will have to go in before term starts for meetings and to prepare lessons and so on.'

'Yes, I know. It's all in the diary.'

'It's not the best time to have made this decision, is it?'

'There would never be a good time.'

'Well you must have some solution. You can't have accepted work without thinking this through.'

'Long term, we will have to find some permanent childcare. I think we agree we don't want an au pair or a full-time nanny, so we need someone flexible and part-time. I may have an answer to that.'

'How? Who?'

'Fiona tells me she is having a Czech girl — a student

doing a masters degree – coming to live with her as a lodger, in return for a bit of babysitting. She thinks she would welcome more work and could help us with child-care. She's late twenties, married, and has a six-year-old son who is looked after by her mother and husband in the Czech Republic.'

'Oh, I see!' said Charlie bitterly. 'Has Fiona put you up to all of this? She struck me as a troublemaker. Anti-men; a ball-breaker. Is this Czech woman a lesbian?'

'Charlie! That's unworthy of you.'

'Okay, I'm sorry. Forgive me. I don't know Fiona, and she may be very nice. She just has an off-putting appear-ance. So what are we going to do next week?'

'I wondered whether we could ask your parents if the boys could go there for a few days until you can take over.'

'They've got Sadie and the girls moving in.'

'Well would that matter? The children would amuse one another and Sadie could look after them. You say that's all she ever wants to do. Be at home with children.' Annie couldn't resist that last remark.

It was not the night that David had hoped for. He sat in the chair in the sitting room under the tartan rug, like an old man in a retirement home, until the early hours of the morning. His asthma attack seemed to have eased and he must have slept, with Roger snoring by his side. He woke cold and uncomfortable in the early hours and went quietly upstairs to join Julia in bed. She lay facing away from him and some time in the night must have put on a pair of pyjamas, white with pink roses. She looked very young and guileless. He gently moved her hair away from her face but she did not stir. She had an amazing capacity for sleep, and even when daylight streamed through the flimsy curtains, she still did not wake.

David got up and went downstairs, needing a pee and thinking about breakfast. He tried the water in the bathroom but found it to be cold, and he tinkered about with the heater on the wall but couldn't make it light. He washed in cold water, cleaned his teeth and boiled a kettle for a shave. He looked grey-faced and old in the bathroom mirror, which was rather what he felt. He tried not to think about Alice, getting ready for work, but wondered instead how his day would be spent. He would have to try and make an emergency appointment to see a doctor and get a prescription for drugs and an inhaler. After that, maybe he and Julia would go for a walk and then he would set off home in the afternoon.

After he had shaved, he opened the front door and looked out. It was a mild morning but there were billowy grey clouds to the west that indicated rain. Roger wandered out and cocked his leg against the garden gate. David supposed that after he had fed him his breakfast he would have to take him up the lane. If he saw the prefect from next door, he would ask her where he could find a doctor's surgery.

He got Roger's food out of the car and went in search of the tin opener, Roger trotting along behind him with an uplifted face and an eager expression. He made his breakfast in the kitchen and fed him in the garden, and then, collecting his coat and a lead, they set off together.

There was no sign of life from the dismal cottage, and by the time they reached the viewpoint from the top of the hill, the rain clouds were overhead and the wind was chilly. It was not going to be a day for walking – at least not for Julia, who didn't appear to have any footwear except high-heeled cowboy boots.

On the way back down the lane, David thought about what had happened between them. On a practical level he couldn't see what he could do to help her. She needed to sort out her whole life in his view – a bit like Sadie – and he knew how hard it was to influence young women to make more sensible decisions.

His visit was unhelpful, in every sense, and he regretted his decision to come. It was insane to have been thrown so drastically off course by the siren call of a young, unstable woman. On the other hand, she was lovely, and being with her had revived something in him that he thought had gone for ever. Although nothing had turned out as they had planned, she had made him feel that there were still possibilities to do things differently.

I shouldn't feel useless and sit back and wait for old age, he thought. Maybe I'll buy the little boat I've always wanted and take up sailing again. Maybe I'll apply to do VSO and go and do something useful in India or Africa where engineering skills are in short supply. And I love Alice, he thought. If nothing else, this escapade has taught me how much I love my wife.

Alice, at that moment, was trying to get an answer from David's mobile, which was sitting on the table in the cottage. His lack of response alarmed her. He had promised to keep in touch and his failure to do so must mean that he was in intensive care in Truro hospital, wired up to machines and maybe breathing his last. She could arrive at no other explanation.

The only thing she could think of was to telephone Edwin's wife and ask for her husband's mobile telephone number. If she could contact Edwin, she could find out what was going on. She went to get the old address book, looked up the name and dialled the number.

'Hello,' said a man's voice.

Alice was flustered. She thought it would be Christine who answered. Maybe she had dialled wrongly.

'Hello?' said the man again.

'Oh, I'm sorry. I wanted to speak to Christine Faraday. This is Alice Baxter.'

'Alice? Hello, this is Edwin!'

'Edwin?' Alice's mind went blank. 'Edwin? What are you doing at home? Is David all right? He's not in hospital, is he?'

'Alice, I can't help you here.' Edwin sounded alarmed. 'I don't know anything about David, I'm afraid. Why do you think he might be in hospital? What has happened?'

'Well I thought he was with you! I thought you were walking together in Cornwall! He telephoned me last night to say that he was having an asthma attack.' Her mind was racing, seeking explanations.

'There must be a mistake. I've been meaning to get in touch with David about walking the coastal path. We had a plan to do it together one day but we've never got it organised. Where did you say he was?'

Alice couldn't find the words she needed. David had lied to her. He had lied and lied. The most important thing now was to finish the conversation and get off the telephone.

'Oh, he's walking somewhere,' she said vaguely. 'I must

have got my wires crossed, because I thought that you were with him. I mean, I thought you were one of the party. I think there are several others. A sort of group walk.'

'Oh, I see. Well, please tell him to get in touch. It would be nice to catch up. Would you like a word with Christine?'

'I'd love to have a chat, but I am just on my way to work. I'll have to go. Sorry, Edwin, to have got it all wrong. I'll tell David to give you a ring.'

'Righty-ho. Goodbye, Alice.'

Alice rang off, relieved that Edwin had absolutely no normal curiosity about his fellow man and had accepted her garbled explanation. She felt strangely empty of feeling apart from disbelief. There must be an explanation, if only she could arrive at it. She must speak to David immediately and find out what was going on. Was he planning some sort of surprise? Was it something to do with the party?

She picked up the telephone again and redialled his number. It was answered almost immediately by a young female voice.

'What on earth is going on?' said Alice. 'Where is David?'

'He's taking his dog for a walk, I think,' said the woman calmly. 'Shall I give him a message?'

'Would you tell him to ring his wife? Thank you.' She rang off and then redialled. Why hadn't she asked the woman who she was? Was she a nurse or something? In the asthma clinic? There was no answer. She rang again. Still no answer. Was she going mad? Was this all some sort of joke, or trick? She sat staring out of the window and felt her heart beating very hard in her chest. There was something going on that she couldn't understand. She needed to think about it in a rational way, and most of all she needed to talk to David.

She tried his number again. Still no answer. She tried to remember him setting off yesterday morning. Had he been exactly the same as usual? Had he said anything that was out of the ordinary? He'd been lying to her all the time about Edwin and yet he hadn't seemed any different. She went over the call from last night, when he was in the middle of the asthma attack. Of course he wasn't well, but he hadn't seemed like a man who was lying to his wife. He had told her that Edwin was there with him and not for one moment had she suspected it wasn't true.

She thought back over the past weeks and could find no clues, nothing to explain what was going on. Then a very faint memory crept into her frenzied brain. She remembered disturbing David at his computer, walking into his room while he was working on something and standing behind him while he shut it down. She remembered thinking that he seemed almost furtive. It had occurred to her that he would rather she didn't see the screen.

Alice went upstairs and opened the door of the boys' room, where David now slept and worked. She went to the computer and switched it on. It required a password to open it up and Alice couldn't remember what it was. She wasn't sure that she had ever known. The computer was a cast-off of Ollie's, passed on when he got a newer model.

Alice ran downstairs and dialled Ollie's number. She might just catch him before he went to work, and she was lucky, because he answered the telephone.

'Hi, Mum! I'm just on my way out of the door. What can I do for you?'

Her voice had to remain normal at all costs. 'Oh, Ollie, I'm glad I caught you. I am trying to access some stuff on

Dad's computer. He's not here – away on a walking trip. Can you remember the password? Oh, that's great. Thanks so much. Sabine? Oh dear. Has Lisa gone to collect her from the airport? Look, let's speak later. Bye!'

She ran back upstairs and sat with trembling hands at the keyboard and typed in the password, guessing that David would not have bothered to change it. Obligingly, the screen flickered and cleared and the menu page came up.

Alice clicked on to e-mail and found the in-box empty. David had deleted everything. She went to the deleted box; he had cleared that too. The mouse clicked over 'sent', and there it all was, the evidence that she sought. In his excitement and haste he had forgotten to eliminate everything.

Alice read all the e-mails passed between David and Julia. She read them again from the beginning. It was like a piece of fiction, too incredible to be the stuff of her own life. But there was no escaping the truth. David, her husband of forty years, sixty-two years old, retired, and generally rather grumpy, not particularly good company of late and not much interested in sex, was having an affair with a woman young enough to be his daughter.

What was she to do, to feel? Alice didn't know. She wandered round the house going through all the rooms, touching surfaces with trailing fingers, noting the layer of dust, straightening beds, picking up papers. She collected dirty clothes, hers and David's, and put them in the washing machine, reminding herself that she had been doing that particular job for forty years.

She should have left for work, but instead she got out the Hoover and vacuumed the sitting-room carpet and dusted the furniture. She remembered the morning that Julia had sat in this room while she drank coffee on her own in the kitchen. Her husband and his lover had planned their affair in this room on that morning. She tried to recall Julia's face but could only remember that she was young and fresh and pretty. No wonder David wanted her. Her own face in the mirror above the fireplace looked ancient, etched with lines of shock and misery.

'I can forgive him the sex,' she said out loud, 'but I can't forgive him the treachery and lies.' It was what wives said when they had been cheated on. But it was silly. It was because of the sex that he had lied. It was lust that had made him disloyal. He was the same as all the footballers and politicians caught out with starlets and lingerie models and nannies.

The telephone rang and she picked it up like an automaton and said, 'Hello?' in a relatively normal voice.

'Alice! I can explain!' It was David, and she felt a rush of relief. He could explain it all, the e-mails, everything, and it would all disappear and fade away like a nightmare in the morning light.

'Alice? Alice?' His voice sounded shocked. 'You see I didn't feel well, as you know, and Edwin said . . .' But she knew it was lies. He was squirming like a worm on a hook.

'Stop it, David! That's enough. I really don't want to talk to you.'

'Alice! Please! Just let me—'

'No thank you, David.' She hung up. The telephone rang again and she left it unanswered.

What now? What should she do? There were women who took scissors to their husband's suits, ran over their golf clubs, crashed their cars, but Alice did not seem to have the anger to fuel revenge. Instead she felt crippled by sadness. If David had gone off and slept with this girl, what did it say about her, his wife, and their marriage?

Upstairs, she pulled a weekend bag out of a cupboard and threw in some clothes, anything really, and some under-wear. Before she turned to leave she saw the red dress and tore it savagely from the hanger and stuffed it in the bag as well. Going downstairs, she left her mobile on the middle of the kitchen table and went out of the front door, locking it behind her.

Chapter Thirteen

THE ATMOSPHERE ON the drive home from the airport was uncomfortable and strange. Lisa had expected Sabine to be upset, but she seemed quite calm and distant and didn't want to talk.

'It's no big deal,' she had said when her mother greeted her in Arrivals, bristling with indignation on her behalf. 'Papa was busy – that's all. I hadn't properly checked with him. It was me who bought the ticket. I used your credit card. He's put the money back in your account, so there's no need for you to get worked up about the money.'

'I can't believe you did that!' cried Lisa. She stopped in her tracks and looked at her daughter in amazement. 'You took my credit card and used it without my permission? Sabine! I simply can't believe it!'

'What difference does it make?' said Sabine in a matter-of-fact voice. 'I knew Papa would pay you back. You wouldn't have listened anyway. You were too busy being hysterical about Sadie's baby.'

Lisa stared at her daughter, astonished by what she was hearing.

'Sabine! Don't speak to me like that! What's the matter with you?'

Sabine shrugged. 'But it's true, isn't it?'

'I might have been upset, but that's absolutely no excuse for you to behave like this.'

'Okay.'

'You can't just say "okay". That doesn't put anything right.'

'Whatever.'

'At least say you're sorry for causing all this trouble to your father and to me. It's the last thing I need – to be back at the airport again today to meet you.'

'Okay, I'm sorry.'

They found the car in the car park and drove in silence for a few minutes, and then Sabine said in a matter-of-fact voice, 'Papa says Agnes and me can go to Pompignac when the baby is born.'

'How can you?' said Lisa in an exasperated voice. 'It will be termtime. That's just typical of him, to say something like that.'

'Fuck school! I'm going anyway.'

'Sabine! Stop it! Stop this horrible behaviour at once! Whatever has got into you?'

Sabine didn't answer.

'I've been trying to get hold of Mum all morning,' Charlie told Annie on the telephone. 'There's no answer from home, or her mobile, and Dad's away walking somewhere, so I can't get anywhere with fixing up about the kids. I'll keep trying.'

Ollie left a message on the answer machine for Lisa to pick up when she got back from the airport. 'Mum telephoned this morning to know something about the computer I gave Dad. I was in a bit of a rush and she was leaving for work so I didn't have a chance to ask about Sabine going there this week. I'll keep trying, but I'm sure it will be fine. I'll let you know. Love you.'

'Mum! Where are you?' wailed Sadie. 'I was going to hire a van to bring our stuff over the day after tomorrow but I wondered whether you or Dad could come to pick us up? It would be so much cheaper, for one thing. Anyway, the girls are really excited about coming to you. See you soon. Byeeee!'

'Mum! Where is everybody?' said Marina into the answer machine. 'Just to let you know that Ahmed's family are going to come and visit us in London instead of us going to Syria, and I have to say that I am hugely relieved. We decided it was just too risky for him to go to Damascus at the moment. I was wondering if we could bring them to your party? They'll be over here that weekend in May and it would be lovely for them to meet all the family. And I've talked to Sadie! Goodness, Mum, poor old Sade. Send her my love. Okay, better go. It's mad here, as usual. Mo is just gorgeous. He's smiling so much and reaching for things now. He loves that mobile you gave him. Longing for you and Dad to see him again. Why don't you come to London and stay for a night? Let me know. Bye!'

'How could you have done that?' David asked Julia. 'How could you have answered my mobile? I can't believe you did that. What am I to say to Alice? She has just rung off when I was in the middle of trying to explain.'

'I don't care what you say,' said Julia dismissively. 'I could have been anyone. A chambermaid, a waitress, anyone. I was pissed off with you anyway. I went into the kitchen to make a cup of tea and then, oh my God! A tin of fucking dog meat on the counter! Chunks of revolting brown stuff in jelly. And the smell of it! You know how I feel about meat products. Honestly, I nearly threw up on the spot. I still feel nauseous now.'

David looked at Julia in amazement. He had never come across anyone quite like her. At that moment his telephone rang again and he seized it hoping that it would be Alice ringing back to apologise for cutting him off. Instead he was surprised to hear Edwin's voice. 'David? Are you all right? I've just had Alice on the telephone. Apparently she thought you were with me and that you weren't well, or some story like that. I'm afraid I wasn't quick enough to provide you with an alibi. Ha! Ha! Only joking. David? David? Are you there?'

All the way home, David drove with exaggerated care. He must remain calm, stay in control, and then this fiasco could be explained away. It was an absurd situation he found himself in, laughable, farcical. What had he been thinking of? What had he done? He had never, not for one moment, thought there would be any consequences. He couldn't believe how things had gone so disastrously wrong, and now Alice was very upset and God knows what she thought he had been up to.

He would have to explain the whole thing, or at least offer her an explanation that she would accept. There was no reason why she should suspect he had been with another woman. It was so out of character that he could hardly believe it himself. Julia answering his telephone could be explained away. He had left it on the breakfast table at the pub and the girl who was doing the clearing answered it when it rang. She had seen him taking Roger for a walk. It all made sense. He almost believed it himself.

He would explain Edwin away too. He would say that when he came to it, he preferred to walk alone. Edwin was a bore. He couldn't face two days in his company. He had told Alice he was with him because she might have been upset by him wanting to be alone – especially when she had suggested coming with him herself. Explanations, excuses, reasoned arguments raced round his head. The most important thing was to make Alice believe him. He couldn't begin to imagine the damage he would cause if she ever knew what he had really been doing. The last thing I want to do is hurt her, he told himself over and over again. I never thought it would come to this. Oh God, what have I done?

He stopped twice and tried to reach her on the telephone, but she wasn't at home and she wasn't answering her mobile. He thought of ringing the surgery but decided that was taking things too far. In two hours he would be home and everything would be explained and smoothed over and life could return to normal. He remembered how glad Alice had been when he brought back the flowers and the sausages. Perhaps he should stop in Chard and get something special from the deli owned by a television cook: chargrilled artichokes and Parma ham, ridiculously expensive bread, that sort of thing. Alice would be pleased and they would have a good bottle of wine over supper. It would be so good to be at home and safely back to normal.

But maybe it won't turn out like that, he thought desperately.

When he pulled up outside the house, he saw that Alice's car had gone. She must be at work. It was a good thing that he could go inside and compose himself before having to face her. He unlocked the door and saw that there was a sheet of paper on the mat. He picked it up and went into the kitchen. Alice's mobile telephone was lying on the table. That explained why she hadn't answered his calls, which was a relief. Perhaps she had left him a note. He opened up the sheet. Puzzled, he realised that it was the itinerary for some sort of luxury Mediterranean cruise. He put it on the table and went upstairs to his room.

He realised at once that he must have left his computer switched on, which struck him as strange, but then he had gone off in such a state of agitation that anything was possible. He sat down in front of it and clicked it from standby to active mode. Instantly the sent box of his e-mail account appeared on the screen. Horrified, he saw the list of all the messages exchanged between Julia and himself.

It must have been Alice. Alice must have found out what he had been up to. He was doomed. Finished. He sat stunned, unable to form any coherent thoughts. He had no idea what he was going to do next. He went downstairs and poured himself a glass of whisky, which he knocked down his throat in one. Putting the glass back on the table and reaching for the bottle, he saw the cruise itinerary. Was that it? Had Alice buggered off to sea and left him?

Margaret's flat was spacious and bright. The room she had allowed Alice to use was painted a calming pale blue and had a comfortable double bed with a white lace counterpane. At the window were blue and pink dotted curtains and the outlook was over a little-used road to a park with swings and climbing equipment, all empty now in the rain of the afternoon.

The flat was very quiet. Alice could hear the fridge switching itself off and on and the clicking of the electric clock on the kitchen wall. Margaret had told her to help herself to anything, but apart from a glass of water Alice hadn't felt like even making a cup of tea. She dragged off the counterpane and folded it carefully, took off her shoes and lay on the bed, flat out, like a corpse, her hands folded and her eyes open.

She felt a bit like a corpse, she thought, because everything that she was had spilled out of her and now she was empty, a nothing person. When I got up this morning I thought of myself as being one thing, and now I am completely another. Everything that seemed true yesterday is a lie today. Everything I thought I had has slipped through my fingers and now my hands are empty. Everything that was solid has given way. Everything I was sure of has proved an illusion.

She felt that some of these thoughts were so profound, so original that she ought to write them down. She imagined putting them in a letter to David, but just at the moment she couldn't think too much about David. In fact she didn't want to think about any of them, not Sadie and the girls, or what Ollie had told her about Sabine, or Marina and Ahmed, or Annie and her job. She didn't want to think about them at all. Neither did she want to telephone her sister and tell her the news. 'Yes! He's been having an affair! With a young girl!' She never wanted Rachel to know. Never. It was her disgrace. Her own wound.

Instead she would lie here and see what happened. Later on Margaret would get back from work and she would have to talk, she supposed. She had given her the briefest of explanations when she had telephoned the surgery and said that she was sick and would not be coming in. 'Could I go to your place, Margaret? I need somewhere to go. I need somewhere to lie down,' and Margaret had said, sensing the import of the question, 'Of course,' and had asked nothing more but told her where a spare key was to be found and that she could use her second bedroom for as long as she liked.

So here she was, a non-person, and it was restful to feel so estranged and adrift and removed from her life, and apart from getting up to go to the bathroom, she stayed quite peacefully where she was, feeling nothing.

Of course this couldn't last. She knew it couldn't because she wouldn't be allowed to disappear quite so painlessly. When she heard Margaret's key in the lock and she saw that the afternoon light was fading, she felt herself being pulled back to the surface of her life again.

Margaret appeared in the door, still wearing her red coat with the fake fur collar. Her face was full of concern. 'Oh, Alice, whatever has happened? I have been so worried about you all day. Your husband's been ringing the surgery. I didn't tell him you were here. I hope I did the right thing.'

'Yes, you did. Absolutely. I'm sorry to put you in this position, Margaret.'

'No, don't apologise. I'd do anything for you, you know that. But what's going on, Alice? He seems to think that you've gone away on a cruise.'

Alice, sitting up on the bed, stared blankly at her friend. A cruise? A *cruise*?

And then she began to laugh.

David had the worst day of his life – easily the worst. He had no idea where Alice was and he felt tormented that he couldn't reach her. Most of all he wanted to comfort her and explain that it all meant nothing, nothing, and that she was everything to him, his whole life, his world. He wanted to tell her that he was unworthy of her and to beg her forgiveness. He couldn't bear the thought that she was desperately unhappy, hurt and alone. 'Oh Alice, forgive me!' he cried out loud as he paced the house. His ears strained to hear her key in the door or her step on the stair but the house remained silent and accusing.

He opened the door of their bedroom and went in. All was tidy and calm within. There was no sign of a rushed departure, no drawers left open or clothes on the floor, but there were two unfamiliar cardboard boxes on a chair and out of one David lifted a pale green and blue silk dress. He held the slippery material to his cheek. It was Alice's party dress, he supposed, and he felt his eyes brim with tears. Alice's garden party! The party that was planned to celebrate their lives together, and he had wrecked it all.

At half past five the telephone began to ring, and each time he seized the receiver hoping that it would be her.

'Dad? Hi! Where's Mum? I left a message for her this morning but she hasn't rung me. Dad, is there any chance you could come and collect me and the girls? It would save me hiring a van. Could you come tomorrow morning? Great! How was the walk? You sound a bit odd. Are you okay? And Dad, I've had a call from Charlie. He wants to bring the boys over to yours for a few days while Annie tackles some article that she's been commissioned to write. I said that it would be fine. You don't mind, do you? I'll do the cooking and stuff. It will be fun for the girls. Where did you say Mum was?'

'She's out at the moment,' said David, casting round for an excuse. 'There's a practice meeting. She'll be late.' I can't tell her, he thought. I can't tell her. I am too ashamed.

'Hi, Dad!' The telephone rang again. 'Did Mum tell you about Sabine? Is it okay for her to come to you for a week while Agnes is away? Yours is the destination of choice, you might be flattered to hear! To tell you the truth, she's been a bit of a worry. She took herself off to France off her own bat, and has been sent back by her father. She's a bit upset and is taking it out on Lisa. You remember teenagers, don't you? So would that be okay? Are you all right, Dad? Have you got a cold? How was the walk?'

'Dad! Hi! Did Mum tell you about Ahmed's parents? Is it going to be okay to bring them to the party? Is Mum there?'

David answered mechanically. How can I tell them? he thought. How can I tell them that everything has changed; that everything our lives are based upon has gone?

'You should try and eat something,' said Margaret kindly. 'I've got some M&S meals in the freezer. I was going to have the salmon en croûte. Couldn't you manage a little?'

'Thank you, but I don't think I can face anything just at the moment.'

'So what now?' Margaret asked, sitting on the end of the spare-room bed. Alice felt strange, lying there as if she was ill. She felt she should be less weak and feeble but she didn't think she had the energy to swing her legs off the bed and stand up.

'I don't know,' she said. 'I have no idea. Is it up to me, do you think?'

'Of course it is!' Margaret went to the window and yanked at the curtains angrily. 'After all these years of marriage! It makes me mad to think of how that man has behaved to you. You can throw him out. Let him see how long that piece of baggage stays with him when he's living in a bedsit and you've screwed the last drop out of his pension.'

'I don't think it's like that,' said Alice slowly. 'I don't think he's having that sort of affair. It seems to me more like an act of carelessness on both our parts that this has happened.'

'Carelessness? This was *planned*! You have the evidence. You can throw him out for a start. And it's not *your* fault!' cried Margaret. 'This is what men are like. It's a cliché, what has happened to you. Look about you. It happens all the time. If you hadn't found out, this would have gone on behind your back while he went on lying to you. My second husband kept it up for three years before he got caught out and I found he'd been shagging our neighbour whenever I worked the evening shift.'

'No, it isn't my fault. I'm not saying that. I don't know

what I think, or what I want to do. I can't face any of it just now. I shall have to see him, I suppose, but I can't do it yet. Sadie and the grandchildren will be arriving at any moment and he'll have his hands full. I don't know what he'll tell them.' It seemed to Alice that with those words she stared into a blank future. The family. What was going to happen to the family? Whatever could be rescued from all of this?

'Oh Alice!' Margaret's eyes, ringed with make-up, filled with tears. 'You don't deserve this, you really don't.' She reached out for her with open arms and the two women embraced clumsily.

The telephone rang and Alice knew that it would be David before Margaret disentangled herself and picked it up. She looked across at Alice and made a questioning face.

'Tell him I'm here,' said Alice in a whisper. 'But I don't want to speak to him. Not yet.'

'So where *is* Mum?' demanded Sadie as she and the girls unloaded the car and carried bursting carrier bags of clothes and toys and books into the house.

'She's away for a few days,' mumbled David, taking two suitcases out of the boot.

'She hasn't left you, has she?'

David looked up sharply but realised that Sadie was joking, as if it was a ridiculous thought that Alice might have walked out.

'Where has she gone? She never said anything about going away. Hey! She's not ill, is she?'

'No, no, she's not ill. She needed a rest. A little break. She's gone on a sort of retreat.' This was the explanation that he had arrived at, the only one that he thought he might get away with.

'A *retreat*! What sort of retreat? It sounds most peculiar. Has she gone to a convent or something? Is that why she hasn't taken her phone with her?'

'That's right. No telephones. No contact with family. Silence and simple food and plenty of sleep. It was something organised through the practice. Holistic well-being. That sort of thing.'

He was becoming such a good liar that he could almost sell this idea to himself. He wished that he could crawl away and find such a place. He had never felt worse, more unhappy, more unravelled. Although she wouldn't speak to him, Alice had told Margaret to tell him that she would meet him tomorrow, *to talk*. Margaret had made it sound as ominous as possible. When he'd asked her how Alice was, she had snorted with contempt and said, 'It's a bit late for that, isn't it? How do you *think* she is? How do you *think* she feels?'

'So when will she be back?' demanded Sadie, going up the stairs with armfuls of stuff. 'It seems so odd she never said anything about it.'

'Oh, in a day or two. I don't think it was planned much in advance. While I was away she just decided that she needed a break herself.'

'Oh look, she's done the girls' room,' cried Sadie from the upstairs landing. 'Come and see, girls! Georgie, Tamzin! Granny's made your room all ready and welcoming for you.'

David lumbered after them with the cases and stood in the doorway. Alice had put soft toys on each of the single beds, which had been made up with pink girlie linen, and there was a selection of children's books on the bedside table. She had found the old fairy mushroom nightlight, and when Sadie pulled open the drawers of the chest, it was evident that Alice had cleared them out for the girls' clothes. Oh Alice, he thought miserably. Oh Alice. She must have been busy doing this while he was at the cottage, intent upon adultery.

'When we've got this stuff sorted out, I'd better go and do a supermarket shop, Dad. Archie and Rory are coming tomorrow, and apparently Sabine too. Ollie telephoned me last night when he couldn't get hold of Mum. She'll have to sleep with Tamzin and Georgie. You've still got that fold-up bed, haven't you? I'll do an enormous spag bol for tomorrow night, and some sort of crumble. We'd better make a list.'

David looked at his younger daughter. Despite her un-happiness and her woeful situation, he could see she was glad to be busy. This reminded him so much of Alice, or rather of her absence, that he would have liked to have crept quietly to their bedroom and closed the door and laid on their bed, on Alice's side, where her body had made a soft scoop in the mattress. Instead he promised to raise the saddle on Georgie's bicycle and then take the girls for a cycle ride to visit the ponies down the lane.

Alice slept deeply and dreamlessly. Several times she woke during the night, and lay staring into the darkness trying to work out where she was, in what strange bed in which unfamiliar room. It wasn't until Margaret tapped on the door in the morning with a cup of tea in her hand that she felt conscious of what had happened and everything came flooding back into her mind with a new and surprising clarity.

Without make-up and in a worn candlewick dressing gown, her hair standing on end, Margaret looked younger and more vulnerable.

'Do you want me to be here?' she asked, putting the cup on the bedside table. 'When you meet him?' Since yesterday she hadn't been able to say David's name. Alice felt touched by her loyalty.

'Of course not, Margaret. He's my husband, not an axe murderer! It's sweet of you, but we ought to be alone, I think.'

'You can stay here, you know, for as long as you like.'

Alice reached out and caught her friend's hand. She wished she did not feel that in a way Margaret was almost glad that David had proved himself to be an unfaithful wretch; not because she wished Alice unhappiness but because it endorsed her view of men.

'Thank you. You are the best possible friend, but I'm already starting to feel that I should be at home. The children will be there. They'll wonder what has happened to me.'

'But you can't just go back as if nothing has happened. You'll never be able to trust him again.'

'Things can never be the same, I know that, but I can't stop believing that David's a good man, really. I've got to make sense of what has happened. We need to talk about it.'

'How can you say he's a good man when he's betrayed you?'

'Easily. I have all the past evidence, as it were, which can't be wiped out. Anyway, he's all I've got. I've invested my whole adult life in him. I'm not like you. I'm not brave enough to be on my own.'

'What will the children say? They'll lose all respect for him.'

'They'll never know. I'm sure he won't have told them, and I won't tell anyone. Only you know, and I'm swearing you to secrecy.'

'But what he's done to you will always be there at the back of your mind. Every time he annoys you, every time you have a row, you'll look at him and remember.'

'He hasn't done anything to me. He has been unfaithful with a foolish and manipulative girl, from what I can tell, but what happens to me as a result is my decision. Don't you see? I can *let* it ruin my life, wreck everything, or we can try to get over it, learn something, pick up the pieces and go on. Unless, of course, he has fallen in love with her and wants to end our marriage.'

It was this thought that struck like an arrow into her heart: that this really might be the end. She knew that it happened. She had read about it – thirty-, forty-year-old marriages running out of steam and new partners being sought. Perhaps David felt like that. Perhaps that was what this girl was all about.

Margaret sighed. 'Well, it's your life. But if it was me, I couldn't forgive him. The thought of them together would make me gag every time I looked at him.'

Alice smiled wanly and closed her eyes. 'I know, Margaret. It's devastating, but unless I find a way of dealing with it, I don't see how I can go on in any way at all. I can understand how you would feel differently. You haven't had one man in your life for so many years that you feel almost the same person, and maybe that's part of the problem – that somewhere along the line David and I have stopped considering each other properly as individuals in our own right, and maybe this girl's attention made David feel like himself again. I don't know. Maybe I am looking for excuses because it makes it less painful and humiliating.' She stared out of the window as if a solution was to be found amongst the trees of the empty playground.

'Also I have other things to remember – a lifetime of shared stuff, like when the babies were born, when he held each one for the first time.' Hot tears welled and she compressed her lips to stop herself from weeping. 'We've been through so much together and I don't want to jettison all that because he has lost his head over a girl. She doesn't seem *worth* it – not to me, anyway.'

'You're too kind to him, too forgiving. It's a weakness in you, Alice. It's like battered wives who go back time and time again for another black eye.'

Alice sighed. 'I've got to deal with it in my own way. And don't worry about me being too forgiving. At the moment I am so angry with him I could kill him. Yesterday I was too stunned to feel anything except deep shock. Today I'm *angry*! I just want to scream at him, "How could you?"'

'Good! Fighting talk!' Margaret patted her arm. 'Now I expect you could manage some breakfast? There's toast and yoghurt and fruit and muesli. Do you want to help yourself while I have a shower? And don't worry about work. I'll say you called in sick and arrange cover.'

'Thank you, Margaret. Obviously I'll be back as soon as

I feel up to it. I'll need to hang on to normality to get through this, and going to work is probably a good thing.'

After Margaret had left for the surgery, Alice took a long bath and got dressed. She felt weak and shaky, like a proper invalid, and so nervous that her skin prickled and the smallest unfamiliar sound made her jump. She had told Margaret to tell David to come at three o'clock and she would meet him in the small park across from her flat, and now she dreaded both the wait and the meeting itself.

She moved restlessly about the flat, marvelling at Margaret's neatness, at the half-empty kitchen cupboards and the ordered shelves. There were a few framed photographs – a young Margaret, with the same big hair, receiving an award from a hoteliers' association, dressed in a tight black suit with an enormous red cabbage rose pinned to her lapel; and one of her parents, posing on a beach with Margaret and her brother as children, sitting side by side on a picnic rug, squinting into the camera. Naturally enough there were none of her discarded, cheating husbands.

Alice thought of the mess and muddle of her own home and realised how she had been crowded out by the accumulation of other people's discarded possessions, things they had no room for in their present lives but which they had left cluttering hers. It's time I did something about it, she told herself. The place needs a spring clean, a radical turnout. The children must take what they want to keep and the rest can go. I want empty cupboards and clean shelves and just my books in the bookcases and my clothes in the cupboards – and David's too, of course, if that is how it turns out.

'So what's going on?' said Sabine to Tamzin after breakfast, sitting side by side on Tamzin's bed, painting their nails in pink and silver stripes. 'Where's your granny, do you think?'

Tamzin shrugged. 'She's on holiday or something. Mum says she needed a break.'

'You don't think they're splitting up, do you? Your grandpa seems a bit weird about it. He goes all peculiar if you talk about when she's coming back.'

Tamzin looked at her step-cousin with fear. 'That's rubbish,' she said. 'Anyway, they're way too old for stuff like that.'

'Yeah, probably. They kind of go together, don't they? You can't imagine them apart. They're not lovey-dovey, but that doesn't mean anything. When I last saw my dad, he got drunk and told me how much he loved my mum – and yet they can't be in the same room without fighting. They can't even talk on the phone without having a row.'

'Yeah,' said Tamzin, nodding her head wisely. She couldn't remember anything about her dad, but she supposed there had been rows, like there had been with Kyle. She could remember her mum crying without being able to stop, holding her hand tightly and pushing Georgie down the street in the buggy, while everybody stared at them. 'I'm never going to love anyone,' she said. 'Well, not boys and all that stuff.'

'Nor me,' said Sabine. 'No way. It's always going wrong. People are always wanting something they can't get, or wanting the other person to be different from how they really are.'

'Yeah,' said Tamzin, not really knowing what Sabine was talking about but recognising something true in what she said. It had been like that with her mum: everything being all right with each new man and then ending with tears and rows. 'Anyway, Grandpa's going to see Granny this afternoon,' she said. 'So why don't we send her something. Make her a card, maybe. A "Come Back Soon" card.'

'Yeah, or a "It's Funny Here Without You" card, because it *is* funny, isn't it? It feels like we're all holding our breath till she gets back.'

'Grandpa said he'll take us swimming later on, when Rory and Archie get here. Five of us! Like a big family. You know my mum is having a baby? That's why Kyle walked out. I don't care, though. I'd rather it was just us.'

Sabine held out her hand, examining her nails. 'I'm never going to have a baby,' she said. 'Personally, I think they're overrated.'

At two o'clock Alice got ready to meet David. She put on some make-up and combed her hair. Her appearance frightened her. Her face seemed to have collapsed into sags and folds. I am an old woman, she thought. 'Pensioner Alice Baxter, 60, prepares to meet her unfaithful husband, David, 62, to discuss the future of their marriage. The couple have been married for forty years and were due to celebrate their wedding anniversary in May.' How foolish this is, she thought sadly. All the human misery and tragedy and natural disasters in the world and we behave like this, David and me. We are foolish and spoiled and self-indulgent.

She was ready far too early and stood by the window that overlooked the park, and at half past two she saw David's old car drive slowly past as he looked for a parking place. She watched him reverse into a space and her heart beat very fast and her hands shook. She saw him get out, forgetting to close the window, and then get in again, and out again, and then fumble to lock the door, and then unlock it and reach for something on the rear seat. She saw him duck back out and this time he was carrying a bouquet of flowers. He stood beside the car door, deep in thought, and then he opened the door again and returned the flowers to the back seat. He is as agitated as I am, she thought. All this is as bizarre and unfamiliar and shocking to him as it is to me.

She watched him walk to the gate into the play area, look round and then go towards the bench by the swings. It must be a warm afternoon because he was wearing only a navy sweater and had no coat. He sat on the bench for a moment or two, looking right and left, and then he dropped his face into his hands in a gesture of despair. When he looked up he stared straight across the road to Margaret's window and Alice, with a shock, found their eyes meeting. She saw his face alter with sudden recognition, and instinctively she raised her hand in a tentative greeting. Equally apprehensive, he raised his hand in reply.

She had to remember how to lock Margaret's door and to take the key with her, and her hands fumbled at the catch, and then she went back for her coat and hurried down the stairs to the front door, which she had difficulty opening. She could see that David had come to the gate of the park to meet her, and she did not know how to look at him as she crossed the road. Her composure left her completely and her breath came in gulps and her shoulders shook.

When she reached him she stood apart and uncertain, her hand to her cheek, looking across the playground, unable to bear the sight of his stricken face.

'Alice, Alice,' he was saying, in a voice weighty with emotion. 'Oh, Alice!'

She allowed him to put an arm round her shoulders but stood stiffly apart when he tried to pull her towards him. Her resistance upset him.

'Oh! Please, Alice! Please! It wasn't what you think. It wasn't. Please let me explain.'

'What I don't want to hear, David, is that you are sorry. It seems to me you are sorry because you were caught. You are sorry that you didn't get away with it, that's all.'

'That's not true. I am deeply, deeply sorry to have caused you this pain.'

She allowed him to lead her over to the bench, where they sat side by side and he tried to take her hand, which she removed from his grasp. She didn't want him to touch her.

'I gather you had only just begun this affair . . .'

'It isn't an *affair*! It's not even a *relationship*!'

'But no doubt it would have been . . . it would have become one.'

'No! It was all a terrible mistake. I don't know how it happened. I just went along with it, without thinking about you at all.'

'Thanks. Your wife of forty years was conveniently forgotten when you met a compliant young woman.'

David sat in miserable silence staring at his hands.

'It was a sort of madness. I knew it was . . .'

'The siren song.'

'Yes, I suppose so.'

'There's something more, David, than you being flattered and all that male ego stuff. What I want to know is, what has happened to us to make this possible? To allow you to lie to me, to feel okay about deceiving me?'

'I didn't feel okay. When it came to it, all I could think of was you.'

'I don't want to hear about what it came to, thank you very much. I'm not interested in you and this girl other than what it says about us. The first question I need to ask is what you intend to do now.'

David looked at her in surprise. 'What *I* do? The ball is rather in your court.'

'I mean, what do you *want* to happen next?'

'I want you back, Alice!' David cried. 'I want you to forgive me and to allow us to start again. I want our old life back.'

Alice felt a huge wave of relief, but she pressed on. 'Our old life won't do, David. Our old life allowed this to happen. We will need to make some changes.' She knew how David hated this sort of conversation, examining feelings that he would much rather leave unexpressed. 'We need to find out why this happened.'

David sighed. 'I suppose I felt you weren't really interested in me. I seem peripheral to all the other things in your life, the children, the grandchildren, your job. I suppose this feeling has grown since I retired and, frankly, I have become a useless old has-been. I loaf about the house feeling in the way and a nuisance.'

He wants me to feel sorry for him, thought Alice, and I'm not going to. I can try to understand but I'm not going to feel sorry.

'But I can't change that!' she said briskly. 'Only you can alter how you feel about yourself and what you choose to do with your retirement. You resent any suggestions I have made about how to occupy your time. You could do voluntary work or get a part-time job, couldn't you?'

David sighed again. 'I have thought of that. It's fairly obvious, isn't it? But I can't do anything until I know what you want to do. And just at the moment it's a good thing I am free to help Sadie.'

'Yes, it is,' acknowledged Alice, 'but that's only temporary. We've let the children rule our lives at the expense of our marriage.'

'Aren't they the most important thing?'

'No. *We* are the most important thing. You and me. We've grown careless of each other. We've lost sight of who we are. We've lost respect for each other's feelings. What are we going to have left when we grow old and are of no use to anyone any more, when we only have each other? What is it going to be like then, unless we can put things right now?'

'Alice, if there is one thing this has taught me it is that I love you more than ever. I may have lost sight of that recently, but it's true.'

Alice allowed David to take her hand. She felt the sincerity of his declaration and it moved her. She couldn't remember the last time he had told her he loved her. Tears started to run down her cheeks. She wiped them away with her free hand and laid her head on his shoulder, and they sat like that for some time. Alice thought how Margaret would be disappointed in her, but all she felt was relief.

'Here!' said David eventually. 'I've got something for you.' He fumbled in his pocket and drew out several squares of folded paper. Alice opened them on her lap, revealing hand-made cards from Sabine and Tamzin and Georgie. 'They're worried about you,' said David. 'I've told them you are away on a sort of retreat, but I'm not sure they believe me.'

Alice smiled wanly. 'How are they all?' she asked. 'Is Sadie all right?'

'Yes. She's in her element, looking after everybody. The boys are arriving this afternoon. I've promised to take them all swimming.'

There was a silence until Alice said, 'I *will* come back, David, but not for a day or two. I need a bit of peace and quiet to sort things out. I need space to think. There are changes to be made.'

'Of course,' said David with feeling. 'Oh, Alice!'

'What about the girl? Has this knocked her further off course? She seemed unstable to begin with.'

'She had no serious feelings about me. I discovered she has been in touch with a number of other men in the department. She had an affair with the principal of the bogus business school she taught in. She's much tougher than she appears. Edwin knew all about it. Contrary to appearances, he is a terrible old gossip.'

'He can gossip about us now.'

'Let him! Who cares?'

David reached into his pocket again and drew out Alice's mobile telephone. He put it in her hand.

'Please keep in touch,' he said. 'Please let me speak to you. I don't want you to think too much and change your mind about coming back to me.'

Alice smiled faintly. 'I won't,' she said. 'I promise you I won't.'

'Would you like to do something? Go for a walk? Have a drink somewhere?'

'Let's just walk.'

They got up, and tucking her hand into the crook of her husband's elbow, Alice allowed herself to be led slowly across the park.

Chapter Fourteen

'W HERE IS SHE? Where's Mum?' asked Sadie, pushing open the side gate of the house with her hip, her arms full of flowers from her garden.

'She's still upstairs getting ready,' said Annie, going forward to meet her. 'We sent her away and told her there was nothing more to do. It looks wonderful, doesn't it, and aren't we lucky with the weather? Not a cloud in the sky!'

The two young women paused to look at the pink and white marquee and the tables covered in crisp white linen. Catering staff in black skirts and white blouses were putting the final touches to the table settings and members of the family had already opened some bottles of wine and were gathered in groups, talking and laughing. David was nowhere to be seen.

'She and Dad have done miracles with the garden,' said Sadie. 'It was looking very wintry and sad when we were living here a few weeks ago. I see the skip is still outside in the road, which slightly spoils the effect.'

'Alice insists that while the family is gathered, there has got to be a clear out of all the stuff that has accumulated over the last forty years. Take it or bin it, she says. The skip's already half full.'

'She's got rather empowered, hasn't she? Ever since she went on that retreat thing,' laughed Sadie. 'I've got flowers here for the tables,' she went on. 'The girls and I picked them this morning. Do you think jam jars will matter? Tamzin is bringing some from the car. All washed and clean, of course.'

'Not a bit. The flowers are lovely. They'll add a personal touch. You look well, Sadie. You really do. Being pregnant suits you.'

'Does it show that much? I'm only four months gone. I'll be whale-sized by October. Talking about looking well – what about you! You've got your London polish back, and some!' It was true, she thought. Annie looked quite different with her shiny bobbed hair and her very high-heeled shoes.

'Thanks. I have to admit that I love being back at work. I've got more articles commissioned. I'm really excited about it and I have to thank you for stepping in and coming to the rescue in the holidays. Charlie found the childcare issue so hard to accept and it was only the fact that the boys could come here that swung it. We've got it all set up now with a wonderful Czech girl, who started after Easter. Charlie can see for himself that the boys are fine. I don't think they miss me being there at all, which is slightly galling. Look at them now.'

She indicated behind the tent where a blue and red bouncy castle had been erected, on which Rory and Archie were leaping up and down, to be shortly joined by Georgie in a pink party dress.

'Actually, I've got something for you.' Annie darted to retrieve her bag, which had been stowed under a table, and produced a glamorously packaged box.

'Oooh! How lovely! I love a surprise present,' said Sadie. 'Can I open it now?'

She unwound the silver bow and carefully opened the shiny turquoise paper. Inside was a small leather box, and when she opened it she found a pair of silver filigree earrings.

'Annie! These are so beautiful! Thank you so, so much! Wow!'

'You deserve them. You really helped us out and it can't have been easy. You're pregnant, your partner walked out, you had to move out of your home and had a houseful of other people's children foisted upon you. And Alice went AWOL!'

At that moment, Tamzin appeared at their elbows with a cardboard box of small jam jars, and using an empty serving table they began to sort out the flowers into posies to fill them.

'Be a darling and go and get a jug of water from the kitchen,' said Sadie, and Tamzin went off obligingly. She wanted to look for Sabine, with whom she was now thick friends.

'Yes, it was uncharacteristic of Mum to take off like that. I don't quite know what it was all about,' said Sadie when she was out of hearing. 'I felt it was better not to ask. I guess it was Dad, being a prat in some way. He went round like a beaten dog while she was away.'

'I suppose there can be tricky times in even the longest marriages. But tell me about you going back to the farm. It sounds as if it has all worked out well,' said Annie.

'Yes, it has. I've been asked to manage the new set-up when the dairy is finally moved. They need someone on site to deal with the migrant workers when the asparagus and soft fruit business is up and running. We will have twenty-five static vans, a club room, a launderette, a games room – even a mini football pitch. We have to accommodate and look after teams of young people, mostly from Eastern Europe, who will come over for the picking season from March through to September. It's ideal for me. I can fit it in round the girls and the baby and it's much better paid. They've even done the cottage up.'

'Oh, Sadie! I'm so glad.'

'Yeah. Things are looking better. I still miss Kyle, of course. He hasn't been in touch, but I'm keeping my fingers crossed that he'll want to know, come October, about his baby.'

'I hope so.'

'There! What do you think?' Sadie stood back to examine their handiwork.

'They look lovely. Let's put them on the tables quick!'

'Here's Marina and her entourage. She always arrives when everything has been done.'

There was a rush of swooping and kissing and introductions as Marina and Ahmed arrived, carrying little Mo in a travel seat, followed by Ahmed's family, beautifully dressed and elegantly coiffed, bowing to left and right as they made their way through the family.

'Where are Mum and Dad?' asked Charlie. 'They ought to be here. Do they know we are waiting for them?'

'They want to make an entrance!' someone called back, laughing.

Ahmed's uncle, Adib, small and square and exotically good-looking, who had an eye for substantial women, caught sight of Mandy, resplendent in a white trouser suit, standing with her parents, and moved swiftly to introduce himself in his excellent English. She blushed like a girl as he kissed her hand.

Sabine, in a new, short dress from Topshop, hung off her mother's arm, her other arm linked through Tamzin's. 'I want this to be the best party ever!' she whispered in Tamzin's ear.

'Me too!'

'Don't do that, darling!' said Lisa. 'Ollie, I'm going to sit down, if that's okay. I'm feeling a bit, you know . . .'

Sabine and Tamzin exchanged glances and giggled.

Standing at an upstairs window, Margaret, dressed in low-cut cream lace with a large pink bow in her hair, gave Alice a running commentary.

'That's your sister and her husband arrived! She looks very smart in a navy suit, matching shoes and bag, and she's had her hair done. She's fatter than you, mind! The kids are all on the bouncy castle, having a great time. Oh, it looks lovely, Alice! The garden, the tent, everything. How handsome your sons are! There's the little wife who's the journalist. She looks happy. Very smart get-up; you can tell she knows about fashion. She's helping Sadie put flowers on the tables. Sadie looks pretty, too. Is that the dress you bought her? Dark green with geometric print?'

'Oh, let me see!' cried Alice, leaving her dressing table, lipstick in her hand. She joined her friend at the window. 'It all looks lovely, doesn't it?'

'Hurry up and put your dress on. Charlie is opening the champagne and they're calling for you and David. Here, let me help you.'

Margaret eased the red dress over Alice's shoulders and slid up the zip.

'There! I'm going on down. I've got my camera ready. You look lovely, Alice. Just beautiful!'

'Thank you, Margaret. Thank you for everything.'

'Alice! Where are you? Everyone's waiting for us!' David called up the stairs.

'I'm coming! I'm coming!'

Out in the garden, Ollie was filling champagne glasses. Even the children were allowed a sip. The next moment there was a movement from within the house. Everyone turned to look and a small cheer went up as Alice and David stepped through the French windows hand in hand, David in an unexpectedly smart cream linen jacket, looking handsome, and Alice, laughing, in a miracle of a red dress.